Mallory couldn't breathe

She could almost feel Em's soft little body hugged tightly in her arms, smell her shampoo, see her twinkling brown eyes and freckled nose. "We have to find her," she said, glancing up at Mac Phearson. Fear made her voice sound slightly off-key. "She's only seven. It'll get dark soon."

"We'll find her." Mac's arms slipped around her reassuringly. "There's plenty of daylight left."

Lifting her head, Mallory looked deep into his gray eyes. The low timbre of his voice bolstered her. He sounded so certain. *Oh, please, let him be right.*

CATHERINE ANDERSON

Catherine Anderson is the award-winning author of over twenty-five historical and contemporary romances.

Catherine Anderson

Switchback

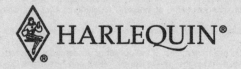

TORONTO • NEW YORK • LONDON
AMSTERDAM • PARIS • SYDNEY • HAMBURG
STOCKHOLM • ATHENS • TOKYO • MILAN • MADRID
PRAGUE • WARSAW • BUDAPEST • AUCKLAND

As always, to my husband Sid, because his support has made it possible for my dream to become a reality. And, of course, to his mother Carolyn, who played a big part in making him the man he is.

To Julie Brinegar and Stella Cameron, because they have been such wonderful friends to me.

To Sue Stone, because she is such a great editor.

And, last but never least, to my niece Gerry, who can always make me smile—even when we're hopelessly lost in the wilderness.

ISBN-13: 978-0-373-47087-7
ISBN-10:   0-373-47087-8

SWITCHBACK

Copyright © 1990 by Adeline Catherine Anderson

This edition published by arrangement with Harlequin Books S.A.

® and TM are trademarks of the publisher. Trademarks indicated with ® are registered in the United States Patent and Trademark Office, the Canadian Trade Marks Office and in other countries.

www.eHarlequin.com

Printed in U.S.A.

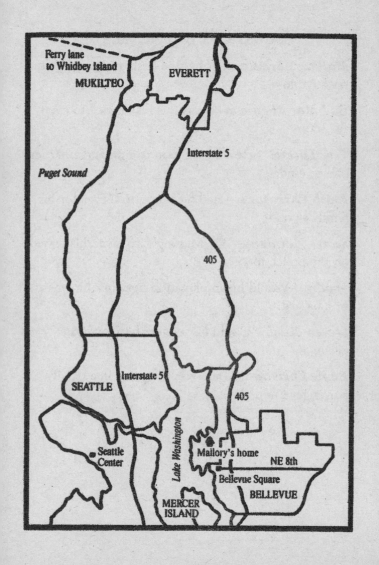

CAST OF CHARACTERS

Mallory Christiani—She was desperate enough to try anything.

Bud Mac Phearson—Was this his chance to even the score?

Pete Lucetti—He's a hard man to find and a harder one to elude.

Keith Christiani—Had he been too clever for his family's good?

Scotty Herman—Was Mac right to avoid his friend on the police force?

Shelby—Would his information network be a help or a hazard?

Steven Miles—Could his ledgers be worth the price?

Emily Christiani—She was the prize in a deadly scavenger hunt.

Prologue

Keith Christiani stared at the telephone, letting it ring three times. As he curled his fingers around the receiver, he gripped the plastic so hard his knuckles turned white. Only a chosen few had the number to his private office line. He knew who was calling. "Christiani here."

Keith could hear breathing, raspy and shallow, underscoring the silence with almost palpable intensity. At last a coarse, cold voice said, "Did you mail the package?"

Keith shifted his gaze to the paperweight on his desk. It was a glass globe with a snow scene inside, a Christmas gift from his little granddaughter, Emily. Knifelike pain cut deep into his left temple. He squeezed his eyes closed. Just a few more hours and this would all be over. He'd fly his family to safety, then notify the authorities of where they could get the key. "Why ask? I know your goons were on my heels all day."

"I have men watching your home as well. That better've been my package you mailed. If it wasn't, that granddaughter of yours will be stretched out in the morgue by Friday. I guarantee it."

Keith rose halfway out of his chair. "You promised if I cooperated, you'd leave my family alone." If they were watching his house, how could he get Em and Mallory out of there? His vision blurred and he sank back into his chair. "You mess with me and I'll call the cops so fast you won't know what hit you."

"*You* mess with *me* and your daughter-in-law and her brat will be dead so fast *they* won't know what hit them. Nobody crosses me and gets away with it. Not even highfalutin' lawyers. You know that firsthand. You went to the bank today. What the hell for?"

Keith gripped the edge of his desk. Anger, white-hot and searing, coursed through his body. "Probate."

"And that was all?"

"I swear it." A long silence followed Keith's lie.

"For your family's sake, I hope so."

The phone clicked and went dead. Keith clenched his teeth to ward off panic. What had he done? He had been crazy to try outwitting Lucetti on his own. Lucetti was so sharp, so fanatical about detail, so paranoid about leaving evidence, that his mind functioned with the precision of a computer. The man was the worst kind of gutter slime, too smart to be caught and ruthless enough to kill a child without hesitation.

With a shaking hand, Keith dropped the phone receiver into its cradle. He had to get help, but now he didn't dare bring the cops into this. Not as long as Mallory and Emily were still in Seattle where the man could get at them. The panic Keith had been holding at bay threatened to engulf him. Then a rush of hope filled him. Maybe, just maybe, Mac had returned. He was due back sometime today. Pressing the fingertips of one hand against his throbbing head he passed a hand over his eyes. He couldn't remember if he'd taken his pills today or not. These past few days, he'd been so strung out, he had scarcely remembered to eat. Keith lifted his receiver and dialed Mac's number from memory. After four buzzes, Mac Phearson's answering machine broke in. Keith nearly hung up, but desperation forestalled him. He waited for the tone and then said, "Mac, this is Keith."

He paused, unsure how much he dared reveal on tape. An excruciating pain shot up the right side of his neck. Licking his lips with a tongue that felt suddenly thick and rubbery, he frowned. Fragments of sentences danced in his mind. He had to remember what he should and shouldn't say.

"There's—um—a man, a man known as Pete Lucetti." Keith blinked. What on earth was wrong with him? He drew a deep breath. "This Lucetti, he's threatening to kill Mallory and Em. I've got to get them out of town. Tonight. I'd—uh—call the police but he's got a couple of cops on the payroll." The room seemed to spin. Keith struggled for balance, propping one elbow on the arm of his chair. "Don't know who I can trust...I'm counting on you, Mac. You're my only—"

The pain in Keith's head seemed to explode. He heard the phone clatter onto his desk. Then there was a shrill ringing in his ears. The room went dark, then flashed bright as if someone had popped a flashcube in his eyes. The next second, he felt himself pitch forward. A funnel of blackness sucked at him, pulling him deeper and deeper into its center. He couldn't die. Not right now. Not before he could talk to Mac.

With all his concentration, Keith dragged himself back to semiconsciousness and reached for the intercom to call for help. His arm weighed a thousand pounds. He couldn't feel his hand. When he opened his eyes, he couldn't see. The ringing in his ears grew louder.

The intercom. Dear God, where was the intercom?

Chapter One

The moment Mallory Christiani stepped into the Intensive Care Unit, she saw the fear in her father-in-law's eyes. He lay propped against two pillows, the weight of his silvery head creasing the starched cases, his sunken face cast in stark relief against white linen. She took a steadying breath, repositioned the shoulder strap of her leather purse, and pasted on a smile.

The click of her heels echoed as she walked toward the bed. She was glad she'd taken extra pains freshening up while she was at the house. Her collarless blazer and matching green skirt were crisp and wrinkle free. Keith would never know she hadn't eaten or slept since he'd been stricken yesterday.

"Dad. It's so good to see you awake." Mallory leaned over to kiss his cheek, holding her amber-colored hair back so it wouldn't trail in his face. As she straightened, she took his right hand in hers. His skin felt cold. The lack of response in his limp fingers shocked her. Until now, she hadn't realized how dearly she had come to love him, how big a part he played in her life now that they shared the same home. Keith was more a father to her than her own had ever been. "You're looking better already, you know? Some of your color's coming back."

A treacherous catch in her voice nearly betrayed her. Why hadn't she recognized his prestroke symptoms? Any nurse worth her salt would have.

Spying tears slipping down his pallid cheeks, she gave him

a careful hug. "Oh, Dad. We're through the worst, right? From here on in, you'll be amazed at how quickly you recover."

Keith's blue eyes followed her as she drew away. Was there something wrong here, something more than anxiety over his paralysis? She glanced at the monitor above his head. It seemed to her his heartbeat was too rapid, but she could detect no irregularities in the configurations. If the fast pulse were anything to be concerned about, the monitor alarm would be going off. Through the glass partition, she could see the ICU nurse sitting at the desk, her dark head bent as she filled out charts. Nothing out of the ordinary, apparently.

Pulling up a chair, Mallory eased her purse to the floor. Spittle ran from the corner of her father-in-law's mouth. Suddenly the nightmare of what had happened to him became a reality. She reached for a tissue and wiped his face, keeping her smile steady, her hands sure.

"Emily will come see you as soon as they move you to a regular room. She can't wait. She lost another tooth, but she won't put it under her pillow until you get home. Holding out for more money, I think. So much for believing in fairies, huh?" She laughed. The sound reminded her of two tin cans clanking. "She's staying with Beth Hamstead until Mother and Dad get home. They're driving back from Texas immediately, but it'll take them an extra day. Dad lost the motor-home keys. Can you believe it? You remember Beth, the lady with all the little redheads?"

Keith's eyes clung to hers, frantic, pleading. His bottom lip quivered as he strained to speak. Spying a flutter of movement, she glanced over to see his left hand twitching, his fingers extended like claws. A low moan erupted from him.

"What is it?" She shot up from the chair. "Are you in pain?" The green graph line was rocketing across the monitor screen. He was clearly agitated about something. Her own pulse began to race as she grabbed the nurse buzzer. "There, there, it'll be okay. Relax, Dad. Take deep breaths."

The approaching swish of the nurse's polyester uniform

eased the tension from Mallory's shoulders. She turned to watch the plump woman hurry to the bed. "Problems?"

"I don't know. He was fine and then—" She broke off. The nurse looked so unperturbed by the racing monitor that Mallory felt foolish. "I was just talking. And he became agitated."

The nurse smiled. "He's just pleased to see you. Right, Mr. Christiani?" She slid her twinkling blue gaze to Mallory. "A little too much excitement, that's all."

Another moan erupted from Keith. The nurse flashed Mallory a concerned glance and lifted her patient's hand. After studying the configurations on the monitor a moment to be certain nothing was wrong, she said, "You're fine, Mr. Christiani. Just too many visitors." Turning toward Mallory, she added, "Why don't you have a cup of coffee? Let him nap for an hour or so. We have a lovely cafeteria."

"Visitors? I thought only immediate family was admitted."

"Yes, but we make exceptions for clergy. Your parish priest got your message and came in about an hour ago. And a few minutes after that, Mr. Christiani's son came in. You're the third in a short period of time. Even brief visits from family and close friends can be wearing the first day."

A prickle of alarm ran up Mallory's spine. "I'm the only relative and we're Methodists. Are you certain you're recalling the right patient? Mr. Christiani's son is—" She hated to remind Keith of Darren's accident when he was so ill. "I'm a widow."

The nurse looked nonplussed. "How odd."

Mallory was beginning to feel extremely angry. Keith shouldn't be having a parade of people marching through his room so soon after a massive stroke. The priest could have come by mistake, but the so-called son had clearly lied to gain admittance. Who had the man been? Why had he lied to see Keith? "What did this *son* look like?"

The nurse pursed her lips. "He was tall, blond, quite good-looking. The athletic type. Mid to late thirties, I'd say. He was wearing scruffy gray sweats and a blue windbreaker. He asked after you, wanted to know where you were. He seemed like a very nice man.''

A very nice man wouldn't have lied to get into Intensive Care. Mallory racked her brain, visualizing all Keith's friends and associates. None she knew fit the description the nurse had just given her. Glancing at Keith, she decided the less said about it in front of him the better. No wonder he was tired.

"If I'm quiet, wouldn't it be all right if I stayed?"

"It would really be better if you gave him a rest," the nurse replied with underlying firmness. "I know he seems distressed about your leaving, but that's quite common the first day. Trust me to know what's best."

"Well... I believe I'll go have that cup of coffee you suggested then." After stooping to retrieve her purse, Mallory touched her father-in-law's hand reassuringly. His eyes seemed to beg her not to leave. She felt as though she were abandoning him. "I'll be back soon, Dad. Okay? You take a short nap while I'm gone. When I come back, I'll read to you for a bit. I found a great issue of *National Geographic* in the hall. Would you enjoy that?"

Keith's reply was a dry sob. She forced herself to smile with a cheerfulness she was far from feeling. Once outside the room she drew the nurse aside and said, "Our minister is Reverend Miller. He should be the only church visitor allowed in. And I'm the only relative except for my daughter, Em, who's only seven." Mallory glanced at her watch. "An hour, you say?"

"Give or take a few minutes." The nurse seemed to empathize with Mallory's difficulty in leaving and gave her a kindly pat on the shoulder. In a low voice, she said, "Thank you for cooperating. I'll put the visitor information on his chart."

The sound of Keith's sobs echoed in Mallory's mind as she left Intensive Care and walked down the long hall. She couldn't remember ever having felt so helpless. She wanted to *do* something for Keith, make him better somehow. The shining floor tiles blurred as she blinked back tears. Seeing Keith so distressed made the visit from his so-called son all the more infuriating. Mallory couldn't imagine who the blond man had been, and it was probably just as well. If she knew, she'd be tempted to strangle him. At least she had the consolation of knowing Keith had a good nurse caring for him, that instructions were being logged on his chart so the visitor flow would be monitored more closely from now on.

A good nurse. There had been a time when she had classified herself as one. Memories rushed through her. Pictures of her husband Darren's face flashed in her mind. *Blood, so much blood.* She lifted her chin and took longer strides. She couldn't let these sterile surroundings get to her. It had been over a year. Long enough for the memories to fade. So why couldn't she put them behind her? When she reached the elevator, she could barely see the buttons. Extending an arm, she jabbed blindly, biting the inside of her lip. Crying was a luxury she seldom indulged in, certainly never in public. *This is what you get for going without sleep.*

"Excuse me, Mrs. Christiani?" a deep voice called.

Because she didn't want to be seen in tears, she almost ducked into the elevator without answering. But what if it was Keith's doctor? He might not make rounds again until tomorrow. She swiped at her cheeks, then turned. The elevator doors closed behind her.

"Yes?"

At first glance, Mallory knew the man loping down the hall wasn't Dr. Stein. He had golden hair, not dark brown, and looked to be about a foot too tall. Gray sweats and a blue windbreaker. Keith's mysterious "son"? Anger flashed through her, and she straightened her shoulders.

As he drew nearer, she saw why the nurse had pegged him as the athletic type. Though she did so begrudgingly, Mallory had to admit she had never seen blue nylon and gray knit filled out quite so impressively. Her gaze fell to a yellow smear on the front of his sweatshirt that looked suspiciously like mustard. Her attention then plunged to his smudged white sneakers. One toe was stained orange.

He shoved a hand into the pocket of his windbreaker and

withdrew a business card. As he extended it to her, he whispered, "I'm Bud Mac Phearson, Keith's detective friend. Sorry I took so long. You must be half out of your mind."

Still rigid with anger, Mallory said, "I beg your pardon?"

The faint aroma of hot dogs clung to him. She had a hazy impression of tanned skin, sharply cut features and full lips. She glanced down at the card but didn't reach out to take it. The words PRIVATE INVESTIGATION stood out in boldface type.

Heaving a frustrated sigh, the man raked a hand through his already disheveled hair. "Keith didn't tell you?"

His eyes unnerved her. They were that rare, light shade of gray that seems to see right through you. "Keith isn't able to speak, so he hasn't told me much of anything. The nurse, however, told me plenty. You're the man who lied to gain admittance to Intensive Care, aren't you?"

She didn't miss the guilty surprise that flashed across his face. Without giving him a chance to speak, she rushed on.

"I suppose you're working on a case for the law firm? I've known a few overzealous investigators before, but this stunt takes the prize. The hospital rules are meant to protect the patients. You can't help but know my father-in-law is an extremely sick man." She gave the elevator button another jab. She was so furious her hand was shaking. "What could be so important that you'd bother him here? See his partner, Mr. Finn. He's handling everything until my father-in-law recovers. Now if you'll excuse me?"

He slipped his business card back into his jacket and stepped closer. "Wait. I have to talk to you. It's urgent."

Mallory, whose escape was thwarted by the slow response of the elevator, found herself meeting his unsettling gaze again. "Nothing you have to say could be *that* urgent. Christiani and Finn handles only civil cases."

"Could we find someplace private where we could talk?" He was already looking around as he spoke and reaching for her arm. "Someplace where we won't be seen or overheard?"

She avoided his outstretched hand. Now that she was studying him, she could see a fine sheen of sweat on his face. He kept looking around, as if he expected someone to creep up on him. Not the kind of fellow with whom she wanted seclusion. He turned to glance down the hall again. As he did, the front of his jacket fell back and she saw that he wore a shoulder holster and gun. Since Darren's accident, just being in the same room with a gun made her nervous.

The elevator doors slid open. Before she could react, Mac Phearson stepped forward to block her path with a set of shoulders that suddenly seemed as wide as a linebacker's. She tipped her head back to glare at him. He topped her five foot five by a good ten inches and outweighed her by at least eighty pounds. Her heart sank when the doors closed again behind him.

"Please," he said. "I realize I'm scaring you, but if you'll just give me a minute I'm sure I can explain."

Mallory inched away from him, growing more uneasy by the moment. "So explain."

"I'm an old friend of your father-in-law's. I've been out of town on a case for nearly a week, got back a day later than I planned. When I called in to check my answering machine this afternoon, there was a message from Keith. He said that he needed me to get you and your little girl out of town. *Immediately.* A man named Pete Lucetti has made a threat on your lives." He paused as if for emphasis. "He must have left that message yesterday, before he collapsed, which means I'm a day late as it is. We can't waste any time."

Of all the things Mallory had expected him to say, this wasn't one of them. She didn't like the way this man was behaving. Terrified was the only word to describe him. Or maybe paranoid, the way he kept checking the halls. "That's preposterous."

"But true. We can call Keith's office so you can be sure I *am* who I say I am, but we can't do it here in the hospital. Right before I went in to see Keith, some guy dressed like a priest visited him, and believe me, he was the farthest thing from a priest you're ever going to see. I saw the guy up close, and I recognized him. The last I heard, he was a strong-arm type who collected on delinquent bets for a local bookie. I watched him through the window and it looked like he was threatening Keith. About what, I have no idea. Do you have any idea how Keith got tied up with Lucetti? Do you know what this is about?''

''I—no—I—'' Mallory swallowed. ''You're really serious.''

''Dead serious.''

''Why didn't Keith simply call the police?''

''He said Lucetti has a couple of cops on the payroll. He must have been afraid, not sure who was safe to talk to and who wasn't. Mrs. Christiani, Pete Lucetti heads one of the largest crime rings in Seattle. He's bad news—*real* bad news.''

Silence fell over them, such complete silence that Mallory could hear herself breathing. Her gaze dropped to the mustard stain on Mac Phearson's shirt. She hesitated. Christiani and Finn was one of the most prestigious law firms in Bellevue. Surely no one associated with the firm would be dressed so scruffily.

The man heaved another exasperated sigh. ''I had a run-in with a kid toting a hot dog. I know I'm a mess, okay? My flight was late getting in. I went directly from the airport to coach baseball—changed into my sweats in the dugout. During break, I went up to the pay phone to call for my messages. After hearing that recording from Keith, I didn't take time for anything. My other clothes are in the car.''

''Do you have any identification? Something besides a business card? For twenty dollars, you can have one of those made up proclaiming that you're just about anything, a snake charmer, an underwater basket weaver, anything.''

An angry glint crept into his eyes and he reached for his wallet. When his hand skimmed the smooth hip of his sweatpants, he rolled his eyes toward the ceiling. ''Mrs. Christiani, if I were some nut case looking for an easy target, would I pick on a woman in a busy hospital? Didn't you hear what I said? An extremely dangerous man has threatened to kill you and your daughter. Do you think Keith would have left me that message if he hadn't believed you were in serious danger?''

"I've no proof that he even called you. Keith and I are very close. If he had been in trouble, he would have told me."

Mac Phearson parted his lips to make a retort, but was cut short by the sharp sound of footsteps as someone came up behind them. Both he and Mallory glanced at the direction of the sound to see a priest rounding the corner up the hall. The priest paused midstride, his gaze coming to rest on Mallory. With a thoughtful frown, he reached a hand under his jacket. Mac Phearson cursed under his breath, seized Mallory by the arm and pulled her between him and the wall. Leaning sideways, he punched the elevator button and then slid his hand under his windbreaker. When Mallory saw that he was pulling his gun, she shrank back.

The priest had drawn a square of paper from his pocket. He studied it a moment, then resumed his pace.

"I thought he'd recognized you and was going for his weapon," Mac Phearson hissed. Hiding her from the other man's view, he whispered, "Don't scream. Please don't scream."

Mallory wouldn't have dreamed of it. This man was clearly suffering from paranoia. He had his gun concealed between their bodies. If he accidentally pulled the trigger, the bullet would go straight through her right breast. She could feel the tension in him, his muscles coiled tightly, his breath coming in short, uneven rasps. She craned her neck toward the priest. The man looked completely harmless to her, just a priest making duty calls to sick parishioners. He had probably pulled the paper from his pocket to check a room number. Mallory watched him, willing him to look her way again. If only he would see what was happening and help her. To her dismay, he walked past, sparing her not a glance.

A heavy ache pooled in her lower abdomen, and she pressed her shaking knees together. Mac Phearson's features swam before her in a dark blur. Her brain kicked into low gear, registering everything in slow motion with super-clarity: his breathing, the drumming of her own pulse, the beads of sweat popping out on her forehead. The chime signaled the elevator's arrival on their floor. The instant the doors slid open, Mac Phearson jerked her half off her feet into the cubicle, releasing her only long enough to holster his gun and hit the lobby button.

Mallory threw a panicked glance at the swiftly closing doors. There hadn't been time to run before Mac Phearson had grabbed her arm again. She stood there in frozen horror and tried desperately to think what to do. If she screamed, would she be heard? How well were elevators insulated? And suppose someone did hear her? Was she willing to jeopardize the lives of innocent people? This man couldn't be sane. He might open fire in the busy lobby.

He threw her a look that seemed to mirror her own feeling of terror. "Look, I'm sorry about this, but right now my first priority has to be getting you out of here in one piece. If that means I have to be a little heavy-handed, it's better than you getting killed."

Hysteria closed her throat. She had read about this kind of thing occurring, but she had never dreamed it could happen to her. *Think. Don't give way to panic.* What was the best way to handle someone who had lost his grip on reality? Appearing calm was a must. Angering or frightening him could prove fatal, not just to her but to others.

She ran a cottony tongue over dry lips. Suddenly, insanely, she wanted a drink of water. Visions of her little girl's face swept through her mind. *Emily.* Mallory didn't want to die. Not yet. She had left too many things undone. She wanted to hug her daughter and tell her one last time how much she loved her. There were some dirty dishes in the kitchen sink. She hadn't finished weeding the violets yet, either. And who would take care of Keith?

Mac Phearson was watching the floor numbers flash on the panel above their heads. Without looking down at her, he gave her a perfunctory pat on the back, which she presumed was meant to comfort her. "With any luck, they're all upstairs, Mrs. Christiani. Maybe we'll make it out of here with no trouble."

Mallory had no idea who *they* were. Pete Lucetti? The name

sounded like something out of an old gangster movie; it had nothing to do with reality. Who was this man? And where was he taking her? She fixed her gaze on the left front panel of his jacket. Having the gun out of sight did little to comfort her.

"Where's your daughter?"

"Sh-she's staying with friends."

"Do they live far from here?"

Mallory could only pray her face didn't betray her. "A long way."

"How long has it been since you spoke with her? Since you knew for sure she was all right?"

"This morning."

He threw her a sharp glance. "Did she attend school today?"

Surely he didn't know what school Emily attended. "Yes."

"Your sitter takes her and picks her up, I take it?"

"She has kids who go there."

"Does she keep a close eye on Emily?"

Mallory was startled. He knew her daughter's name? Of course, he could have learned it in a dozen different ways, not necessarily through an association with Keith. Indecision held her paralyzed. His gray eyes locked with hers, compelling her to answer him. "I—yes, she watches her closely."

The floor panel light indicated that the elevator was approaching the lobby. Mac Phearson took a deep breath. When the elevator stopped and the doors opened, he looped an arm around her shoulders and propelled her forward into a short hall that opened into the lobby. The lean, hard ridges of his body pressed against her arm. She felt him grow tense, and her heartbeat accelerated.

What if he were telling the truth? As she watched his gaze dart suspiciously around the waiting area, she couldn't help wondering. He seemed as scared as she was, which meant he truly believed they were in terrible danger. Her thoughts flew to Emily again. Mac Phearson was either totally immersed in make-believe or on the level. Her skin prickled. Had someone really threatened to kill her and her daughter? Mac Phearson *had* reached for his wallet earlier, presumably to show her his

ID. It wasn't beyond the realm of possibility that he *had* forgotten his wallet in his street pants, just as he had claimed. And there *had* been a priest in the ICU visiting Keith.

What if? She recalled the terror she'd seen in Keith's eyes, the feeling she'd had that he'd been trying desperately to tell her something.

They were halfway across the lobby. Time was ticking by, second by treacherous second. If she was going to scream and try to get away, it was now or never. The click of her shoes against the tile resounded inside her head as her captor led her through the milling people. She fastened her gaze on a toddler fleeing from his mother. If Mac Phearson was unbalanced, he might pull his weapon and fire indiscriminately. On the other hand, what if he was perfectly sane and telling the truth? What if there were killers in the hospital? *Now or never. Now or never*, her mind taunted. A few more feet and they would be out of the building.

Mallory couldn't be sure what it was that finally decided her. Perhaps it was the firm but somehow gentle pressure of Mac Phearson's grip on her arm. Or the way he walked, turned slightly toward her, as if he were trying to shield her. She only knew she couldn't risk being wrong. It was broad daylight, after all. There were bound to be people in the parking lot. If he was telling the truth, he had identification in the car. She would simply demand to see it before going anywhere with him.

A sea of parked automobiles stretched before them as they left the loading area. Mac Phearson never broke stride as they crossed the parking lot. His arm felt unnervingly strong vised around her shoulders. He was a tall man, heavily muscled and agile. If he wasn't who he claimed to be, she was in big trouble. *Just as far as the car.* If he didn't come up with identification then, she'd scream so loudly that people on the next block would hear.

He drew her closer to his side. "Lean into me and look down, Mrs. Christiani."

"What for?"

"To hide your face. *Just do it.*"

Mallory almost refused, but the urgency in his voice compelled her. She dropped her chin to her chest and pressed her shoulder against his ribs.

He quickened his pace. "Be sure you don't look up."

"Is there really someone out here?" Now that was a brilliant question. If he was lying, would he admit it?

"In a car to our left, two rows over. Three men. Listen to me and listen close. If I tell you to get down, I want you to drop right where you are. Understand? Don't try to run."

Surely this wasn't an act. Fear inched up her spine.

"They may have a perfectly legitimate reason for sitting there. But it pays to be safe, and they look suspicious. If they have guns, I can't see them. My car's not far." He fished in his jacket pocket for his keys. "Just a few more steps. You're doing great."

He drew to a stop and reached across her to unlock the door of an old, blue Volvo. As he opened the door, he took hold of her elbow and shoved her forward, giving her no time to protest.

"Fasten your seat belt," he ordered, as he slammed her door.

On the floorboard was an array of tools, including a hefty screwdriver and a tire iron. An investigator might use such things. On the other hand, so might a killer. Mallory reached for the door handle. She threw open the door, but before she could get out, Mac Phearson had climbed in on his side.

"What are you doing?" he snarled. "You don't seem to understand, lady. This isn't a game we're playing."

He seized her arm, jerked her back into the automobile and leaned across her to slam the door. He glared at her as he fastened his own seat belt, then reached over to buckle hers. The clasp clicked with finality. Mallory dropped her head to avoid eye contact. What if she looked into his eyes and saw madness gleaming back at her? What if there weren't any hoodlums in the parking lot? What if the priest had been just that, a priest who had visited Keith by mistake?

The car engine leaped to life and Mallory leaped with it. Her head shot up and she fastened a terrified gaze on Mac Phearson's taut features. He threw an arm over the seat and craned his neck to see behind them as he backed the Volvo out of the parking space. Despite the mustard-stained sweat suit and tousled hair, he was an extremely attractive man. Were madmen good-looking? She remembered seeing the infamous Ted Bundy's photograph, remembered thinking how incredible it was that he'd murdered so many women. The police claimed he had convinced some of his victims that he was a police officer and coaxed them into his car. Like Mac Phearson had just coaxed her?

As the car surged forward, she turned to look back at the parking lot, not sure whether or not she wanted to see a carful of men pursuing them. Either way, she was in a mess. He was driving too fast and the slanting sun reflected off all the windshields. "May I see your ID now, Mr. Mac Phearson?" she asked as calmly as she could manage.

"Now?" He threw her an incredulous look. "It's there in the back seat, but I'd really rather you didn't undo your belt. As soon as we're someplace safe, I'll get it for you."

Someplace safe? she thought. Safe for who? Him or her?

Chapter Two

For an endless moment, Mallory stared at Mac Phearson's profile, acutely aware that their car was picking up speed, heading west. Buildings flashed by. Air whished in around her door. She inched sideways in the seat to face him. He was too busy driving and checking his rearview mirror to notice her.

"I can't see anyone following us. Why should it hurt if I unfasten my seat belt?"

Distracted by the question, he glanced her way. "Give it a few minutes so I can be sure they aren't coming. Right now, ID is the *least* of our worries. Where's your daughter staying?"

Mallory gnawed the inside of her lip, a bad habit of hers when she was upset. His act was convincing, she had to admit, but there didn't appear to be any villain on the scene. "Mr. Mac Phearson, I want to see some ID. *Now.*"

He ignored her, his mouth pressed into a grim line.

Mallory unfastened her seat belt and turned as if to get out of the car. "Either you come up with some ID or I'm taking a quick exit."

His hand shot out to grab the front of her jacket. "Damn, are you crazy? Don't you *dare* open that door."

"Take your hand off me."

"We're doing forty-five, in case you haven't noticed." He checked his mirror again, then narrowed his eyes. With a curse, he released her and grabbed the wheel with both hands. "That's them. Hold on."

He floored the gas pedal. She stared through the windshield at the heavy traffic, horrified, as he switched lanes and cut off the car behind them. Brakes squealed as he swung across an oncoming lane to reach the north 405 exit ramp.

"You're going to kill somebody!"

"I've got to make the exit."

A blue Lincoln swerved into the guardrail to miss them. Mallory had a death grip on the dash. "We're going to crash!"

"They're on our tail."

They? She couldn't tear her eyes from the brown Bronco that bore down on them. Its steel bumper and winch seemed as formidable as a tank. More brakes squealed. The Bronco skidded sideways and brought the exiting lane of traffic behind it to a quick halt, causing a chain reaction of fender benders. The Volvo careened onto the access road that merged with 405.

Once on the freeway, Mac Phearson darted the car in and out of lanes, driving far faster than was safe, to put several miles between them and Bellevue. "I've only gained us a couple of minutes' head start. They probably doubled back to the exit to follow us. We've got to switch over to southbound."

"Across the divider?"

He flashed his blinker and forced his way over to the middle lane. "It's not a divider once we get down past the bridge, just a sloping ditch. Cops cut across there all the time."

Mallory, unable to believe any of this was happening, saw the overhead bridge coming up fast. She didn't see how Mac Phearson could get over through all this traffic. They zoomed under the bridge and had to travel several more miles before he could manage to squeeze over.

She threw an arm up to shield her face when he finally gained the inside lane. The next second, she felt their tires lose traction on the gravel shoulder. The car bottomed out, bounced, and was airborne. They landed with an ear-shattering clunk that jolted her so hard she bit her tongue. Pain exploded through the roof of her mouth. She clung desperately to the dash as the underbody of the Volvo grated its way up the incline to the southbound lanes.

When she felt smooth highway caressing the tires again, she noticed that the glove box had popped open. She reached to close it and froze. A manila envelope in the glove box had come open and spilled an array of glossy plastic squares. Washington drivers' licenses and ID cards, several of them, all with Mac Phearson's snapshot and other names. *Aliases?* She shut the glove box. She was in big trouble. This man didn't work for Christiani and Finn. He was either an undercover man or a crook, and right now, the latter seemed most likely. As yet, she hadn't seen anyone following them. And if no one was following them, everything he had told her was a lie.

Tiny beads of sweat glistened on his forehead. "I don't see them coming yet," he said, "but even so, it'd be a good idea to get off this freeway. We'll be sitting ducks out here."

Visualizing a lonely dirt road and a gun pressed to her temple, all she could think of was getting out of the car while there were still people around. Sudden inspiration hit her. "Pull over. I'm going to be sick. Oh, hurry. Pull over now."

She clamped a hand to her mouth, gagged, and bugged her eyes at him. He swerved into the parking lane and brought the car skidding to a stop. Throwing open the door, Mallory snatched up her purse and made her escape.

"Here they come!" he yelled just as she gained her feet.

Grabbing her arm, he spun her around and jerked her back into the car. She sprawled facedown on the seat as the car lurched forward again. She crooked an arm around his thigh to hold on, too shocked to scream. The door swung inward scraping her calves. When the car swerved back into traffic, all that kept her from spilling out was his hold on her.

"Get in!"

She didn't need to be told twice. With nothing but open air between her and the blur of road, sixty seemed much faster than usual. Scrambling for purchase, she clawed her way in.

"Shut the door." He held her wrist in a steely grip. "I'll hold you."

As she leaned out to reach for the door handle, she could only pray Mac Phearson didn't let go of her. Wind blasted her face and whipped her hair flat against her head. Her fingertips curled on the chrome. *Just one more inch.* She angled her body farther forward.

With the wind pushing against it, the door slammed shut so easily when she pulled that she was propelled backward against him. She felt his muscles tense under his jacket sleeve as he fought for control of the car.

"You okay?"

"No, I'm *not* okay."

"Get that seat belt back on."

She sat up and rammed the buckle together. "Where *are* they? You crazy idiot, you nearly got me killed."

"They're coming up on our left."

There *wasn't* any highway on their left, only a dividing strip. She looked back, not expecting to see anyone. Her heart skipped a beat. Sure enough, there came a cream-colored car, bouncing and swerving inside the ditch, gaining on them at an alarming rate. A man poked his head out the rear window. He held something black in his hands. She couldn't be seeing what she *thought* she was seeing. "They've got a gun!"

In grim silence, Mac Phearson inched up behind an old woman in an equally ancient Ford.

"Step on it! Didn't you hear me? They've got a gun!"

"I can't step on it! We're bumper-to-bumper!"

"Then hit the ditch! You did it before. They're gaining."

"It's too dangerous. I took it at an angle last time. Now I'd have to side-hill. We'd roll."

The cream-colored car was within five car lengths. A rapid splat of bullets riddled the back of the Volvo.

Mac Phearson checked his side mirror. "Hold on."

Swerving to the left, he entered the emergency parking lane and floored the gas pedal. Twisting within the confines of her safety belt, she peered out the rear window. "They're shooting at us! They're actually *shooting* at us."

His only response was a scowl. Mallory saw the pursuing car hit a chuckhole, do a nosedive and send up a spray of dirt. The Volvo gained several car lengths. Mac Phearson jerked the steering wheel hard to the right and smacked a green Honda broadside. The terrified driver slammed on his brakes, his tires grabbing pavement and spitting blue-black smoke. Mac Phearson took advantage of the open space and managed to move over two lanes. He swiped at his forehead with his sleeve and blinked trickles of sweat from his eyes. He looked as terrified as Mallory felt. "They're trying to follow us over."

Hardly able to believe her own ears, Mallory heard herself say, "I—I could switch places and drive so you could shoot back."

"That's an *Uzi*, lady, not a popgun."

"Wh-what's an Uzi?"

"It puts out about a thousand rounds a minute, *that's* what."

A thousand rounds a minute? Turning, she saw a flash of cream-colored paint in the whizzing traffic. "Who *are* they? Why are they doing this?"

"Lucetti's thugs is my guess. They haven't gotten close enough for me to get a make on any of them and I'd like to keep it that way." He punctuated that statement with a screech of tires. "Scoot down."

Mallory inched down just far enough to hide, but not so far she couldn't see as he took the exit. The Volvo rocked on two wheels around a corner. She saw a red light coming up fast and braced herself. She knew without asking that they were going to run it. As they hit the intersection, she opted for oblivion and closed her eyes. When nothing happened, she lifted her lashes.

He darted a glance her way. "What happened to your cheek?"

She touched her cheekbone and winced, remembering how she'd hit the edge of the seat. "Just a little bump. I'm fine." Sliding up in the seat, she glanced through the back window. The cream-colored car was blocked in traffic. "Can we lose them?"

"We've got the advantage."

"We do?"

His mouth quirked slightly at one corner. "It's called motivation."

"I see your point."

He turned left into a residential area and drove aimlessly for several minutes. Mallory couldn't take her eyes off the rear window even though she soon became convinced there was no longer a car following them. He reduced his speed to twenty-five.

"I think we've lost them," he told her.

She sighed and swept her tangled mass of whiskey-colored hair back from her face. At the end of a cul-de-sac, he parked behind a center island of tall shrubs that would hide them from passersby on the intersecting street. To Mallory's right was a brown house with a lazy cocker spaniel sunning on the lawn. She wished they could go inside, lock all the doors and hide. "Why are we stopping? Is that wise? If my daughter's in danger, I want to go get her."

"We have to stay out of sight for a while. Besides, I need to get my stomach back down where it belongs." He leaned his head back against the rest and closed his eyes. His hands remained clenched on the steering wheel. "As for wise? If I were wise, lady, I wouldn't be here."

Now that she knew he was telling the truth about Keith's message, Mallory was plagued with more questions. "Why, exactly, *are* you here then?"

"Keith's a good friend. He asked, I'm here."

Bitterness laced the words. After several uncomfortably quiet minutes had dragged by, he released the catch on his seat belt and rose to his knees beside her. She turned to watch him sift through piles of assorted junk in the back of the car. She'd never seen such a collection. Boxes, baseball bats, rumpled clothes, a battered suitcase and various fast-food cartons. After a search that led him clear to the bottom of the pile, he lifted a white plastic case and a spray container.

"What's that?"

"First aid. For your scrapes." He gestured to her legs.

She hadn't even noticed. "I'm fine. Please, can't we go get my daughter now?"

"I told you, we have to give them time to get off the scent. Might as well take advantage of it." He crooked his right leg under himself and sat down, motioning her to turn sideways as he gave the can a shake. "Hand me a foot."

Catching hold of her skirt to cinch it tight, she lifted her legs and swiveled on her bottom to put her feet on the seat. Her eyes widened when she saw she was minus a shoe. It must have fallen off when she was dangling from the car.

"No great loss. High heels spell nothing but trouble anyway. I'll get you something practical. No fashion shows where we're going." He ripped a larger hole in her nylon and doused the back of her leg with cold spray. "Your ankle is pretty bruised."

He made it sound as if he thought fashion was the be-all of her existence. Mallory shot him a glare, then leaned forward to assess the damage to her legs. "And just where are we going?"

"Eastern Washington. A cabin in the mountains. You and Emily will be safe there until I get to the bottom of this."

Capping the spray can, he tossed it in a careless arc into the back seat junk pile. Her spine went ramrod straight when he pursed his lips and blew softly on her skin until the disinfectant dried. The play of muscle in his shoulders stretched the cloth of his jacket taut. His hands were gentle as he smoothed stick-on bandages over the worst of her scrapes. He'd obviously done this before. Perhaps he had children? He wasn't wearing a wedding ring, but that didn't always mean anything.

She watched his bent head, feeling suddenly ashamed of herself. Most men would have dumped her from the car and said good riddance when she'd faked being sick. "Mr. Mac Phearson, I—I didn't mean to call you names back there. I was just so scared, they popped out."

"Names? Crazy idiot, you mean?" He raised his eyes to hers, his mouth twisting into a humorless grin. "I've been called worse, believe me." He snapped the first-aid case shut and threw it over the seat. "You weren't really sick, were you?"

"When I saw those fake IDs, I thought—" Mallory broke off and licked her lips. "Well, I—"

His gaze flew to the glove box. A slight frown pleated his forehead. "I can't always go by my real name in my line of work."

"Yes—well—investigators for Christiani and Finn don't usually go undercover. And if not undercover investigators, most people who use aliases are—"

"Crooks?" He grabbed his street pants from the pile of stuff on the back seat, fished for his wallet and tossed it in her lap. "Christiani and Finn isn't my only client, you know. In my line of work, I've even worn a chicken costume to catch a thieving employee at a fast-food joint. Believe it or not, if people know who I am, I don't always get the answers I need. I'm Bud Mac Phearson, just as I said. You almost got us both killed pulling that stunt back there." When she didn't open the wallet, he snapped, "Go ahead and check me out. Blood type, political affiliations, licenses, permits. It's all in there."

"I don't really need proof, you know. After all that's happened, how could I not believe you?" But even as she said it, to satisfy him and herself, Mallory opened the wallet and glanced at his identification. She couldn't afford mistakes.

"I'm glad to hear it." He flopped back down behind the wheel. "If we're stuck with each other, a little trust can't hurt."

A heavy silence settled over them. "I said I was sorry."

"Yeah, me, too."

From his tone, she couldn't be sure if he was sorry for something he'd done or if he just regretted his entanglement with *her*.

"I should have had my ID with me. I was stupid to forget it in the car. When I lecture on crime prevention, I warn women never to—" He swiped at a hank of hair that waved across his forehead, getting in his eyes. "Let's just forget it, okay?"

Mallory offered his wallet to him. He took it and shoved it into his jacket pocket. She studied him for a moment, then said,

"I feel as if I'm having a bad dream and can't wake up. Why are those men doing this? I can't understand it."

"For now, I'm not going to worry about why. A gun in my back has a way of dampening my curiosity. As for dreaming, I wish."

She rolled down her window and inhaled a bracing draught of spruce-scented air. The sound of children's laughter came to them from up the street. The sound reminded her of Emily and unbidden tears welled in her eyes. "Shouldn't we be going? I'd like to get my daughter."

He stuffed a rumpled handkerchief into her hand. "In a few more minutes. They'll comb the streets for a while. Let's make sure we're safe."

Mallory searched for a clean spot on the handkerchief.

"Sorry. Toby's hot dog and orange slush is all over it."

"Who's Toby?"

"My pitcher." He grabbed a dog-eared notepad off the dash, unclipped the Lindy pen attached to the bent spirals and jotted something down. "Was that a Buick they were driving? An '88?"

"There was a *gun* hanging out the window. That's all I noticed."

He didn't even look up. "It was at least an '88. I think the first three letters on the plate were LUD."

"Are we going to the police?"

"Keith said no."

"Then why write the tag number down?" She stared at his taut face. "Every cop in King County can't be working for Lucetti."

"Do you want to take a chance on trusting the wrong one?"

"Do you know what you're saying? That there are policemen who know about this and aren't doing anything to stop it."

He tossed the tablet back onto the dash and braced his arms on the steering wheel. "That's right."

"This is Seattle, not Miami Vice."

His eyes locked with hers. She had the feeling that he thoroughly disliked her.

"You say *Seattle* like it's smack dab in the middle of *Disneyland. Most* cops are on the level, probably ninety-nine-point-nine percent, but it only takes one. Bellevue, with its manicured streets and fancy houses and fifty-thousand-dollar cars, isn't the real world. I know that's hard for you to digest, but take a stab at it."

"Just what *are* we going to do then?"

"We're going to go pick up your kid and then get out of town." He gave her a challenging glance. "Unless you can come up with a better suggestion?"

For the life of her, Mallory couldn't think of a single one.

Chapter Three

The ride to Beth Hamstead's house, where Emily was staying, took thirty minutes, during which Mallory felt the tension in her neck and shoulders beginning to ease. She couldn't think of any way anyone could know where Emily was. That thought and the peaceful country scenery along the Woodinville-Duvall Road soothed her as nothing else could. Leaning her head back against the rest, she watched the green hillsides whiz by, relishing the cool caress of the early-evening breeze as it rushed in through her open window. In a few more minutes, she would have her daughter safely in her arms, and Mac Phearson would spirit them away to a safe place where they could wait together until he could find out what was going on.

Turning her head, she watched him as he maneuvered the car, one shoulder propped against his door, one hand loosely curled around the steering wheel. At a glance, he appeared relaxed. Only his eyes gave him away. They darted continually from the road to his rearview mirror. His watchfulness reminded her that the nightmare from which they'd just escaped was far from over.

"See anyone?"

"Not yet. Mrs. Christiani—"

"Mallory, please. Mrs. seems so formal."

"Mallory," he corrected. "I want you to think back over the last few weeks. Has Keith said or done anything odd?"

She shook her head. "He's been horribly tense, that's all."

"Any strangers been calling the house? People who've never called before? It's extremely important."

Again she shook her head.

"Has Keith been gone at odd hours? Has he, um, had a sudden increase in income?"

Mallory stiffened. "Just what are you implying?"

"Nothing. I'm just trying to—" He narrowed his eyes. "Get something straight, okay? Keith's like a father to me. I'm not maligning his character, just looking for answers."

"He *isn't* dealing in anything criminal, not Keith."

"Has he had an increase in income?"

"No!"

"Don't just say no, *think*. Like it or not, he's tied up in something pretty nasty and there has to be a reason for it. Not everyone runs in your circles, you know. Keith didn't meet Lucetti over a friendly game of handball at the athletic club."

Mallory sat straighter in the seat. He made affluence sound like a sin. It wasn't as if she were one of the rich and famous, after all. Her dad was an ex-congressman—so what? She had been raised in a town where the wealthy greatly outnumbered the middle-income families. Again, so what? People didn't pick their parents, after all.

"You don't like me, do you?" she ground out.

His jaw tensed. "I just met you. Why wouldn't I like you?"

"You tell me."

He turned his attention from the road to give her a lazy perusal. "If I had to describe my feelings toward you, I'd have to say I'm indifferent. I haven't known you long enough to form a personal opinion of you. I'm here as a favor to Keith. Which brings us back to my question. Let's stick to that."

He didn't sound indifferent, he sounded contemptuous. And for the life of her Mallory couldn't see what it was he found so revolting. Her expensive green suit was a mess, no doubt about it, but he wasn't going to take any fashion prizes himself. In frustration, she decided to let the issue drop. Indifference could be mutual.

She forced her mind back to his question, Keith's income.

Could her father-in-law have become involved in something shady? No, she couldn't believe it of him, not for an instant. "There's been no increase in income that I'm aware of. No strangers calling. Nothing. He's been tense...that's all."

"How about strange cars in the neighborhood?"

"No, not that I noticed. Our neighborhood is pretty quiet."

He frowned. "There has to be something we're missing."

Mallory had no answer. "Keith's a good man, an honest man."

"I know that." He squinted to see out the dirty windshield. "You said to take a left at two hundred and twenty-sixth, right?"

She nodded and tried to read the street signs. They still had about a half mile to go before their turn. "It's not finished yet, is it? They could still find us."

"Assuming Lucetti doesn't already know where we're heading. It's possible that he's been having you followed."

Sweat sprang to her palms. So much for her calm assumption that Emily was safe. Thank goodness they were only a short distance from Beth's. "You think that he might've?"

"It's possible. But let's not borrow trouble."

He was right. She had problems aplenty already.

He glanced over at her. "You look exhausted. How long since you slept and ate?"

"I'm fine."

Remembering the bitterness that had crept into his voice earlier, she fastened a curious stare on him. One minute he sounded almost as if he hated her, the next he took her off guard by being kind. Did he have some particular reason for disliking Bellevue people? He seemed loyal enough to Keith, referring to him as a surrogate father, which meant he must have grown up in the Seattle area. Intercity, probably. But what part? She shifted her gaze to the pile of junk on his back seat. The baseball bat caught her eye. "I take it you like kids?"

"They're okay."

"You must think they're a little better than okay or you wouldn't coach ball."

He checked the rearview mirror again. "We can't all do our good deeds at fancy charity dinners."

She ignored the dig. "Still live in your old neighborhood?"

"My mom does."

"Is that where you coach?"

He hesitated before answering. "That's right."

"Is it a school team?"

He looked over at her. Something flickered in his eyes, something so cold it almost made Mallory shiver. "You want to know what part of Seattle I'm from, right?"

"Is there something wrong with that?"

"Nope. Just predictable."

It was several seconds before she realized he hadn't answered her question. *Just predictable.* What was that supposed to mean? He took the sharp left turn off the Woodinville-Duvall Road. She pointed through the trees toward Beth's two-story, white house. "It's the third right, up there on the hill." Glancing at her watch, she added, "The kids are probably out in the pasture with Lovey. It's not quite supper time yet."

"Lovey?"

"The Shetland pony."

Mac Phearson steered the car up the narrow, winding driveway. Trees blocked Mallory's view of the house. She strained her neck to see the upper pasture, hoping to spot her daughter. When she looked back at Mac Phearson, he was staring straight ahead, his eyes flat and hard. He braked to a stop.

Mallory immediately knew something had to be wrong. Her heart leaped when she saw the police car angled across the driveway. Beth Hamstead was standing beside a tall policeman out in front of the garage. Mallory threw off her seat belt and wrenched her car door open. Mac Phearson cut the engine, pulled the emergency brake and piled out his door after her. She felt his hand clamp down on her arm. "Be careful what you say."

Mallory jerked away from him. Beth's brood hovered around their mother. But where was Emily? Mallory searched for her daughter's amber-colored braids among the bobbing redheads.

Oh, dear God, where was Emily? A call came over the police car radio, and the officer left Beth to go answer it.

Beth stiffened when she spotted Mallory running up the steep driveway. "Oh, Mall, thank heaven you're here. I've been out of my mind, trying to call you. Em's wandered off."

It felt to Mallory as if the ground had disappeared from under her. She didn't realize she'd nearly fallen until a hard, strong arm caught her around the shoulders. *Mac Phearson.* Forgetting that she barely knew him, no longer really caring, she leaned into him for much-needed support. "Wh-what do you mean, she's wandered off, Beth? How long has it been since you saw her?" Mallory dreaded hearing the answer.

Beth lifted both hands, blue eyes apologetic. "I only turned my back for a few minutes. The phone rang and I ran inside to answer it. That's all, I swear it. You know how closely I watch her. She was right here playing with the others and then—then she was just gone." Running her fingers through her red hair, Beth flashed an unconvincing smile. "I'm sure she's just lost her way in the woods. No need to panic. In this thick brush, it happens sometimes. I can't count the times my kids have gotten turned around. Of course, they're more familiar with the area, so they've always gotten back before I felt it was necessary to call the police."

Fear sluiced down Mallory's spine and pooled like ice at the small of her back. An image of her daughter's face swam through her head, and she felt a scream welling in her throat. She clamped her arms around her middle, clinging desperately to her self-control. Mac Phearson's hand clasped hers where it rested at her waist and she threw him a pleading look. The dismay she read in his eyes only intensified her fear. "Lucetti?" she whispered.

"Let's not jump to conclusions," he cautioned in a low voice. "It doesn't add up."

He threw an uneasy glance at the policeman to make sure he wasn't listening.

Ignoring his warning glance, Mallory continued her questions. "You don't think Lucetti took her then?"

Mac Phearson's gaze slid to Beth before he answered. The redhead was busy speaking with one of her children, not listening to them. "When professionals make a hit, they do it quick and clean, Mallory. They couldn't have found a more ideal place than here, remote, no witnesses. Why take her someplace else and risk being seen while they—" He broke off and swallowed.

Mallory knew what it must be that he had left unsaid, but she couldn't let herself dwell on it. What he *had* said was what she must concentrate on and that was bad enough. If Lucetti was out for blood, he couldn't have found a better place to spill it. Which meant what?

The police officer turned away from the car, his face lined with concern. He stared at Mallory's torn stockings and bare feet for a moment, then lifted his gaze to Mac Phearson's smeared sweatshirt. "I assume you're Mr. and Mrs. Christiani?"

"I'm Mrs. Christiani. This is my friend, Mr. Mac Ph—"

"Pleased, I'm sure," Mac Phearson said, cutting the introduction short and extending his arm for a handshake.

"I'm Officer Maloney. It looks as if your daughter has wandered off into the woods, ma'am."

"Did you already question the children?" she asked.

"Yes, but they weren't much help. It seems they left Emily holding the Shetland's halter while they ran into the barn to get some oats. Evidently the pony isn't a very cooperative riding mount unless she's bribed. They had trouble getting the feed-room door open and took longer than they meant to. When they came back out, Emily was gone. Mrs. Hamstead had gone inside and wasn't watching them, as I understand it."

Beth approached, her eyes taking on a glint of anger. "I *was* watching them. I just went in to answer my phone."

The officer cleared his throat. "I don't think there's any cause for alarm. She's been gone less than two hours. We have four squad cars on the roads, three officers on foot. We've asked all the neighbors, and no one has seen her. But most people are busy this time of day preparing dinner, so that's not really odd. We'll have her home for her own dinner if my guess is right. Too many roads around here for her to wander far.''

Mallory nearly groaned in exasperation. Em wouldn't take off without permission. The child *knew* better. And Mallory never left her here without cautioning her against leaving the yard. In one direction, there was a busy highway, and in the other, a lake.

There was a horrible, quivery feeling in the pit of Mallory's stomach, a feeling that seemed somehow connected to her throat. *Emily?* She searched the faces of the other children, willing her daughter to appear. This was every mother's nightmare, the sort of thing you read about in the paper but never dreamed would happen to you. *Oh, please, God, not my baby.*

''It's not like my daughter to leave the yard without permission,'' Mallory said, struggling to keep her voice calm. ''Have you considered the possibility that she might have been kidnapped?''

Mac Phearson stiffened and cast Mallory a warning glance, which she presumed was meant to silence her. She lifted her chin and met his gaze head-on before returning her attention to the policeman.

''Kidnapping is always a possibility, Mrs. Christiani, but we've no reason to suspect that at this stage. Mrs. Hamstead hasn't noticed any strangers hanging around. This is a quiet area, not much off-the-highway traffic. Who'd be up here to spot an unattended child and take her that quickly?''

''*Unattended?*'' Beth protested. ''What are you implying? I watch the kids more closely than most mothers, especially with a lake so close.''

Mallory doubled her hands into fists. Her nails bit into her palms. Her daughter was missing. This was no time for Beth's ego to get in the way.

''I— Don't misinterpret what I'm saying, Mrs. Hamstead,'' the officer said patiently. ''I didn't mean that you were neglecting the child. Kids will be kids. They forget rules sometimes and wander farther than they realize. Unfortunately a turn of the head is all it takes and they're gone. Especially in a wooded area like this. Emily probably didn't intend to go more than a few steps and simply got turned around. Where is this lake?''

''Right up the road.''

The alarm that flashed across the officer's face was impossible to miss. ''Did Emily know about the lake?''

''Yes!'' Mallory cut in. ''I've warned her about it.''

''Does your daughter like the water?''

Mallory stared at the policeman, scarcely seeing him as she pictured Em standing on the diving board at home, poised to do a back flip. *Mommy, look at me!* The memory made her eyes burn with unshed tears. The trees in her peripheral vision seemed to be closing in, spinning. ''Yes, she loves the water.'' Her voice sounded as if it belonged to someone else, calm and reasonable, completely at odds with the panic churning inside her. She wanted to charge off into the woods—scream, cry— beg someone to tell her this wasn't really happening. ''We have a pool. She's an accomplished swimmer. She's already in intermediate lessons.''

''Excuse me just a moment.'' The policeman walked back to his car and leaned through the open window to grab the mike to his radio. After talking a few minutes, he strode back to them. The expression on his face spoke volumes.

Mallory couldn't breathe. It felt as if a thousand-pound weight had hit her square in the chest. *The lake.* Em *was* a good swimmer, but what if she had fallen in? Her woolen school uniform and shoes would soak up water like a sponge and hamper her.

Mallory began to tremble. She could almost feel Em's soft little body hugged tightly in her arms, smell her shampoo, see her twinkling brown eyes and freckled nose. ''We have to find her,'' she said, glancing up at Mac Phearson. Fear made her voice sound slightly off-key. ''She's only seven. It'll get dark soon.''

''We'll find her.'' Mac Phearson's arms slipped around her reassuringly. ''There's plenty of daylight left.''

Mallory nodded and sucked in a breath of air, holding it until her temples throbbed. Exhaling with a shaky sigh, she forced herself to relax. She had to stay calm. Think. Where might Em have gone? She glanced over the bushy hillsides, trying to see it from a child's perspective. What could have enticed Em from the yard? A squirrel, perhaps? A pretty bird? Mallory couldn't imagine her daughter disobeying the rules on a whim.

"Better?" Mac Phearson's arms loosened and she felt him smoothing her hair. "She's okay. Count on it."

Lifting her head, Mallory looked deep into his gray eyes. The low timbre of his voice bolstered her. He sounded so certain. *Oh, please, let him be right.* Again she turned to stare in indecision at the semicircle of trees that hemmed the property. Emily's name ached in her throat. Could Lucetti have tailed them here last night, as Mac Phearson had mentioned? What if he had? What if he had taken Em? If he had, they'd be wasting time searching the woods.

But what if Lucetti doesn't have her? Em *might* be lost. They had to search for her here first—just in case. She might panic, fall and hurt herself. That thought spurred Mallory into action. She took several steps toward the trees, only to be dragged to a stop by Mac Phearson's strong grip on her shoulder.

"You can't take off on foot, not without shoes."

"I have to. She'll be getting scared by now." She tried to slip out of his grasp. "She'll come if she hears my voice. Hearing a bunch of strange men yelling her name might frighten her. She could start running and fall or—"

His grip on her wrist tightened. "We'll take the car. You can drive up and down the roads while I search the brush. If you keep your window down, she'll be able to hear you just as well as if you were walking, and you can cover more ground that way. She's bound to stumble out to a road sooner or later, right?"

Mallory glanced at the car, anxious to start searching. If Em did come out onto a road, she would surely stay on it. Mac was right. Looking for her in an automobile might prove to be the fastest way to find her.

The policeman turned to Beth. "Someone should stay here."

Beth nodded. Glancing at Mac Phearson, the officer said, "We're sweeping up from the highway in this direction. As soon as the men get here, we'll go on up the road."

It went without saying that "up the road" meant the lake. Despite Mac Phearson's reassurances, Mallory's stomach lurched.

"Then that's where we'll head first," Mac Phearson replied.

AN HOUR LATER, Mallory stood beside the car. Mac wove his way toward her through the thick brush, never taking his eyes off her. Standing there barefoot in the dusky light with her tousled hair framing her face, she looked like a scared twelve-year-old. The bruise along her cheek was a dark shadow against her white skin.

His stomach tightened as he drew closer. The fear in her sherry-brown eyes reached out and coiled itself around his heart.

He had hated Mallory Christiani so venomously for so many years that the sudden wave of pity he felt for her confused him. Time after time today, he had found himself forgetting who she was. Now he was getting to a point where he didn't much care. She wasn't at all as he had imagined her. Admitting, even to himself, that he might have been wrong about her didn't sit well. But the truth was staring him in the face. She wasn't the empty-headed, spoiled little rich girl he'd expected. She had more guts than most.

And now he had to kick her when she was already down.

The news he had wasn't good. A few minutes ago, he had run into one of the policemen beating the brush. The general consensus was that if they didn't find Emily soon, there was only one place she could possibly be, in the lake. There were so many houses and fences peppering the woods that they didn't think the child could have wandered past them into open country.

After beating the brush as thoroughly as he had this past hour, Mac was inclined to disagree with the lake theory. He'd circled the body of water himself, and there wasn't any sign that a child had been playing along the shore. After leaving the lake, he had worked his way back toward the Hamstead place.

He'd found a dirt road above the property that looked down on the Hamstead house, a cul-de-sac where some new homes were being constructed. There were tire tracks on the road's shoulder where a car had been parked. Judging from the scattered cigarette butts, someone had sat there a good long while, chain-smoking. There were also a man's shoe prints in the dirt going from the car toward the pasture where Emily had been playing right before she disappeared.

Mac knew what must have happened to Emily. But he still didn't know why. Lucetti must have taken her. Who else? Like the cop had said, there was no throughway up here, no random passersby who might have taken the opportunity to snatch a child.

Now, after having assured Mallory that Lucetti probably wasn't involved, Mac hated to have to tell her he had been wrong. And, boy, did he dread the confrontation he knew was coming when he told her he didn't want the cops involved.

Being afraid your child might be dead was bad. But to know she was alive and probably in the hands of a heartless criminal? That would be enough to send anybody over the edge. There was a steep bank at the shoulder of the road. Mac paused below it and gazed up at Mallory. In the next few minutes, he would find out just how much strength Mallory Steele Christiani really had.

Most people would be basket cases after the day she'd been through, but she stood with her chin lifted, mouth set in a grim line. When he looked closely, he could see that she was shaking, but she hid it well, arms crisscrossed over her small breasts, trembling hands tucked out of sight so they wouldn't give her away. She had grit, he'd give her that.

"Anything?" Her voice quavered as she spoke.

He tried to shake his head in reply to her question and found he couldn't. A shiver ran the length of her, and she hugged herself more tightly, hunching her shoulders against the cold breeze blowing in off the water. Mac knew she was thinking of her child, wishing she had her arms around her. He'd never had a kid of his own, but he could imagine the agony she felt. There was nothing he could think of to say or do. Not one damned thing.

She turned her pale face toward Lake Tuck. Her mouth worked for a moment, no sound coming forth. "D-do you think th-they'll drag it?"

He sighed and raked a hand through his hair. "She isn't in the lake, Mallory."

"Then where is she?" She lifted her hands in supplication. "It's been three hours." Her voice grew shrill. "There are so many houses around here, how could she have gotten lost? Where is she?"

Mac squared his shoulders. "I think Lucetti has her."

Dead silence fell between them, broken only by the breeze whispering through the tall spruce and fir trees that crowded the hillsides. The sky had darkened to slate. The wind-twisted evergreens in the background loomed like black sentinels, casting Mallory and the light blue car in stark relief.

As briefly as he could, Mac told her about the car tracks and footprints he had found.

"Lucetti." Her voice rang hollow now. "But you said that didn't make sense. That he would have—have just done it here." Her voice broke and a low cry erupted from her throat. "You said you thought she was just lost."

"I was wrong. Don't misunderstand and start thinking she's dead. If he took her—and I'm pretty certain he did—I don't think he did it so he could kill her. He must have had other reasons. Like I said earlier, this is the perfect place if he meant to—" He sighed and gestured behind him. "There are houses in every direction going away from Beth's. She couldn't have stayed lost this long. The cops think she's in the lake, but I don't buy it. They have no reason to suspect foul play, so they probably didn't take notice of the tire tracks up above. If they did, they more than likely thought it was one of the home builders' vehicles that had been parked there."

"Then why didn't you call their attention to them?"

"I didn't feel I should, not until I had spoken with you—explained the possible consequences."

"Consequences? My daughter is missing. We should tell the police everything so they can find her. If someone took her, we've no proof it was Lucetti. It could have been anyone, couldn't it?"

"I'd say that's unlikely. Extremely unlikely. Knowing what we know, we have to assume it was Lucetti."

"This is my *daughter* we're discussing. I don't want to assume anything. I *can't*. We should go back to Beth's and tell the police."

"They're convinced she's in the lake. To convince them otherwise, we'd have to tell them *why* we think the tire tracks are significant, *why* we feel the footprints going off the road might indicate a kidnapping."

"So we'll tell them!"

"About Lucetti? Mallory, if they once get wind of it, they'll be in on this case for the duration. We can't risk that."

"But—" She stared at him, no longer able to conceal how violently her body was trembling. "You're supposed to get help from the police when things like this happen. That policeman—the one at Beth's—he looked really concerned. I'll bet he's got a little girl of his own. He's not one of Lucetti's men. He'd help us, I know he would. They won't let Lucetti know the police are involved. They're trained to handle things like this."

Mac wiped his mouth with the back of his hand and stared into the woods for a moment, trying to consider the situation from all angles. "I'm sure you're right and the cops we've met tonight are all on the level. There are probably only a couple in the whole county who aren't. Finding men we can trust isn't the problem. One of my best friends is on the King County force. I could trust him with my life, Mallory. But not with this. It's the grapevine *inside* the police force that we're up against. Stop and think about it. No cop likes to believe the cop next to him is on the take. They *have* to trust one another to survive. Even my friend Scotty might be working with someone who's crooked and not realize it. If we turn this matter over to them, the wrong cop could get wind of it. And if he clues Lucetti, it could be dangerous for Emily.''

"Dangerous?"

"If Lucetti thinks the police know she's missing, he'll dispose of—of any evidence.''

Even in the dusk, he could see the pupils of Mallory's eyes dilating. "K-kill her, you mean? You're saying we should tell the police nothing, just leave? And what if someone besides Lucetti took her?''

"I don't think that's the case.''

"You don't *think*? I don't want you to think, I want you to know. My little girl could die.''

"Mallory, whoever has her will have to call if they want ransom. If it isn't Lucetti, we can contact the police then. Sometimes you have to weigh everything and go on gut instinct. I'm telling you what I feel our next move should be. No cops, period. I told them I was taking you home to get some rest so you wouldn't see them dragging the lake, and I think that's exactly what we should do.''

"And what if you're wrong? What if we don't go to the police and Lucetti just kills her? That's what Keith said he had threatened to do.''

"That's the key word, *threatened*. Men like Lucetti don't bother with threats, not unless they're trying to coerce someone. So we have to assume Keith either had something Lucetti wanted or that he was in a position to do something Lucetti needed done. Now Keith's in the hospital and your daughter is missing. Like I said earlier, if Lucetti had wanted to kill her, he would have had it done here. There's a lot of cover for a sniper to hide in and several back roads to use to get out of here afterward. It's the perfect place for a hit. But instead, they took her? They wouldn't have bothered unless they needed her alive for some reason. That convinces me that Lucetti believes *you* can do whatever it was he needed Keith to do. You see what I'm saying? He's taken Em to use as leverage against you.''

"How can you be so sure you're right?"

"I don't *know* I'm right. I'm only making an educated guess. I grew up on the streets. I know the kind of people we're dealing with, how they think."

Her eyes widened. "You're saying you're one of them?"

"In a sense. I used to be."

"What did Keith do, post your bail once? Get you off on a lesser charge? What?" The words shot out of her mouth before she could call them back, then hung there like a cloud between them.

She saw something flicker in his eyes. Pain? "I—" Running a hand through her hair, she averted her face for a moment. "I'm sorry, Mac Phearson. I didn't mean that. I'm just so scared."

He sighed and switched his weight from one foot to the other. "It's your decision. She's your child. I could be wrong. My theory makes sense, but that car chase today doesn't back it up. If Lucetti wants you to do something or give him something, he needs you alive."

"Maybe he was just trying to scare us."

"That's a risky way to scare someone. If I'd lost control of that car, we both could have been killed." The torment in her expression was so pronounced, Mac could almost feel it. "Mallory, it's your daughter who's missing. It should be you who weighs the risks and makes the decisions. If you want to drive back down to Beth's and tell the police, I'll go with you."

She thought for several seconds before she replied. "No. Keith trusted you. For now, at least, I'll do what you say." Her eyes sought his. "You don't think Lucetti will hurt her, do you? If we don't call the police and we cooperate?"

Mac could scarcely bear to look at her. There was no gentle way to tell her the truth, so he chose to say nothing at all. Before he realized his feet were moving, he was nearly up the bank. Two more steps and he was standing over her, feeling like a cumbersome clod as he grasped her shoulders. She wasn't a very large woman. Her collarbone felt fragile under his hands. The flood of tears he was expecting didn't come.

Instead of leaning against him, Mallory pulled back. Taking a deep, shaky breath, she raised her chin.

"If he touches a hair on her head, I'll kill him," she said evenly. "Come on, let's go."

Mac took a moment to respond. For some reason, he'd always equated small with weak. Now he realized he couldn't have been more wrong. "Where?"

"To find him."

There was a deadly gleam in her eye. If it hadn't been such an awful situation, Mac might have laughed. "Mallory, people like Lucetti are roaches. They crawl out of the woodwork after dark. We can't just drive into Seattle and look him up in the phone book. He keeps an extremely low profile. He's renowned for it. I've never even seen him. I don't even know anyone who has."

"Then how do we find him?"

The question took him off guard. She was serious. If he pointed her in the right direction, she would take off without hesitation. "We have two choices. We can hit the streets. Start asking questions, which could take days and might get us nowhere, or we can wait for him to find us. That would probably be a lot quicker, judging by what happened this afternoon."

"In other words, we should stay extremely visible?" She turned decisively toward the Volvo. "Then I'm going home. I can't get much more visible than that. You don't have to stay involved in this, Mac Phearson. She's not your daughter."

He grabbed her arm, steering her away from the driver's door. "It's my car, remember? Where it goes, I go."

"You'd be wiser to walk back to Beth's and call a cab. They'll be watching for the Volvo. I'll leave it parked at the hospital and you can pick it up after things have calmed down." She looked up at him. "I'm serious, Mac Phearson. Why should you risk your neck? This isn't your problem."

"Nobody ever said I was smart." He studied her face for a moment, then shook his head and gave a halfhearted grin. "Keith asked for my help. He's my friend so I'm making it my problem, okay? You can't do this alone."

"And why should you care? You scarcely know me. You've never even seen Em. Keith wouldn't hold it against you if you backed out now. He isn't that kind of fellow."

"You forget I know what kind of fellow he is, probably better than anyone does." Mac felt a strange tightness rise in his throat. "He did me a favor once, a big one. I owe him."

"That's ridiculous. No matter how big a favor Keith did for you, you don't owe him your life."

"Oh, I owe him, all right. There are some things you can't put a price on. Let's just leave it at that. Besides, you and I were nearly killed together this afternoon. You don't go through something like that with someone and then just walk away."

"If it was me, I wouldn't be *walking*, I'd be running."

"I doubt that." Mac was surprised to realize he really meant it. "If it was my kid, you wouldn't rest until we had her home."

"You're crazy, Mac Phearson," she said softly.

"So you've been telling me most of the day." He gave her a little shove and stepped toward the car. "And *please*, stop calling me Mac Phearson?"

"Bud?" °

His gaze met hers over the top of the car. "My friends call me Mac."

She paused by the passenger door, peering at him through the gloom. His friends? All day long, she'd been getting the distinct impression that he didn't like her. She tried to read his expression, but he was standing in the shadow of a tree, which made it impossible. Perhaps it was just as well. If he was making an overture, she should accept it and leave it at that, not wonder what had happened to change his mind. "All right, Mac it is."

Once they were inside the car, she leaned her head back and closed her eyes. Again he braced himself for a deluge of tears. Shoving the shift into first, he eased the car forward, casting uneasy glances her way. "You okay?"

"No." She straightened. "I—want to thank you."

"For what?"

"For staying."

"No big deal. A few thrills every once in a while keeps life interesting."

From the corner of his eye, he saw her wiping a tear from her cheek. He pretended not to notice. She pressed the back of her hand to her mouth for a moment, then dropped her fist onto her lap. "I'm going to get her back. If it's the last thing I do…"

"Correction. *We* are going to get her back. I told you earlier that I'd find her for you. That's a promise I intend to keep." He sighed and adjusted his side mirror. "The way I figure it, Lucetti will get in touch if we make ourselves available, probably by phone."

"To make a ransom demand?"

Mac frowned. "My gut instinct tells me it's not money he's wanting."

"Earlier, you said you thought he needed me to do something, that he'd taken Em to use her as leverage against me. What could he need done that only I could do?"

Shaking his head, Mac threw her a puzzled glance. "I wish I knew."

"Whatever it is, I'll do it. When it comes to my daughter's safety, the word no isn't in my vocabulary."

"Then broaden your vocabulary," he retorted softly. "No may be the most important word you can utter. We can't let him bully us. When he calls, you'll have to insist on speaking to Em, so we know she's all right. That's her life insurance. Unless you insist on that and keep insisting, he has nothing to gain by keeping—" He broke off and looked uncomfortable.

"No reason to keep her alive?" Mallory finished for him. Fear rushed through her, but she refused to give in to it. "Don't pull your punches, Mac Phearson. I need to know exactly what to expect."

"If we don't talk to her, he can get rid of her without our realizing it," he said hollowly. "There's no way we can second-guess what he wants or what he might say, but on that one point—assuring ourselves that Em is safe—we have to stand firm, no matter what he threatens. Think you can handle that? He's liable to get nasty.''

"I can handle anything if Em's life might depend on it."

She sat quietly for a moment.

"You know," she added thoughtfully, "I have a phone that's equipped with a speaker. We should probably turn it on when he calls so both of us can hear. If we listen closely, perhaps the background noise will give us a clue as to where he is keeping Em."

"Good idea. We also need to find out everything else we can manage while you're talking to him. What he wants. Why he needs you. How Keith became involved with him. Any tidbit of information you can get out of him may help us find Emily."

She murmured her agreement. In the darkness, he saw her face crumple before she turned to gaze out her window. He gripped the gear shift until his knuckles hurt. His first inclination was to stop the car and take her into his arms to comfort her, but he instinctively knew it wouldn't be wise. She wasn't the type who wept easily. Before she would break down in front of him, her pride would have to go. And right now, her pride, and fear for her child, were all that held her together.

Chapter Four

Mallory was quiet as Mac Phearson pulled his Volvo into her driveway. The windows of the house yawned black against the white siding. A shiver raised goose bumps on her skin. Without Em and Keith here, the place looked as lonely as a tomb, an impersonal mass of wood, plasterboard and brick. As they climbed out of the car, he shot uneasy glances over his shoulder to check the cul-de-sac. Her heart lifted with hope. Surely Lucetti knew where Keith lived. Coming home had to be the smartest move.

"Got a key?"

As she climbed the steps, she unzipped her bag and became so engrossed in her search she stubbed her toe. Mac snaked an arm around her waist and steadied her. Too tired to care, she leaned against him, letting him guide her up the remaining steps. "My keys aren't here."

"What?" He released her and grabbed the purse. After rummaging a moment, he swore and dumped the contents of her handbag onto the porch. He sorted through the pile and then said, "Well isn't that great. Did you leave them in your car?"

"No. The alarm goes off if I leave them in the ignition. I know I had them when I went into the hospital. I do have a spare set in the house for all the good it does me." Mallory groaned and plopped down on the top step, hugging her bent knees. "I've heard of Murphy's Law, but this is too much."

"I can get in. That's not what bugs me. Was there an

opportunity for someone inside the hospital to have had a moment alone with your handbag?''

Mallory pursed her lips in thought. ''I left it for a couple of seconds—right before I went into the ICU to see Keith, I stepped up the hall to a sitting area to get a *National Geographic* that I had seen earlier, lying there on a table. I wasn't gone but a second, though. And there wasn't anyone else in the hall.''

''A second is all it would take if someone was watching you, waiting for the right moment.''

''What makes you think they were stolen? I could have dropped them by your car when we left.''

''No, I would have heard them fall. Let me go check the floorboard.'' He left her for a moment to search his car. As he walked back up the steps to the front yard, he called, ''Nothing.''

''They could have spilled out when we were on 405. When the door was open. My purse might have gotten dumped.''

He leaned over to eye the assortment of odds and ends. ''Pretty selective dumping. Besides, you had it zipped.''

''I could have zipped it while I was driving around the lake tonight. I remember looking for a tissue.''

''I still say that if the keys fell out, other things would have, too. Someone's rifled your purse. Look at all this stuff. And there's not a scrap inside the car.''

He lifted a wad of tissue and several other pieces of paper as if to use them to prove his point. One of them was a small photograph. He stared at it a moment and then dropped it onto the pile, but not before Mallory glimpsed her daughter's face. Her hand flew toward the photo. A small cry escaped her before she could bite it back. *Emily.* Mallory could almost hear her giggle, smell her hair and the curve of her neck where silken curls escaped her braids. Was she alive? Hungry, cold? Not knowing was awful. Funny how clearly she could remember her first smile, her first tooth, her first step. And, oh, how the memories hurt. Like a knife twisting in her guts. Wrapping her arms around her waist, she rocked forward until her chest nearly touched her knees.

Mac sighed and crouched next to Mallory, placing his hand on her hair at the back of her neck. The warmth of his touch was nearly her undoing. Tears burned in her throat, forming a huge lump that suffocated her. Closing her eyes, Mallory clung to what little self-control she had left and conjured a vision of her mother to put some starch back into her spine. Crying in front of a stranger would be the unforgivable sin in Norma Steele's books. *Ladies* didn't make spectacles of themselves, *not ever.* And her mother was right. How could she help Emily if she was falling apart.

Keeping her head bowed, she straightened her shoulders. "I'm handling this badly. Just, um, give me a second. I'll—"

"You'll what? Pretend everything's fine for another hour? I think you're handling this better than most people could."

"No, I'm not."

Her voice floated up to Mac no louder than a whisper. He studied her bent head and wished he knew what to say to her. There was no shame in tears, after all. But she seemed to think so. Who had done this to her? Beneath his hand, he could feel her shaking, feel the brittle tension in the column of her neck.

"I'm not real good at comforting people, but I've got a great shoulder to lend you. Absorbent, anyway." Mac watched her, feeling inept. Why couldn't he just say what he meant, that he wouldn't mind holding her? The words caught at the base of his throat. "I—Mallory, come here."

She shook her head emphatically. "Crying never solved anything. In my family..." Her voice trailed off.

With a heavy sigh, he cupped her chin and lifted her face. His touch felt sandpapery and warm against Mallory's skin, so strong and solid that she wanted to lean into it. In the moonlight, his eyes shimmered silver, delving so deeply into hers she felt as if he knew her every thought.

"Crying may not solve anything, but it sure can make you feel better sometimes."

"How would you know?"

"Experience. When my little brother—" He broke off and shrugged one shoulder. "There have been a few times. Over in Nam. Here. We all have to let go sometimes." He tightened his grip on her chin. "The point is, you don't have to pretend with me, okay? There's no sin in having feelings."

Drawing away from him, Mallory dragged in a deep breath of air, acutely conscious of his other hand where it still rested against her hair. "It's just that I feel so helpless, so alone. When something happens to your kids, you expect to have the other parent to share it with. You can lean on each other, you know? I'm so *scared*. I wish it was me instead of her. If only it was."

He slid his hand to her shoulder, draping his other arm across his bent knee. He studied the brick pattern of the porch for a long while. "I know I'm a poor substitute for your husband or Keith, but you're not alone. And if you need that shoulder I offered, I won't think any less of you for it."

"I'm afraid that's not saying a lot."

He looked up at her. "What's that supposed to mean?"

"That you don't think much of me anyway."

She felt his thumb rasp along the arm seam of her jacket, saw the corners of his mouth quiver with a repressed smile. "It's a bad habit, I guess, judging people by their addresses."

A peculiar awareness electrified the air between them. Not sensual, but powerful just the same, a drawing together, a feeling of having known one another always. It frightened her. They had been thrown together by crazy circumstances, then shaken up for most of the day like the dried seeds in a *maraca*. There hadn't been time for the usual proprieties, and now it seemed too late for them. Her emotions were roller coasting out of control. She wanted him to set her world right again, to put his arms around her, to hold her, to stroke her hair, to make everything better. It was stupid, ridiculous, childish, but she wanted it with such an intensity she ached. The fact that he was a complete stranger made that realization pretty scary.

He seemed as uneasy as she with the feelings erupting between them. She was relieved when he broke the building tension by giving her shoulder a pat and standing.

He gazed down the street, his expression thoughtful. "It's scary to realize how close you came to trouble today. Before I ever got to the hospital, one of Lucetti's men got near enough to you to go through your purse."

Until this moment, Mallory hadn't thought of it that way. She had been in danger and hadn't even known it. She threw an incredulous glance at the pile of junk from her purse. "I wonder why they wanted my keys? To strip the house? Steal my car?"

"Lucetti isn't into small-time theft. My guess is, he wanted to get into the house to search for something. Or he thought you might have the key to something he needs opened."

"Like what?"

"Beats me." He turned and patted all his pockets. Pausing next to her, he said, "I need my lock picks. Be right back."

Lock picks? Mallory watched him lope to his car. After rummaging in his trunk for a moment, he returned, carrying a key ring with a number of small tools attached to it. She watched him select and try three picks before he found the right one. Seconds later, she heard the door latch assembly click.

"Do you have any idea how much money we invested in that lock?" she asked.

He smiled and pocketed the key ring. "If it's any consolation, the average burglar probably couldn't pick it. It's a high-quality lock."

"Which you just opened in a matter of seconds."

"Dead bolts are a better investment. For night security, I recommend the type that locks from the inside and doesn't have an outside keyhole."

She scooped everything back into her purse and stood, not at all sure she was pleased that he was so adept at breaking and entering, or that he knew so much about locks. What kind of man was he? As she walked toward the open door, she realized that it didn't really matter to her what kind of person he was, not as long as he would help her find Emily. "I don't suppose I should ask where you learned to do that."

He stepped back so she could enter. "Probably not." Pausing behind her, he glanced around the large entry. She sensed a sudden wariness in him. "Come back out to the car a sec. I want to take another look for your keys. I need you to hold the light." He motioned toward the porch. Once they were outside with the door closed, he whispered, "Another reason just hit me why he might have wanted your keys. To plant bugs. With your keys, they could get right in without alarming any of your neighbors by picking the lock or breaking the door."

"Listening devices? In my house?"

"I should have thought of it immediately. If he's going to hold Em for ransom, he'll want to be sure you don't call the cops. The best way to do that would be to listen to everything you say. Which puts us in a spot. We can't let him know who I am."

"Why?"

"I'm a professional. He won't like me being in on this."

"Then maybe you'd better leave."

"No way. We'll just have to be careful."

"But if he learns who you are, it could endanger Em."

"And if you do the wrong thing, it could endanger her even more. You need my help, Mallory. There has to be a way."

"Like what?"

He thought for a moment. "We'll be lovers."

"We'll be *what?*"

He clamped his hand over her mouth, then slowly lowered it. "Lovers. Say we've been seeing each other for six months. Things have gotten cozy. It'd seem natural for me to be here. Keith's in the hospital, your kid's been snatched. I'd hang around, stick close, give you moral support. All it'll take is a little playacting."

"How *much* playacting?"

"Enough to be convincing." He caught her shocked expression and rolled his eyes. "Not *that* much, for heaven's sake."

"It's not that. It's just that I'm afraid I can't do it."

He pressed his fist against her chin jokingly. "Hey, it'll be easy. Just don't call me Mac Phearson. He might recognize the name. Mac or Hey-You, but not Mac Phearson. I'll do the rest."

The front door swung open beneath his hand with a loud creak. He preceded her into the entry, the soles of his sneakers grabbing the tile.

For some reason, the thought that there might be monitors in her house was the final blow to her self-control. She began to shake and couldn't stop. All evening, she had fought off tears and hysteria, telling herself there would be time for that later. Now she realized there wasn't going to be. Her only sanctuary had been invaded.

Mac must have seen her trembling. He paused and curled his arm around her to draw her against him. Being closer to him helped somehow. The tremors running through her body subsided. She pressed her face into the hollow of his shoulder. Soap, cologne, leather, and the faint aroma of hot dogs—a nice smell, ordinary and comforting. The steady beat of his heart lulled her fears. His arms were hard and warm. He ran a hand over her hair and she felt his callused palm catch on the strands. He was wonderfully sturdy when nothing else was, and she dreaded the moment when he would move away from her.

"You okay?"

She found the strength to nod. He gave her back a pat and left her again, disappearing into the shadows. Sudden light blinded her. She blinked and tried to focus. With detached curiosity, she watched him move about the hall, running his hands along the door frames. When she realized he was searching for hidden microphones, she began to help, sliding her fingertips under the edge of the table, behind the painting of the Puget Sound, through the dried flowers. They found nothing, but that still didn't mean there weren't bugs in a nearby room.

"I really appreciate your staying over," she said, praying

she didn't sound too stiff and formal. "Good friends make times like this bearable. Are you sure it's not too much trouble?"

She saw a gleam of approval flicker in his eyes. "I wouldn't have it any other way, sweetheart."

They walked the length of the entry into the kitchen, which adjoined a breakfast nook to the left, a formal dining room to the right. Mac hit the light switch as they passed through the doorway. Mallory turned to stare at the rose-and-cream tiles on the counters, at the oak cupboards and trim. Day before yesterday, she had made breakfast in here. Em had stood chattering at her elbow. Now it seemed like a lifetime ago.

Mac motioned toward a chair in the breakfast nook. Then, shrugging out of his jacket, he draped it across the bar. He took quick stock of his surroundings and began to check the kitchen for hidden listening devices. Taking her cue from him, Mallory ignored his signal to sit down and searched the two adjoining rooms. This *was* her house, after all. She would notice if anything was out of place when he might not.

When she returned to the kitchen, Mac was just stepping through the hall doorway. She guessed that he had been checking the remainder of the first floor. It had been a long while since either of them had spoken. Afraid that the silence might strike an eavesdropper as odd, she said, "It's amazing how much better I feel knowing you're staying over for the night." No sooner had the words passed her lips than Mallory realized she sincerely meant them. Having Mac there *was* a comfort. "With Keith in the hospital and my folks gone on vacation, I would have been alone."

"Maybe you can be there for me sometime," he replied. "That's what friends are for, right?"

He jabbed a finger toward the ceiling to let her know he was going upstairs. She followed him up, searching the rooms off of one hall while he checked the ones off the other.

Nothing. As Mallory slipped silently from Keith's bedroom into his upstairs study, a deluge of memories swept through her mind, pictures of Keith and Emily together, laughing, playing, filling the rooms with sounds of happiness.

Now, with nothing but silence around her, Mallory could appreciate how truly blessed she had been. Had the refrigerator always hummed so loudly? She could hear it, even from up here. Had the floors always creaked like this when someone was walking? The horrible sense of emptiness inside the house made her feeling of loss all the more acute. She might never again see Keith sweep his granddaughter into his arms, never hear Em's carefree giggles or see her eyes light up with excitement at the sound of her grandfather's voice when he came in at night. The list of losses seemed endless.

When they had finished searching the second floor, Mac met her on the landing. Together, they returned to the kitchen. Grabbing a notepad and pen off the bar, he wrote, "Nothing that I could find. As far as I could tell, the house hasn't been searched, either."

Mallory lifted her hands to let him know that she hadn't found anything, either. Then she took the pen from him and wrote, "Maybe they wanted my keys for something else? To open something, perhaps?"

He scanned her response, his frown deepening. Shrugging one shoulder, he motioned for her to sit at the table. He seemed more relaxed as he opened the refrigerator. She sat down and watched him, too heartsick to care what he was doing or why. She even forgot to worry about his gun, despite her fears. Em's voice rang in her ears. *Mommy, will you cut my toast into hearts? With jam on top?*

Mac's voice sliced through Mallory's memories like a knife through tinfoil. "How do eggs sound? Eggs and toast."

"I'm not hungry." She closed her eyes and tried to sort the voices in her head, Em's, Mac's, her own. "A drink, maybe."

"Just because you don't feel hungry doesn't mean you shouldn't eat. My cooking may not be up to your usual standards, but it'll fill your hollow spots." He located a skillet and placed it on the stove. Flashing her an encouraging smile, he began taking food from the refrigerator. "You'll be surprised how much better you feel once you've eaten. Take it from me. When things like this happen, you make it through one minute at a time. When you can't do anything else, you fuel up for the next round and rest.''

"I—I really don't feel like eating."

"I want you to try, sweetheart."

Mallory gazed at his broad back, at the crisscrossed leather strap of his shoulder holster. The endearment unnerved her for a moment. Then she decided he must still think it was necessary to keep up the pretense that they were lovers. She watched him move around her kitchen with practiced ease. Clearly he was a man with many talents, as adept at acting and cooking as he was at picking locks and tending scraped legs. He located the silverware drawer and pulled out a fork to whip the eggs he had cracked into a bowl. Seconds later, she heard a loud sizzling sound, followed by the methodical scraping of the spatula against the cast-iron pan.

The cooking smells reached her and turned her stomach. She fastened her gaze on the tabletop. In the reflecting light, she could see smudges on the polished surface. *Fingerprints.* Tiny ones. Everywhere she looked, she saw something to remind her of Emily. She could hear Mac taking plates down, sticking bread in the toaster. Everyday sounds. She wanted to scream at him to stop. She couldn't eat. Couldn't even think about eating. Was Em hungry? Had someone fed *her* yet? It was past her bedtime, and Mallory didn't know if she even had a blanket.

A ringing sound pealed through the room. Mallory stared at the telephone on the bar, her body frozen. Mac jerked the skillet off the burner. "Answer it," he urged.

She pushed up from the chair and took a halting step. The phone clamored again, the sound running along her nerve endings, making her skin quiver. "Do you think it's him?"

"I don't know. Just answer it." Mac strode across the floor and seized her elbow to pull her forward. "Just play it by ear."

By the third ring, Mallory was standing directly in front of the phone. For some reason, it seemed to have taken her much longer than usual to cross the room. She stood there and stared, willing herself to move, so filled with dread of what she might learn that she couldn't. Mac flipped the panel control on to intercom. She lifted her arm, forcing her fingers to curl around the receiver and lift it. Trembling uncontrollably, she pressed it to her ear. "H-hello?"

There was a long silence. Then a voice crackled over the speaker and filled the room. "Mrs. Christiani? I have your daughter. If you want to see her alive again, listen very carefully."

Mallory clutched the phone with both hands, like a lifeline. It was her only link to her daughter. "Where's my little girl? Who *are* you? What have you done to her? She's just a baby!" Her voice broke. "Please, don't hurt her, please—"

"Get a grip on yourself, Mrs. Christiani," the man snarled. "I have no time for hysterics. Whether or not I harm your daughter is entirely up to you."

Mallory held her breath until her temples throbbed. She could hear Mac whispering, "Stay calm—stay calm." The words eventually sank in and she exhaled in a rush. "What do you want? Money? How much? Just name a price. I'll get it for you. Anything. I'll do anything."

"Not money, just a package."

"A package?" Incredulity swept through Mallory. She hadn't expected him to say that. "What kind of package?"

"The day your father-in-law collapsed, he was supposed to have mailed it to me. Unfortunately for you, the package I received was a fake, filled with nothing but blank sheets of paper. I have reason to believe he put the documents I had requested in his safety-deposit box, hoping to retrieve them later."

"What makes you think that?"

"Shortly before he collapsed, he was seen entering the vault at the bank with a package under his arm. He reappeared without it. I have tried, without success, to find his deposit box key. That leaves me with no options. I want that package, Mrs. Christiani. I need you to get it for me."

Someone had stolen her baby to get a package? Hysteria swelled in her throat. "A package? Why did my father-in-law even have it? What connection does he have to you?"

To Mallory's dismay, the man ignored the questions. "It's a large manila envelope. At the upper left corner, you'll probably see the name Steven Miles, Accountant, with the return address stamped in red ink. Inside you will find several sets of ledgers with the same accountant's name in the headings. You don't need to know anything more. Find that key and get the package, Mrs. Christiani. When you return it to me, you get your child."

"B-but I don't know anything about a key."

"You'll find it, Mrs. Christiani. You have access to your father-in-law's files, his belongings. You know what his habits are and where he might have hidden something important. Oh, yes, you'll find it. If you don't, your little girl will die."

For an instant, all Mallory could see was Darren's face after his accident, the blood in his hair, his empty eyes staring up at her. She heard Mac curse beneath his breath, felt him tighten his hold on her. "Y-yes, I'll find it...I'll find it. Let me talk to Emily. I want to talk to my daughter."

"You'll talk to her when I have the package, not before."

"But how will I know she's all right? That you haven't—"

"I guess you won't," he replied coldly. "Now put your friend on the line."

Mallory glanced up at Mac and handed him the phone. For a horrible moment, it occurred to her that he might be in on this, that he had duped her from the start. She gazed up at his chiseled features, at the grim set of his mouth. His eyes locked with hers, as if he had guessed what she was thinking.

Averting his face, he said, "Hello?"

"Let's cut right to the heart of the matter, shall we, Mr. Mac Phearson? I ran a make on your car. I know you're a private investigator. Take this as fair warning. Don't mess with me. I don't care if you hold your little friend's hand, I don't care if you help her find the package for me, but don't interfere. If you call the local police or the Feds in on this—or even *look* like you're going to—your girlfriend's child is dead. Have I made myself clear?''

''Perfectly clear.'' Mac's eyes darkened to a cloudy, turbulent gray. ''Is the child okay?''

''Yes, and she'll stay that way as long as you cooperate.''

''You're going to have to do a little cooperating yourself.''

''You're in no position to make demands.''

''I think that depends on how you look at it.''

A long silence crackled over the speaker. ''What are you asking?''

''Two things. Number one, call off your thugs. We can't find the key, package, or anything else while we're dodging bullets.''

''I don't know what you're talking about.''

''Then *find out* what I'm talking about. Three men tried to kill us this afternoon.''

''A man in your profession is bound to make enemies, Mr. Mac Phearson.'' A horn honked in the background. Thus far, that was the only external sound Mallory had detected. ''I can't be held accountable for that. Whoever those men were, they have no connection to me.''

Mac's eyebrows drew together in a scowl. ''I want the kid put on the phone.''

''That's impossible.''

''No, that's just good business. No kid, no package.''

Mallory held herself absolutely rigid. She knew Mac had to take a firm stand. They'd discussed the fact that it would ensure Em's safety, but that didn't make it any less frightening. Mac glanced over at her, his face unnaturally pale, the only sign that he, too, was afraid. ''So do we speak to the child or not?''

''Tomorrow morning, eight o'clock.''

The phone clicked and went dead. Horror flooded through Mallory, and she grabbed the receiver from Mac's hand. ''No—oh, please—don't hang up!''

Silence hummed over the intercom. Mac felt Mallory's body go limp. As she slumped against him, only her hand on the phone seemed to retain some life. He had to pry her fingers loose to return the receiver to its cradle. He had done his best. And it hadn't been good enough. It was going to be a long, miserable night for her, an eternity—wondering if her daughter was alive.

Chapter Five

Mac didn't like the expression on Mallory's face after he pried the phone from her hand. Her eyes had a blank, dazed look. Her skin was chalk white. She stared at the phone, her head tipped to one side as if she was listening for something. "Mallory?" he whispered.

For several seconds she didn't seem to hear him. Then she lifted her liquid brown eyes to meet his gaze. He could tell that she wasn't really seeing him. He stepped behind her and grasped her shoulders to steer her back to the table. Like a lifeless doll, she sat when he told her. Hunkering at her feet, he gazed up at her and tried to reconcile this woman with the one who had been so resilient all day, surprising him at every turn. She still hadn't really cried. A few stray tears, but she hadn't broken down. He had a feeling that was coming, though—probably soon.

How could he have been so wrong about her all these years? Mallory Steele, wife of the promising young attorney, Darren Christiani, the daughter of a wealthy congressman, a woman who had it all. Self-centered, shallow, as cold as ice. That was how he had pegged her. As useless as a paper dress in a downpour. A pretty little darling with charm-school manners who went every week for a fifty-dollar manicure, who drove a brand-new sport Mercedes around town with the top down, her salon-conditioned hair flying in the wind.

The Mallory he was getting to know held no resemblance to

that imagined girl-woman. Hadn't all day. And now? An ice maiden didn't love this deeply. Her hair hung in a tangled mass of whiskey-colored curls that reached her shoulders. Her clothes were wrinkled and soiled. Her stockings were torn. Her legs were scratched. She looked like an abandoned child, eyes bruised, mouth quivering, hands limp in her lap. Not even Mac could dredge up resentment toward her.

He cupped the side of her face, brushing his thumb along the fragile contour of her jaw. The blue smudge along her cheekbone was turning a darker color. Her gaze shifted but didn't focus. It was as if she had slipped into another dimension, a nightmarish place that wouldn't release its hold on her. "Mallory, come on, sweetheart."

Awareness at last flickered in her eyes. He could almost see her picking up the threads of her self-control. He had never been good with crying women, but this was one time he would have welcomed tears.

With a sigh, she said, "Well, now we know why he stole my keys, to see if the safety-deposit-box key was on my ring."

He sat back on his heels, still concerned about her pallor. "Which means I was probably wrong about the bugs. At least we don't need to be so worried about what we say now." Weariness weighed heavily on his shoulders, ached behind his eyes. "I want you to listen up, okay? Look at me and listen. Emily is Lucetti's ace in the hole. He won't hurt her. Not if he wants that package."

"What if he already has? He wouldn't put her on the phone. If she's all right, why wouldn't he let me speak to her?"

"Scare tactics. She's leverage, Mallory. He's deliberately trying to make you come unglued so he can be sure you'll do as you're told. I know it's hard, but try to think positive. Without Emily, he can't bargain for the package. He'll handle her with kid gloves, believe me."

She passed a tremulous hand across her brow. "Do you really think so?"

Mac nodded with far more certainty than he felt. "He said

we could speak to her in the morning. Now would he have promised that if he couldn't deliver?''

"No, I guess he wouldn't. A package? He took my little girl! Why would anyone want a set of ledgers that much?''

"I don't know. Maybe the information in them is incriminating. Mallory, I don't know. I wish I—''

"Then why would Keith have them?'' Her voice was shrill, quavery. "Keith doesn't handle criminal cases.''

"I assume that Steven Miles, the accountant, gave them to him.'' Mac frowned. "That name rings a bell. I wonder why.''

While he was lost in thought, she pushed up from her chair and went to open the top drawer in the cabinet under the breakfast bar. He watched her rummage through it, her slender fingers sifting the smaller items, her gaze intent.

"What are you doing?''

"Looking for that key.'' She glanced over at him, her lips set with determination. "Keith might have kept it here in the house. It's certainly a possibility, anyway.''

A very slim one, Mac thought, but he hated to say so. Searching for the key would give her something to do tonight, give her hope. Personally Mac thought Keith would have been more likely to keep the key someplace where it would have been more readily accessible to him during the day while he was at work. Lucetti's people had seen Keith going into the bank vault with a package shortly before he collapsed. Could he have returned home after leaving the bank and left the key here? Or was it at his office? In his car, perhaps? Surely he wouldn't have been so careless as to hide it in a junk drawer at home.

Mallory had worked her way down to the third drawer. There was a feverish look on her face, a desperation in her eyes. Mac finally joined her and began searching the cupboards. "You know, to search everywhere in a house this size could take days. We should at least go about it systematically.''

She nodded. "Like Lucetti said, I know Keith's habits, how he thinks. Tonight, we'll look in the most obvious places first.''

"But, Mallory, it stands to reason he probably would have

hidden it if he didn't want Lucetti getting his hands on it. Someplace no one would ever think of looking.''

"Not Keith. He deals in human nature, remember. He has always maintained that people usually fail to see things that are right in front of their noses. If he really wanted to hide a key, he'd probably put it someplace so obvious that Lucetti would look everywhere else first.'' A faint smile touched her mouth. "Think of all the places no one in his right mind would hide an important key. *That's* where we'll find it.''

Mac rocked back on his heels, his gaze coming to rest on a ginger jar on top of the refrigerator. It was a short drive to the house from Keith's office. He *might* have brought the key home and hidden it here. And a ginger jar was pretty darned obvious. After all, Mallory did know Keith better than anyone. Beginning to feel hopeful, Mac stood and went to check the jar. Next, he looked on the key rack by the back door. None of the keys there were for a deposit box.

While Mac wandered from room to room, Mallory finished searching the kitchen and moved on to the dining room. Even though she was busy looking for the key, her mind was filled with pictures of Emily. There was an ache inside her chest the size of a melon. *Hold on, darling,* she thought. *I'll come through for you. If it's the last thing I do, I'll come through for you.*

With each passing minute, Mallory searched a little more frantically. Room by room, she eliminated every hiding place she thought Keith might have chosen. *Nothing.* She headed upstairs, praying Keith's rooms would turn up something.

After searching fruitlessly for four hours, Mallory and Mac returned to the kitchen. Mac shook his head, his eyes filled with discouragement. Mallory sank onto a chair, fighting off a wave of disappointment so acute that she could scarcely bear it. Without that key, she couldn't get her daughter back. She had to find it. And she had to find it soon.

Mac hunkered beside her, gazing up into her pale face. He wished he could think of something to say, something that would make her feel better, but there was nothing. Taking her hand, he asked, "Hey, you all right? Would you like something? I could get in touch with your doctor. He could prescribe something to help you sleep. We wouldn't have to tell him why—just that you're upset."

Mallory shivered. "How could I sleep? No. If I took pills, I couldn't wake up. Something could happen and she might need me and I wouldn't be able to—"

"Okay, okay," he interjected. "No pills. Just a thought." He gave her cold fingers a squeeze. "How about something to eat now? You're running on sheer willpower."

He returned to the stove to finish making the meal he had begun earlier. He didn't like this, not a bit. He had dealt with distraught parents before, managed to keep them glued together when things got tough, but he'd never been with the parent of a small child right after a disappearance, never seen that horrible fear in a mother's eyes or heard the desperation in her voice. Television didn't come close to depicting the agony of it. Watching Mallory, touching her skin and feeling her clammy fear, made him feel physically sick.

What kind of a man did something like this? That question frightened Mac more than anything. Lucetti would clearly stop at nothing to get what he wanted. The day's events kaleidoscoped in Mac's head, bits and pieces that jostled for position, none making sense. Those three men who had chased them today had been professionals. To believe, even for an instant, that they were connected to him and had nothing to do with Lucetti stretched credibility to the maximum. Mac had been in his line of work too many years without having any complications. Why would he suddenly be on someone's hit list? Mac had a few enemies, but they weren't after blood.

And that wasn't the only thing. The voice on the phone hadn't rung true, either. Born and raised in a poor section of Seattle, Mac knew a two-bit hood when he heard one. Lucetti might have climbed the ladder to the top, he might be rolling in dough by now, but unless he had attended college somewhere along the way and changed his circle of friends, he would still slip into old speech patterns, especially when tense.

Mac knew he did himself, probably more than he realized, though he tried not to.

The man on the phone hadn't.

Granted, Mac had never seen Lucetti. But the man was a known racketeer, and Seattle lowlifes weren't renowned for being articulate. Which meant—what?

It meant trouble, that's what. And he didn't know for sure what kind. Stabbing the knife into the butter, he turned from the stove and slanted a concerned glance at Mallory. From the looks of her, he had trouble enough already. She was just sitting there again, staring at nothing. Shock, maybe? He hoped not. Striding to the table, he slid a plate in front of her and cleared his throat to get her attention. She didn't even look up. He poured them both some milk, then slid her plate closer.

"Come on, eat up," he said gruffly. "You won't be any good to Emily sick. And sick's what you'll be if you don't eat."

She turned on the chair and picked up her fork. Giving the steaming scrambled eggs a tentative poke, she whispered, "I have to find that key."

"Yeah, but first you have to eat." He straddled a chair and scooted forward, propping an elbow by his plate. Watching her from the corner of his eye, he took a bite of toast, tucked it aside in his cheek and said, "Come on, just a few bites. Then you can go upstairs and maybe grab a shower, get some sleep. We can't do anything more tonight."

She stiffened, her fork hovering midway to her mouth, a clump of eggs perched precariously on the tines. "Sleep? I can't sleep. I have to keep looking. Can't you understand that?"

Mac swallowed the lump of toast and grabbed his milk to wash it down. "Name me a place we haven't already looked."

"There are hundreds."

"But is it likely Keith would hide a key there? No. The best thing to do now is get a little rest. After we speak to Emily in the morning, we'll be free to leave the house. We can search the office and Keith's car. If we come up empty-handed, *then* we'll tear this place apart again. That's a promise."

"If you think searching here for the key is useless, then shouldn't we be trying to find Lucetti?"

"Pete Lucetti isn't an easy man to find, Mallory. I've told you that. You have to understand the sort of person we're dealing with. He's the man behind the scenes, faceless, impossible to nail, a fanatic about never leaving evidence. If the cops can't find him, how do you think you can?"

"Won't you help? You're good at finding people, aren't you?"

Her voice held a pitiful note of hope.

"Drink your milk."

She lifted the glass to her lips. When he glanced at her, he found that she was watching him over its rim with the most vulnerable brown eyes he had ever seen. Shoving the remainder of his toast into his mouth, he concentrated on chewing and tried not to look at her.

When the toast was finished, he said, "The smart thing for us to do is to wait for that phone call. Eight in the morning isn't so long to wait." *Just an eternity of not knowing.* "After that, we'll have a better idea what we're up against. Right? You don't know. We might find that key and have Emily home by noon."

"Do you really think so?"

Mac hated liars, but he managed to put some assurance into his voice to help her through the night. "Absolutely."

She studied him until he wanted to squirm. "I think you're just saying that to make me feel better." That empty, dazed look had crept into her eyes again. "What are the odds? On the level."

"Mallory—"

"I want to know the truth. The odds of getting her back alive aren't good, are they?" After watching him a moment, she set her glass down with a thunk. "That's what I thought."

An uncomfortable silence rose between them. Mac saw a glint creep into her eyes. Rage. He couldn't blame her. But, even so, he felt uncomfortable, as though he might take the brunt of her anger if he said the wrong thing.

After an endless moment, she cried, "I can't accept that. Pete Lucetti may be slick, but he can't be that slick. I'm going to find him, just you watch. He's going to be sorry he ever did this."

A tremor ran the length of her. Mac tried to imagine how frustrated she must be feeling and realized no one could truly understand without having first lived through it. She looked completely drained.

"Maybe what you need is a long, hot shower," he suggested softly. "I know it'll be hard to lie down, but you have to think of Emily." Mac felt like a heel for using Em's welfare as a bargaining chip, but it was the only way he could think of to convince Mallory she needed sleep. He would have been willing to bet she hadn't so much as napped since Keith's collapse. And he doubted she had eaten much, either. "If you aren't rested tomorrow, you won't be able to think clearly. And you're going to need your wits about you. Why don't you go on upstairs. I'll clean up here."

Though clearly reluctant, she nodded and stood. He watched her as she left the kitchen. How many times had he wished that Mallory Christiani and all women like her would get their comeuppance? Well, he was getting his wish. Daddy's money couldn't buy her way out of this one. Mac crushed the napkin in his hand.

GEORGE PAISLEY cocked his gray head to one side and stared at the crumpled napkin in his plate, considering what his friend, Paul Fields, had just said. In a low whisper, he replied, "The problem is, I don't like wasting broads. Call it what you like, but it doesn't sit right. It's one thing when you get a direct order to rub out some whore no one cares about. It's another to decide to do it on your own, especially when the victim is a—"

"Lady?" Paul supplied in a snarl. A compulsive stirrer, especially when he was nervous, he clanked his spoon in his cup, driving the other two men at the table and everyone else in the restaurant half crazy with the noise. As always, he ended the stirring with two loud thunks on the edge of his cup. "Will it sit better if it's you who gets it? If the boss sees what's in those ledgers, we're all three goners. Do you think I've come this far to get caught because you're feeling chivalrous? I say knock her off. Better her than us. It's the only way I can see to stop her. Look at the facts, man. The boss has her brat. She'll do anything to get that kid back. Nothing will stop her, not as long as she's alive."

Dennis Godbey sighed and propped an elbow on the table, his blue eyes sliding from one of his friends to the other. "My vote is to take her out tomorrow. I'll do it if George can't."

"It's not that I can't handle it!" George snarled. "I just think there ought to be another way, that's all."

Paul laughed softly. "Right. Why don't we simply call her and tell her our problem? I can hear it all now. 'You see, Mrs. Christiani, we were in cahoots with Miles, cheating our boss. Those ledgers you have will finger us. If that happens, we all die. The way we see it, it's your daughter's life or ours.' Come on, George. Do you think she's going to care? He's got her *daughter*. We have to take her out. When the old man leaves Intensive Care, we'll get rid of him, too. End of problem until after everything goes through probate. When the box is finally opened, we'll find out who gets the contents and arrange to steal the ledgers before anyone reads them. It's simple, clean, and we come out smelling like roses."

"Just like the boss would do it?" George said softly. "No loose ends. Don't you ever get sick of it? That's why we got ourselves into this mess in the first place."

Paul began stirring his coffee again, his hazel eyes intent on the swirling liquid. "Oh, I'm sick of it. We're all sick of it. But I'm not so fed up that I'm willing to go swimming in the sound with bricks tied to my ankles."

"I vote we do it from a distance," Dennis inserted.

"I'm game," Paul replied. "And you won't hear any more

arguments from George, either." He gave his spoon a final
clank, skewering Paisley with a meaningful glare. "Right,
Georgie Boy?"

AFTER MALLORY went upstairs, Mac placed two phone calls,
one to the King County Police and one to Beth Hamstead. He
hated lying, but he had to be sure well-meaning cops or friends
didn't unwittingly do something to panic Lucetti. Emily was
home, safe and sound, Mac told them. They had found her
wandering one of the back roads. No more searching necessary.
He apologized profusely for all the trouble that had been
caused. Kids would be kids. Seven-year-old girls didn't always
stay in the yard as they were told. There was another call Mac
wanted to make, to his best friend, Shelby. He needed to find
out who those three men in the cream-colored car were. *Fast.*
Shelby could do the legwork for him. What if Lucetti had
tapped the phone lines, though? A call like that could be dis-
astrous. He'd have to phone Shelby from a booth in the morning.

Once Mac felt certain he didn't have to worry about the
Hamsteads or the police complicating matters, he did the
dishes, one ear cocked toward the stairs to listen for Mallory.
When twenty minutes passed and he hadn't heard water running through the pipes, he began to worry. Was she all right?
He hated to go up. If he caught her half-dressed, they'd both
be embarrassed, but if he didn't go up and she was sick or
something…

He dried his hands and tossed the towel on the countertop.
Indecision held him rooted for a moment, then he moved
through the entry hall until he stood at the bottom of the stairs.
The house was eerily silent now that he had stopped rummaging around. No, not completely silent. He turned his head
slightly and listened. There it was again. She was up there
someplace bawling. And trying very hard not to be heard.

Mac put a hand on the banister, took a step up, hesitated. If
he were smart, he'd stay down here and let her cry. He took
another step. He was lousy at mopping up tears. He took an-

other step. Then another. He might be clumsy, but nobody else was around to take care of her.

The house was like a maze. Two long halls when most places had one. Doors everywhere. He homed in on the soft sounds. At last he found the right room. The door was closed. From the other side, he could hear the sobbing clearly, not quite so soft now that he was so close. He stood there and shifted his weight from one foot to the other. Then he raked his hand through his hair. *Here goes nothing.*

He opened the door and peeked inside. The shaft of light from the hall spilled across Mallory, who knelt by a canopy bed. Pink ruffles and lace. A little girl's room. She held something clutched in her arms. Mac couldn't see what. She was rocking it like she would a child. His guts twisted. He had seen a lot of heartache, experienced his share, but never had he seen anything like this. The raw, jagged sounds coming from her chest sounded as if they might tear something important loose.

He didn't feel himself move toward her. Suddenly he was just there. Going down on one knee behind her, he placed a hand on her back. She jerked away, surprised, then averted her face and shrank from him. Now that he was closer, he could see that she had a tattered stuffed dog in her arms.

"Mallory...."

"It's Ragsdale," she sobbed.

"It's what?"

"Ragsdale. She c-can't sleep w-without him."

"Oh, Mallory. Come here."

Mac thought she might resist. Instead he got an armful of woman and stuffed dog. He caught her to his chest and buried his face in her hair, shocked because some of the tears flowing were his own. He had never felt anyone shake the way she was shaking. He could almost feel her pain.

"My baby. They're going to kill my baby." She clung to him as if she were about to plunge off a cliff. "I love her so much. She's afraid, I know she is. How can he do this? Oh, Mac, I can't bear it. Not my little girl. They can have everything—all of it. But not my baby... Sh-she never did anything to anyone.''

''I know.''

He wrapped his arms around her. Now it was him doing the rocking. There was a first time for everything. Mac dipped his head to wipe his cheek dry on her blouse. She smelled like the lilac bushes that bloomed in his mom's backyard each spring. He closed his eyes. ''You listen to me, okay? I'm going to do everything I can to bring Emily home. You hear me? Safe and sound. Back to you. Back to Ragsdale. I promise you that.''

''But you said Lucetti can't be found.''

''No, I said he would be hard to find. There's a difference. I'm good at what I do, Mallory. Give me a chance to prove it. If he can be found, I'll find him.'' Catching her face between his hands, Mac set her away from him so he could look into her eyes. ''I'll do everything I possibly can to bring Em home. Trust me, okay? Just trust me.''

He felt some of the tension drain out of her. She hiccuped and sniffed. ''D-do you r-really think you can?''

''Of course I do. You and I are going to find that key and get the package. We can find it. After that, getting Emily back will be simple.''

He drew her back into his arms and after a long while, she quieted. When she did, he rose to his feet and pulled her up with him. She swayed sideways and he caught her, tucking in his chin to look at the tattered toy between them. A little girl smell drifted up from the lop-eared dog, shampoo and powder and fresh-washed flannel. He could picture Emily fast asleep with the toy nestled in the crook of her arm. Moving toward the bed, he whipped back the covers and lowered Mallory to the mattress. For an instant, she looked startled to find herself lying down, then she peered up at him through the gloom, her eyelashes fluttering. Mac knew exhaustion was about to take its toll. As he straightened, he hit his head on the canopy frame. He bit back a word that should never be uttered in a little girl's bedroom and shot a glare at the ruffled contraption above him.

The child obviously had no father, or he'd have gotten rid of the darned thing.

With the back of her hand, Mallory made a halfhearted swipe at her nose and sniffed. There weren't any tissues on the nightstand. He felt for his handkerchief and couldn't find it. Sighing, he drew the covers over her and sat down. She sniffed again and made another swipe. He wasn't sure where a bathroom was, and he was afraid to leave her just yet. Tugging up one corner of the sheet, he mopped at her face. She was beyond caring, and so was he.

"Blow."

She made a snuffling noise into the sheet and he gave the tip of her small nose a careful squeeze.

Mac sighed and smoothed her hair back from her cheek. The strands were every bit as soft and silken as he had always imagined.

Her eyelashes drifted downward, wet and spiked. He watched as her lips parted slightly and her breathing changed. Her hand relaxed its hold on Ragsdale and slid partway down the dog's back. Mac touched her hair again. Rubbing it between his fingers, he smiled to himself. Definitely salon-conditioned, he decided. Hair didn't come that soft naturally.

His gaze dropped to the unused half of her pillow. Weariness and the soft sound of her breathing made him yawn. There was room enough for two. If he slept beside her, he wouldn't have to worry about her getting up in the middle of the night. The house was locked up. He stripped off his shoulder holster and laid it beside the bed. Just for a few minutes, he thought, as he stretched out next to her. An hour, tops....

Chapter Six

Just before dawn, Mallory awoke alone in Emily's bed. In the farthest reaches of her mind, she remembered the feel of Mac's body stretched out beside her during the night, the heavy warmth of his arm slung across her waist, his other hand cupped beneath her head. She lifted her lashes slowly, aware of the relentless ache in her chest before she fully opened her eyes. She had escaped the pain for a few hours, but now she had to face it.

She didn't want to. Part of her longed to stay unconscious until Em was home. Ah, but that was the catch, wasn't it? There was no guarantee that Em would ever return. Mac's reassurances had worked their magic last night, giving her hope, but now that her head was clear, she had to accept facts. The odds weren't good.

Determination filled Mallory. It was up to her to tip the scales in Em's favor. And she would. Somehow… No price was too dear, not even her own life, if it came to that.

The room was cast in shadow. As she rolled over in bed, the covers slipped down her arm and exposed her to the predawn chill. She had forgotten to turn up the thermostat. Passing a hand over her eyes, she blinked to clear her vision. As her surroundings came into focus, she spied Mac's silhouette at the window, his shoulders delineated against the charcoal gloom of the sky. She lay there and studied him, making no sound.

It made no sense, but seeing him there was a comfort. At a

time like this, Mac should seem a poor substitute for Darren or Keith, but strangely enough, she no longer felt so alone. Mac had been there for her in all the ways that counted last night. Many men would have been incapable of that kind of tenderness, especially with someone they scarcely knew.

As if he sensed her watching him, he glanced over his shoulder at her. Even in the dim light, she could see the clear gray of his eyes, feel their impact. Eyes like his touched. She knew it had to be her imagination, but that was how she felt—touched. Yesterday at the hospital that had unnerved her. Now she wasn't certain how it made her feel.

"What time is it?" she asked.

"Five. We have another three hours to get through."

Three hours...one hundred and eighty minutes...forever. She swung her legs over the edge of the bed and planted her feet on the floor. Glancing down at herself, she saw that her blouse had come partially undone and that her skirt had twisted until the sideseam was in front. She stood and quickly straightened her clothing, aware that Mac's eyes never left her, that he was watching her fumble with the buttons. She wondered what he was thinking, but when she looked up at him, she could read nothing in his expression. All she knew was that the closeness they had shared last night had evaporated. That left her feeling strangely desolate.

Mac leaned against the window frame, aware of the woman behind him with every pore of his skin. What would she say, he wondered, if he turned to her right now and told her he was Randy Watts's half brother. Because of the different last name, she probably didn't know; not unless Keith had mentioned it. And even if Keith had at some point, Mallory probably didn't remember. Fourteen years was a long time.

But Mac remembered....

Judging by his behavior last night, perhaps he hadn't remembered quite vividly enough. If he closed his eyes, he could see that cheap headstone of Randy's as clearly as though he were there, feel the rain pelting his face, hear the wind whistling. A very lonely place, that graveyard, Randy's eternal reward for having dared to believe in the great American dream…that the sky was the limit, even for poor boys. When Randy was at last forced to accept that he wasn't quite good enough in some people's eyes, the disillusionment had killed him. Mac wouldn't make the same mistake. Women like Mallory were lethal.

"Mac?" Mallory could see the rigid set of his shoulders, the knotted muscle along his jaw. He looked angry and remote. She didn't mean to sound pitiful when she said his name, but her emotions betrayed her, making her voice tremble. "I—are you—is something wrong?"

"No."

The word hung there between them. *No.* Sometimes, no meant yes, and she sensed that this was one of those times. Her first thought was that something had happened while she was asleep, that Mac was trying to work up the courage to tell her. *Emily.* She clasped her hands and pressed them against her stomach. Words slid up her throat and caught right behind her larynx, words she couldn't utter. *Emily.* Mallory felt as if she might be sick. Cold sweat trickled from her armpits down the sides of her breasts.

"It's Em, isn't it? Something's happened."

Mac shot her a puzzled look. "No. Why?"

Mallory stared at him. Running a hand through his hair, he moved away from the window. "I was just thinking, that's all. This time of morning does that to me, makes me gloomy. I didn't mean to upset you."

"You—there's nothing—they didn't—she's not—" She could hear herself babbling, but couldn't stop, couldn't sort the words once they began to erupt.

Mac laid a hand over her mouth. "She's all right, Mallory," he whispered. "I'm sorry if I frightened you."

She had an unbalanced feeling, very like when waves washed the sand out from under her on the beach. She was losing her grip, and this was how it felt to go insane. She could feel her body twitching. Taking a deep breath, Mallory quit breathing and clamped her mouth shut. Little black spots bounced in front of her eyes. She wondered if she might faint.

Mac slid a hand behind her neck to pull her face against his shoulder. He kneaded the spasm-stricken muscles in her shoulders. "You're all right, Mallory," he murmured. "It happens sometimes. Happened to me once, in fact, after a grenade hit near our foxhole. The old muscles go crazy. Stop trying to control it and just let go."

After a minute, her body began to respond to the gentle massage of his hands. The twitching slowly subsided. She stood there with her face buried against his shirt and wished she didn't have to lift her head. She had *never* in all her life acted like such a complete idiot. What was happening to her? What must Mac think? She had to get a hold on herself. She'd be of no use to Emily or anyone else if this continued.

Forcing her head up, Mallory pushed against his chest and took a wobbly step back. "I don't know what's gotten into me. You must think—I'm really sorry."

His eyes probed hers. "I think you're a mother who loves her child, that's what I think."

Hugging her breasts, Mallory averted her face and avoided looking directly at him again. "I'm going to take a shower and dress. Keith's room is down the hall. You're welcome to use his things. He's a little shorter than you, but his shirts might fit."

"I still have my luggage in the car, remember?"

"Oh, yes. Your trip. Baseball practice." Her gaze shifted to the mustard stain on his shirt, then to his sneakers, and she managed an anemic smile, remembering her first impression of him. What a great judge of character she had turned out to be. "There's a bathroom two doors down, or you can use Keith's."

She turned and walked to the doorway.

"Mallory?"

She glanced back, one hand on the doorknob. "Yes?"

His eyes locked with hers. After a long moment, he said,

"She's going to be home before you know it. Try to remember that."

She nodded. "See you downstairs."

AFTER TAKING THEIR SHOWERS, Mac and Mallory utilized the time until eight o'clock to search both of Keith's studies, this time looking everywhere, even going so far as to remove the covers from the furniture cushions. Their thoroughness turned up nothing. At seven-thirty, they headed for the kitchen to await the phone call.

Stepping to the sink to fill the coffee maker's reservoir, Mallory said, "We should be thinking of alternate places to search, don't you think, so we don't waste time once we talk to Em."

Mac drew a chair to the table and sat down. "I'm not so sure where we search is as important as *how* we go about it. There aren't that many places he might have stuck a key, are there?"

"Here," she replied. "Or in his office. Possibly his car. Other than that, I can't think of anyplace, unless he rented a locker somewhere or put it in still another deposit box."

"Let's not borrow trouble."

She flipped the brew switch on the coffee maker, and turned to face him. "He probably won't give us much time, will he? So *how* we go about looking will be crucial. Let's face it. Something as small as a key could be hidden almost anywhere. Under some loosened carpet. Inside a book. In his mattress. We could spend weeks looking."

He nodded.

"Then I say we use the process of elimination. Let's search only in the likely places first, so we can make an initial sweep. If that turns up nothing, we can backtrack and take rooms apart, piece by piece, if we must. His office first, then his car, then back here."

Mac glanced around the kitchen. "You're right. In this room alone, we could spend hours. For all we know, he could have stuck it in a cereal box or something."

"So we're agreed, a superficial search first in the obvious places, then we go deeper?"

"Agreed."

When the coffee was made, Mallory poured them each a cup, then joined Mac at the table to wait. It seemed to her that each minute was an hour long. She watched the clock. Fifteen before the hour. Then ten. Then five. Her breath began to catch as she measured off the remaining seconds. At last, the large clock hand moved forward onto the number twelve. She braced herself, her nerves raw with expectation. Nothing happened. The silence seemed deafening. And the minutes crept by.

When it became apparent that Lucetti had no intention of calling at the agreed time, Mac leaped up from his chair and let loose with a string of expletives that expressed Mallory's sentiments exactly. Then he began to pace. She counted the steps he took. Back and forth, his fist smacking his palm each time his right heel hit the tile. Just when she felt sure that the sound would drive her mad, he stopped and turned to look at her, his blond head cocked to one side, his gray eyes almost blue with anger. Leveling a finger at her nose, he said, "He'll pay for this, I promise you that."

Mallory believed it. He looked furious enough to rip someone apart. He was a big man, lean of waist and hip, with heavily muscled shoulders and arms. Sunlight poured in the sliding glass doors and surrounded him with a golden aura, creating an almost mystical effect. Even in pleated gray slacks and a fresh blue shirt with tie, he managed to look formidable. His anger surrounded her and emanated an almost electrical charge, tingling on her skin. She was glad he was in her corner; she wouldn't have wanted such a man as an enemy.

By this time, Mallory felt as if she had been injected with a gigantic syringe of novocaine. In a hollow voice, she asked, "Do you think she's dead?"

He planted his hands on his hips. "It's a mind game. He'll call. We'll talk to Em. But he wants to make us sweat first."

"But why?"

"So we'll jump when he tells us to, that's why." He grabbed

a chair, turned it around and straddled it, folding his arms across its back. After studying her with a fierce intensity that unnerved her, he said, "I know I've stressed this once before, but it's worth saying again. You can't let him bully you. Emily's life might depend on it. Insist that you be allowed to speak to her, not just this time, but every time you talk with him until we find that package. Ask her at least one question each time. We don't want him playing us a recording. He'll want to refuse. For one thing, he'll be afraid we'll put tracers on the phone. No matter what he threatens, you remember four words. *No kid, no package.*"

"But—what if he gets angry and kills her?"

Mac lifted an eyebrow. "Mallory, you and you alone can deliver that package to him. Whatever's in it, he wants it so badly that he's nabbed Emily to get it. He's desperate or he never would have done it. You *have* to remember that. You can't let fear do your thinking for you. If you want your daughter back, you're going to have to get tough."

She knew he was right. To get Em back, she would have to maintain control, bargain, threaten if she had to. She couldn't let Lucetti sense her fear. If she did, he would use it against her, and Em would be the loser. "Right. Tough, I'll be tough." She ran a hand over her hair. "I just wish he'd call."

Mac reached out and caught her hand. His fingers closed around hers, warm and strong. "Just for the record, I think you've done great so far."

Heat crept up her neck. "After last night? And then this morning?"

A slow smile lifted one corner of his mouth. "Yeah, before, during and after. Believe me, I wouldn't say it if I didn't mean it. I don't dish out praise much, especially not to—"

His eyes darkened. He let go of her hand and turned his head to gaze out the sliding glass doors at the pool deck. Mallory watched him and wondered what it was he had left unsaid. Especially not to *who?* Her? She nearly asked, but something about the rigid set of his shoulders forestalled her.

An hour passed. Then another. When the clock in the hall

chimed ten, Mallory knew firsthand what hell was like. She also knew now that you didn't have to die to go there. There was nothing Mac could say to make her feel better, so neither of them said anything. They just sat there at the breakfast table and stared at the phone on the bar. And they waited....

Mallory thought of little else but Emily. It was strange, really, the things she found herself remembering about her daughter, silly things that she scarcely noticed day to day. The way her mouth drew down at the corners when she felt disappointed, the dimples in her plump elbows, the silken hair that shimmered like gold on her upper lip when she stood in the sunshine. She remembered how it felt to snuggle with Em beneath the warm folds of her Winnie the Pooh sleeping bag on Saturday morning, their fingers sticky from eating hot Pop-Tarts, attention glued to the cartoons on television. Silly things...the sort of things only a mother would recall, things Mallory knew now she might never do again. She found herself wishing she could do them all just one more time—just once—so she could memorize every precious moment.

When the clock struck ten-thirty, the phone rang almost simultaneously. Both of them leaped from their chairs and whirled to stare at it. Then sanity returned. Mallory crossed the room, made sure the speaker was on and lifted the receiver. "H-hello?"

"Mrs. Christiani? I trust you slept well?"

The voice on the other end of the line was so smug that anger flashed through Mallory. She tightened her grip on the phone. "I slept quite well, thank you."

The silence that followed her cool reply gave her a sense of satisfaction. Mac had been right. Lucetti had delayed calling to gain an emotional advantage. For once, she was grateful to her mother. She might sweat, but Lucetti would never know it.

"Listen carefully. I have reason to believe that—"

"Excuse me," Mallory cut in. "You're forgetting I requested that my daughter be put on the phone. First things first."

"Have you ever visited the King County Morgue to identify a body, Mrs. Christiani?"

Mallory's legs quivered. She glanced at Mac, licked her lips and said, "Yes, as a matter of fact. I'm a retired nurse and I've worked in the hospital morgue." Mac's eyes locked with hers and he gave her a thumbs-up signal as he walked toward her. A proud grin slanted across his mouth. She pressed a trembling hand to her throat. "I think perhaps we've reached a stalemate. Mr. Mac Phearson made our position quite clear last night. Call back when you can put my daughter on the phone."

With that, Mallory hung up. For a moment, absolute silence resounded in the room. Then Mac let out his breath in a rush. Mallory threw him a frightened look.

"Oh, Mac—" She clamped a hand over her mouth and closed her eyes.

Mac came over to stand beside her. "You did the right thing. He'll call back, honey. And when he does, he won't play mind games."

Mallory nodded and made an odd little sound behind her palm, half sob and half hysterical laughter. She prayed he was right, that she hadn't just signed Em's death warrant. The phone rang again, making her jerk. Her eyes flew open. Mac put an arm around her and held her clasped to his side as she reached out for the phone.

"Just stay cool," he whispered.

Mallory gulped down panic and lifted the receiver. "Hello?"

"Mommy?"

Joy welled within Mallory, so intense that she couldn't speak for a moment. She moved closer to the phone, as if somehow she could get closer to her child. That precious little voice ran over her like sunshine. "Em? Oh, Em! How are you, princess?"

"Fine. Mommy, why didn't you tell me I had to stay someplace new? I felt awfully angry with you at first. Is Gramps better yet? I'm tired of staying places. I wanna come home. I miss you, Mommy. And you forgot to bring me Ragsdale." She made a clucking sound with her tongue. "You promised you would when we found out I forgot him, remember. I've had bad mares for two nights now.''

The scolding note in her daughter's voice brought a fresh rush of tears. "Nightmares, you mean? Not bad ones, I hope? I wanted to bring you Ragsdale, darling, but something came up and I—I couldn't. Em, are the people there treating you nice?''

"Yes, but I'm—" Emily's voice broke off "—homesick. I can't talk more, Mommy. We don't got enough quarters.''

"Em? Em!''

"Satisfied, Mrs. Christiani?''

Mallory leaned heavily against Mac, drawing strength from him. "For the moment, yes.''

"I'll call back with the instructions.''

The phone clicked and went dead. Mallory threw Mac another panicked glance. "He's afraid to stay on the line too long in case we're trying to trace him," he explained. "It'll be a few minutes. He'll call from another phone so he can't be located.''

Mallory grabbed the back of a bar stool and swung into it. "That was the hardest thing I've ever done in my life. The very hardest.''

"I know, but you didn't show it. That's what counts. I thought you were the lady who couldn't act?''

Mallory leaned her head back. "That wasn't an act. It was just—" She broke off and licked her lower lip. "You'd have to know my mother. A regimental upbringing comes in handy.''

Mac lifted an eyebrow. "Regimental?''

Mallory met his gaze. "How long before he calls?''

He glanced at his watch. "Another five minutes, probably. So we wait again." He studied her for a moment. "I'm curious. What is a regimental upbringing? Tell me about your mom.''

Mallory hesitated, but something in his expression—she had no idea what—made her start talking. When she finished, she couldn't remember exactly what she had said, but Mac's expression, which had started her talking in the first place, had subtly altered. "Do you like your mother?"

"Of course I do. I love her."

"That isn't what I asked."

"I admire her."

"But do you like her?"

Mallory frowned. "That's a terrible thing to ask."

"Only when you can't say yes." He caught her by the chin, his eyes searching hers. Then the phone rang and interrupted them. Mallory turned on the bar stool, her heart slamming.

"Wait for the third ring so we don't appear too anxious."

Her hand shook as she reached for the receiver. "Hello?"

"Listen carefully," the now-familiar voice hissed. "As I mentioned last night, I have reason to believe your father-in-law put the package in his safe-deposit box. You find that box key and get the package. Once you have it, return with it to your home. I'll phone you there to arrange a meeting place for the exchange."

"How will you know when I've gotten the box opened?"

"I have you under constant surveillance, so I'll know."

"And what if I can't find the key?"

"For your child's sake, find it. You have twenty-four hours. Countdown begins now."

The moment the phone went dead, Mallory dropped the receiver and made a fist in her hair. "Twenty-four hours! He can't expect—what kind of miracle worker does he think I am?"

"That's not what has me worried. Are you on the safe-deposit contract at the bank?"

"The what?"

"The contract. It just occurred to me that if you aren't authorized to open that box, key or no key, they won't let you touch it. Did you ever go in to the bank and sign a release?"

Pressing her hand to her forehead, Mallory tried to remember. "I—I don't know. I've signed so many things. After Darren died, there was so much red tape, so many contracts and releases and affidavits. Keith, being a lawyer, was relentless about having everything done to the letter.''

"Let's hope he didn't forget any minor details, like giving you access to his deposit box. If you aren't on that contract, it would take a court order to get the box opened even with a key.''

Mallory's hopes lifted. "But, Mac, if I *am* on the contract, couldn't I have the box drilled myself?''

"Sure. But it might take too much time. One locksmith is authorized by the bank chain to drill their boxes, and it'd be our luck he'd be in Spokane or someplace. Let's see about the contract first.''

Mac leafed through the phone book, ran his finger down a page, then punched out a phone number. A woman's voice came over the speaker, "Good morning, Ann speaking.''

"Yes, Ann, this is Keith Christiani. I'd like to do some checking on my safe-deposit box contract. I need to find out if my daughter-in-law, Mallory Christiani, is down as an authorized user?''

"One moment, please.'' When the woman came back on the line, she said, "No, Mrs. Christiani's signature isn't on file. If you'd like for her to be, it's a simple matter of signatures.''

Mac closed his eyes for a moment in disappointment, then angled a meaningful look at Mallory. "I might do that. Well, um, thank you.'' Dropping the receiver into its cradle, Mac turned and leaned a hip against the counter. "That's not good news.''

Mallory could feel her blood pounding in her temples, hear the pulse beats going *swish—swish* in her ears. "But we *have* to open it. What are we going to do? Does that mean that even if we manage to find the key, we can't get the package?''

A distant, thoughtful look crept into his eyes. "No, it just means we can't get it legally.''

"Meaning?''

"Meaning that once we find the key, I'll have to forge Keith's signature and pray I'm good enough they don't suspect.''

"Couldn't you get in trouble? What if they caught you? Someone there might know Keith on sight. He isn't exactly a nobody in town, you know! If they're that strict about who can open those boxes, you could be arrested or something."

"It wouldn't be the first time." He chucked her under the chin. "Don't look so horrified. It isn't a hanging offense."

"You mean it, don't you? You'd actually risk jail."

"Don't pin wings on my shoulders. You can't pass for Keith, so I'm elected, simple as that. So where do we start? His car or the office? We have to start searching. Like you said, a key could be almost anywhere."

A key. A cold prickle began at Mallory's nape and crept up to her scalp. Keith's face flashed before her. She remembered how his hand had clawed the air when she had mentioned that her father had lost the motor-home key. Now she realized what he had been trying to tell her. "Mac!"

He glanced over at her. "What?"

In a rush, she told him what had occurred yesterday. "Do you suppose we could set up some kind of signal to question him?"

Mac shook his head. "It's no use. I tried that yesterday before you arrived. He hasn't got enough control over his body. If he could open and close his eyes upon command—anything like that—we could set up a signal, but he can't. Trying just frustrates him. Unless he improves dramatically, we're on our own." He sighed. "Well? Where do you want to look first?"

"My vote is his office. He was there when he collapsed, so it seems the most logical starting point. And if the key isn't there, maybe we'll find a clue to lead us to it."

Chapter Seven

The moment Mac and Mallory stepped into the lobby of the law firm, they froze. The elegant room looked as if a quake had hit: furniture upside down, plants dumped on the rug, paintings hanging askew. Trudy, the secretary, sat at her rifled desk speaking on the telephone with the insurance adjuster, one hand buried in her graying blond hair. Her tortoiseshell eyeglasses were perched on the end of her nose so she could see over the rims to assess the damage.

"Nothing valuable was stolen, and nothing seems to be missing from our files." She rolled her eyes. "And how long will that take? I can't leave things like *this*, you know."

"What on earth happened?" Mallory asked, the moment Trudy hung up.

"Vandals," she replied with a groan. "This is how I found it this morning. Awful, isn't it? All three offices. Keith's got it the worst." She shrugged one shoulder. "I wasn't going to tell you. I figured you had enough on your plate."

Mac stepped over a pile of potting soil and the wilted remains of a fern. "How many offices in the building were hit?"

"Only ours. I guess we were the most convenient."

Mac's gray eyes met Mallory's in silent communication. Turning simultaneously, they headed for Keith's office. The mess in the lobby didn't prepare Mallory for the destruction that greeted them. Nothing of Keith's had been left unmolested. Even his law books lay scattered on the floor. His files had been dumped, his desk gutted, the phones disassembled. The top had even been pried off the IBM Selectric. His sofa and chair had been slit open, the stuffing strewn everywhere on the rug. With a grim scowl, Mac planted his hands on his hips and surveyed the wreckage.

"Well, I wonder if they found it."

Mallory could only stare. The photos of her and Em had been taken apart. Keith's snow globe was shattered. Clearly the intruders had been searching for something small, like a key. "What if they did? Why is he doing this? I don't understand."

"Doesn't make sense, does it?" He sighed and gave the room another once-over. "From the looks of things, they didn't miss anything. That's a good indication."

"It must be Lucetti. It has to be. Who else could it be?"

"That's a question I can't even start to answer. And, given the time schedule, I don't have time to find out. Tunnel vision, Mallory. We have to stay focused on one thing, finding that damned key." He scattered a pile of papers with the toe of his loafer. "Why is he undermining you like this?"

She walked to a file. "Looking now will be twice as hard. He must realize that. Maybe it wasn't even Lucetti who did it."

"And if not, then who?" He shook his head. "No point in even bothering to look here."

She knew he was right, but desperation made her refuse to admit it. "They might have missed it. A key is so small."

"Mallory." Mac's voice was low pitched and persuasive. "Come on. It's hopeless. They put everything through a sifter."

"Let's check his car, then."

"Where is it? We've got to get ahead of them."

"Out back."

Trudy was on the phone rescheduling appointments when they returned to the lobby. She excused herself and said, "Awful, isn't it?"

"Sure is," Mac agreed. "Did you call the police?"

"First thing."

He gave a brisk nod. "We'll be in touch, okay?"

"Tell Keith I'm thinking of him. I hoped to go see him today if they moved him from the ICU, but this—" she waved her hand at the mess "—has changed my plans." Her green eyes rested on Mallory's pale face and clouded with sympathy. "Keep your chin up, honey. He'll pull through."

Guilt washed over Mallory. She hadn't given poor Keith much thought since yesterday. Not trusting herself to speak, she slipped out the door ahead of Mac. Leading the way down the hall to the front exit, she blinked back tears. Tears wouldn't help Em. Like Mac said, she had to get tough. If only it were her in danger instead of her child. She felt so helpless. All her maternal instincts were screaming at her to do something. As she drew near the door, it seemed to her that the tapping of her heels sang, *The key, the key, you have to find the key.* If someone else had found it, how could she ransom her daughter? How much of their twenty-four hours had been wasted by coming here? Time was slipping away, each second taking them closer to deadline. Her mind stumbled on the first half of that word. *Dead.* Oh, Em, I love you. I couldn't bear losing you.

She felt Mac come up behind her, felt his sleeve brush the back of hers.

"You okay?"

Mallory sighed and glanced over her shoulder at him. How many times had he asked her that since last night? Concern lined his face. Well, that was all about to change. A person could only become so scared. Then numbness set in. After that came resignation. Lucetti had Em, and there was nothing she could do to change that. But that didn't mean she couldn't fight back.

When she stepped outside, the morning breeze touched her cheeks and whispered softly through her hair. Above her in a gnarled elm, a pair of birds twittered and hopped from branch to branch, celebrating the sunshine. Tipping her face skyward, Mallory absorbed the warmth and parted her lips to take a bracing draught of fresh air. The expanse of blue overhead was the color of robin eggs, the clouds fluffy wisps of white. "Do you believe in God, Mac?"

He studied the branches silhouetted above them, the azure sky, as if the answer to her question lay there. "Not the way you probably do. I don't attend church and go to pancake breakfasts, that kind of stuff."

Her gaze rested on his upturned profile, on the crooked bridge of his nose, the tiny scar above his eyebrow, the rock-hard line of his jaw. He was incredibly handsome, but not in a refined way, more rugged and rough, like one might expect an ex-boxer to look. She tried to imagine him at a stuffy church brunch and found herself smiling the first real smile in days. Did he really think the sum total of her life revolved around linen napkins and place settings? "But you do believe?"

His gray eyes fell to hers, eyes so clear, so transparent that a reply wasn't necessary. "He watches out for fools and children, you know. She's going to come through this okay."

Taking another deep breath, she stuffed her hands deep into her blazer pockets. "Yes, I think she is, too. I *know* it. I've already lost my husband. It wouldn't be fair if I lost Em."

"Nope, sure wouldn't."

"Besides," she added lightly, "we have you on our side. I'd say that stacks the odds in our favor."

With that unsettling vote of confidence, she turned and struck off down the walkway toward the corner of the building.

Spying a pay phone, he asked her to wait.

She slowed her pace and fell in beside him to walk to the booth. Mac quickly scanned the area, then left her outside, digging in his pocket for a quarter. Dropping the coin into the slot, he punched out Shelby's number. *No answer.* With a sigh, he hung up and left the booth, shrugging one shoulder.

"It figures. Good ol' Shelb. Never home when I need him."

He trailed her to the back parking lot, his gaze shifting constantly, alert for movements between the cars, in the shrubbery. He didn't want to remind Mallory of the men who had tried to kill them yesterday, especially not right now when she seemed to be rallying, but it was something he couldn't afford to forget. Someone else searching for the key might prove to be the least of their problems. She led the way to a silver Lincoln, then stopped to stare at it in dismay.

"What is it?" he asked.

"Keys! My set was on the ring that was stolen yesterday."

"I carry a master key in my car. Be right back."

She watched him take off at a lope toward the client parking area on the other side of the building. A master key? Until now, she hadn't known such a thing existed. Moments later, he returned with two long pieces of flat, flexible metal with yellow handles at one end and cutout hooks at the other. "Slim Jims."

"I thought those were illegal unless you worked for a company that had uses for them."

"I'm a company, and I definitely have a use for them." A flush crept up his neck as he worked the pieces of metal through the crack of the car window and fished with the hooks for a hold on the lock switch. "Mallory, there are two things you need to learn. Turn your head and don't look if I ask you to, and don't say the word *illegal* loud enough for a cop to hear. Even when I'm completely legitimate, it makes me nervous."

A grin curved her mouth. "Then they *are* illegal."

Teasing laughter lit up his eyes. "Only if I get caught or someone yells *illegal* at the top of her lungs in a public parking lot." He stepped back and opened the car door. "The end justifies the means. Scouts honor, I don't steal stereos."

He muttered something else under his breath as he leaned inside the car. "Pardon me?" she queried. He muttered it again and she moved closer. "Sorry...what?"

He threw her a glare. "I said I don't, anymore." He was fanning his arm under the driver's seat, so the words came up from the floorboard muffled.

"You don't what anymore?"

"Steal stereos."

Mallory's grin disappeared. "Oh, come on, you've never robbed people's cars with those."

"It's called thugging, not robbing. And no, not with these. My old set had black handles. Yellow would show up after dark like a beacon. *These* are legally in my possession and I only use them for legitimate purposes. In my line of work, getting into cars is often a necessity. I've cracked a lot of cases from clues I found in locked automobiles." When he straightened, he hit his head on the steering wheel and cursed under his breath, rubbing his temple as he fell back against the seat. He hesitated when he saw her staring at him, and his scowl deepened. "What's the matter? Did I just lose my angel wings?"

Was that hostility she saw flaring in his eyes? She avoided looking directly at him. "Not at all. I'm simply curious. You're saying you were a thugger of automobiles?"

"A *thugger*? Mallory, thugging is something you do, not what you are. And I really don't want to get into my history."

Her eyes flew back to his. "That isn't fair. Why say something like that if you don't want to elaborate?"

"Because I didn't want to give you a false—" He broke off, his jaw muscle knotting as he clenched and unclenched his teeth. "Elaborate? You spew big words like a walking dictionary."

She hadn't imagined the hostility. It glowed like banked embers in his eyes. What had she said or done to set him off?

"You know what bugs me the worst about people like you?" he snapped. "You're *relieved* I got the car open, *glad* I had the Slim Jims, but you'll still stand there and look superior because my having them may be on the shady side of legal." He pressed the panel button to unlock all the Lincoln's doors, his eyes narrowed. "I'm sorry if I offend your refined sensibilities. Don't worry. I'm not breaking the law, okay?"

The contempt in his expression was unmistakable. Since *sensibilities* wasn't exactly monosyllabic, she wondered what his problem was. "What do you mean, people like me? Just what kind of a person am I?"

"Let's just drop it." He slid out of the car and loomed over her, the Slim Jims dangling from his right hand. In slacks and a sport coat, he looked too respectable to have ever engaged in street theft. "We've got a key to find, remember? No time to discuss your character faults." He slanted her a look that spoke volumes. "Or *mine*. Don't worry. I won't rub off on you. Hopefully the same will hold true in reverse."

She felt as if she had been slapped. He was already back inside the car, running his hands along the underside of the dash. She went around to the passenger side. As she rifled the glove box, she said, "You think I'm a snob, don't you?"

He jerked down the visor. "You said it."

She slammed the box closed and nearly stood on her head to check the underside of the seat. "Well, I'm not. You shouldn't judge people before you know them."

"If that isn't the pot calling the— Oh, never mind. I don't want to argue with you, Mallory, okay? We have enough trouble."

"When have I behaved like a snob to you? Name one time?"

"You need me right now, though. Naturally you'll treat me nice. Let's see how thick we are when this is over, shall we?"

"Are you implying that I'm *using* you? That I'm only being civil because I need you?"

He made no reply. His silence was all the answer she needed. He opened the rear door on his side of the car. She did likewise and watched him pull on the back seat. When she realized he was trying to remove it from the car, she grabbed handholds to help him. "One question, Mr. Mac Phearson. If you dislike people like me so much, why are you doing all this?"

Stony silence was his only response.

"Are you going to answer me? Why put yourself out for a Bellevue *snob* that spews words like a walking encyclopedia?"

"*Dictionary*." He tipped the seat at an angle so it would fit through the door opening. Seconds later, he pulled it free. "I told you, I owe Keith. Isn't that good enough? Or don't you people repay favors?"

He made it sound as if she came from another planet. "Someone *did* try to kill us yesterday. I suppose that's an everyday occurrence to *you* people.'' It gave her a perverse satisfaction to see him flinch. Served him right. There was such a thing as reversed snobbery, and he had a bad case of it.

She marched around the rear bumper, her heels snapping smartly on the asphalt to emphasize her anger. Unfortunately Mac was too busy looking the seat over to notice. That infuriated her all the more. In the back of her mind, she knew she was overreacting and tried to calm down. Grabbing an end, she helped him turn it upside down. ''Hold your side up higher,'' he ordered.

She obliged, watching as he poked and prodded the springs and frame. ''It must have been a big favor Keith did for you.''

''Big enough.''

''Well, I'm not sure I like being a payback. Especially when you so clearly dislike me.''

His eyes lifted to hers. ''Have I said I don't like you?''

''Yes.''

''I have not.''

''Yes you di—'' A hissing pop filled the air, and a *twang* resounded as something hit the metal framing inside the seat. Bits of leather and cotton batting pelted her face. She stared at the gaping hole in the upholstery where an instant ago there had been gray leather. There wasn't time to wonder what had made the hole. Before her brain could register what her eyes and ears took in, Mac sacked her in a football tackle, his arms locked around her waist as they fell. Mallory landed on her back, Mac sprawled on top of her, the force of his weight flattening her. Lights flashed before her eyes, then black spots. She couldn't breathe. When her vision cleared, she saw Mac above her, his upper body supported by his elbows, his eyes scanning the parking lot. He focused on something and went pale.

''Son of a—'' He sprang to his feet, back hunched, knees bent, and jerked her up beside him. Mallory's rubbery legs failed her and she slid along behind him on one knee, ripping her panty hose, scraping herself from shin to ankle. The sheer force of his forward momentum finally hauled her to her feet.

He shielded her with his body as they ran the length of the car. "Stay down! When we reach those shrubs, make a dive for them and roll until you're covered by branches."

Another muffled pop. Air whooshed from one of the Lincoln's tires and the car rocked. A gun? In her terror, even with a silencer, it sounded more like a cannon. *Oh, please, God...* "Someone's shooting!" Another bullet splattered asphalt right in front of them. "Dive!" he cried. She saw the shrubs looming ahead of her. *Safety.* She dived, landing chest first on the lawn two feet short of her mark, and did a third-base skid on her stomach into the bark chips and juniper needles. Pain washed through her. Clawing for purchase, she slithered farther into the foliage, unaware of Mac beside her until she felt his arm across her back.

Mallory inched her head up. At the end of an adjacent building, she glimpsed a man as he eased out from around the corner to point something long and dark brown in their direction. Sunlight glinted off something shiny. Before she could react, Mac pushed her down hard.

"Keep down," he whispered.

"You don't have to be so rough."

"You'll know what rough is if half your head gets blown off. That's a high-powered rifle he's taking potshots with." Two more muffled shots rang out. He took a shaky breath and let it out slowly. "Do a Marine crawl to the corner of the building."

"A what?"

He threw her a look that plainly said any idiot should know what a Marine crawl was. "A belly crawl. Dig your elbows into the dirt to pull yourself. Use your knees and toes to push." With a nod of his head, he indicated that she should go first. Mallory pushed off. The next instant he smacked his palm on her bottom. "Keep your butt down!"

She threw him an incredulous glance over her shoulder. Nobody had dared to slap her on the behind in over a quarter of a century, but this wasn't the right time to argue with his methods. Burying her elbows in the bark dust, she pushed forward with her toes. Just as she did, there was another explosion of noise and the ground ahead of her geysered in her face. She stared at the crater left in the dirt. Suddenly it hit her that the noises exploding around them were *real* bullets being fired, the kind that blew holes in you, and one had just missed her by mere inches. Fear held her rooted.

"Move!" Mac snarled behind her. "Now!"

His snarl prodded her forward. She could feel him crawling next to her, keeping his body between her and the sniper. She kept hearing a strange noise—a panting, whining sound. After several feet, she realized it was her. She clamped her mouth shut, not wanting to give their position away, but the noises came out through her nostrils. Her blouse had either ripped or come unfastened, and every time she dragged herself forward, bark scraped and poked her bare skin. A sheared off branch jabbed her collarbone.

By the time they made it to the corner, she felt certain all her hide had been rubbed off. A sharp piece of wood had gotten inside her bra, but she didn't dare rise to remove it. They crab-walked around the building and inched their way toward Mac's Volvo.

"You stay put," Mac whispered. "I'll bring the car to you."

Mallory didn't have a chance to protest. Mac lunged to his feet and sprang forward in a zigzag run. Another shot rang out and a bullet zinged through the air where he had been only a millisecond earlier. It plowed into the building, spraying mortar and bits of brick. She dug her fists into the loose bark and held her breath, terrified for him. Two more shots rang out.

In all her life, she had never seen anyone move with such precision, powerful legs thrusting his body from side to side, eating up distance at an incredible speed even though he took an indirect path. This wasn't the first time he had dodged bullets. His military training? She closed her eyes for an instant to send up a fervent prayer. And not just because she needed him. He was a very special man. In the past day, he had proven himself to be a loyal friend to Keith—and to her—at least a dozen times.

In the distance, she heard police sirens. Someone must have heard the shots despite the silencer. Probably poor Trudy. Mac reached the Volvo, threw open the door and literally dived inside. The next instant, the car engine roared to life. She stared through the juniper and watched as the car bounced onto the walkway. When he cut the tires toward the shrub beds, she realized that when he had said he would bring the car to her, he had meant exactly that. He was coming straight at her. The front grill snowplowed through the evergreens and bent a small fir tree double. Mallory jumped up and out of the way just in time, not sure even then that he wasn't going to drive right over her. The car swerved at the last second. He leaned sideways to throw the passenger door open, his harsh "Get in!" nearly drowned out by the roar of the engine.

She scrambled to obey. The moment she hit the seat, she slammed the door closed. A pop rang out, and a star-ringed hole splattered the windshield. She slipped down between the seat and the dashboard. The Volvo scraped bottom over another twenty feet of shrubs, then grated over the walkway curb as it dropped to the asphalt.

Grabbing the dash, Mallory eased her head up. Mac was guiding the car deftly in and out around parked vehicles. She knew what to expect this time and wasn't surprised when they careened into westbound traffic and headed toward Hunt's Point.

Several minutes passed before either of them realized they weren't being pursued. The sounds of the sirens had become more distant. Mac eased up on the gas pedal and blew air like a surfacing whale. "They must have decided to back off when they heard cops coming. You can get up now."

She slid back onto the seat and fastened her belt with shaking hands. "Who do you think they are? Lucetti's men?" She raked a hand through her hair. "It's bad enough that he gave me only twenty-four hours. Does he have to complicate matters by trying to kill us?"

Mac said nothing. From the frown that pleated his forehead, she knew he was trying to think. He drove aimlessly, taking a narrow road around the lake. After several miles, he relaxed. When he glanced over at her, he did a double take. "You're cut."

She glanced down and saw blood on her chest. She also saw that her top had indeed come unfastened and she was sporting scrapes from her waistband to her collarbone. She plucked the sharp piece of wood out of her bra and tried to do up her blouse, only to find that three buttons were missing. In defeat, she tugged her blazer together in front and buttoned it instead.

He looked over at her and chuckled. "If you could only see yourself. A day in my company and you're ruined for life."

She glanced down. "You're not exactly a prize winner yourself, you know."

Their eyes met and held for an instant, then he returned his attention to his driving. Perhaps coming so close to death was making her magnanimous, or maybe it was simply the bond of friendship that she sensed was developing between them, but their recent quarrel suddenly seemed ridiculous.

"Mac, I—" She licked her lips. "About the Slim Jims. I didn't mean to be judgmental. And I'm afraid I overreacted."

One of his eyebrows arched as he executed a left turn. "Slim Jims? Judgmental? What are you talking about?"

He reached over and placed his hand over hers, his grip warm and all too fleeting. He said nothing more, but he didn't need to. Whatever it was that she had done to rile him, he seemed as sorry as she about what had been said. She took a deep breath and sighed. "So what's our next plan of action?"

"I say we go back to the house. The office is out. We've checked the car. It's time to execute Plan B."

She didn't miss the troubled expression that lined his face as he made a U-turn. "What's wrong?"

"I'm not sure. It just doesn't make sense. You're cooperating in every way possible, right down to not calling the cops. So what's Lucetti stand to gain by having you killed?"

"Nothing," she agreed. "In fact, I'm the most likely person to succeed in finding the key and getting him the package. I know more about Keith's habits and personal affairs than anyone.''

"Exactly. If you're out of the picture, he may never get that package. That's what bothers me.''

Mallory considered that a moment. "Maybe it has nothing to do with Lucetti. It could be someone connected with your work.''

"No way. For one thing, I don't have any deadly enemies. And for another, those fellows have pro written all over them. They're sharp. This whole mess has Lucetti's stamp on it. Besides, if it *was* someone after me, why would they ransack Keith's office? Doesn't make sense.''

"Maybe there's someone else involved, someone connected to Lucetti, who doesn't want me to give Lucetti the package.''

"You took the words right out of my mouth. All we have to do is figure out who. And why. Which is an impossible order, considering we have so little time. We're caught between a rock and a hard spot. The only option we have that I can see is to continue searching and be more careful about guarding our backs so we stay alive while we're doing it. Meanwhile I'll keep trying my friend Shelby. If I can get in touch with him, he can run some feelers out for me and, with some luck, find out who the people after us are.''

"And then?''

"Well, if we're right, and they're somehow connected to the racketeering, we can give Lucetti some names the next time he calls, have a little more fact to back us up. Then maybe he'll get them off our backs. As it stands, he doesn't believe me, thinks they're connected to my work. We won't have much luck convincing him to take care of the problem unless I can convince him we *have* one.''

Chapter Eight

The drive back to Mallory's went without a hitch. With the sun shining and the wonderfully warm air gusting through the open windows, it seemed like any of a hundred May days when she had driven home through downtown Bellevue. Business-people emerged from the mirrored skyscrapers and hustled along the sidewalks. Shoppers from Bellevue Square juggled packages as they scurried across the streets. The world continued its regular schedule. While Mac stopped to make another unsuccessful attempt to contact his friend, Mallory waited with a feeling of unreality. It didn't seem possible that someone had tried to kill them.

Before turning into the cul-de-sac where Mallory lived, Mac drove up and down the adjacent streets. They saw nothing suspicious. A few minutes later, when Mac pulled the Volvo into her driveway, the house looked so cheerfully ordinary she almost expected Em to come bounding down the steps. She could picture her against the rose-pink rhododendrons, tendrils of hair slipping out of her braids, eyes twinkling. After Mac parked, they sat there in silence and listened to the crackle-pop of the cooling engine. There was no through traffic here at the end of the cul-de-sac, so they felt safe enough to take a moment's rest.

He turned to look at her, his gray eyes gentle. A muscle in his jaw flickered as he touched the cut on her collarbone. His hand drifted up the side of her neck to lift her hair. She loosened her grip on the door handle as he traced the hollow of her temple where her pulse had suddenly begun to throb. Maybe it was almost dying, or maybe it was simply a need to be held, but she felt like a wax figure that had been placed too close to a furnace. She let her eyes almost close.

Behind the veil of her lashes, she studied him, remembering how he had looked dodging bullets. A potent combination of good looks and rugged, old-fashioned masculinity, that was Mac. Nothing like her father in his expensive suits and silk ties. Garrison Steele would have lain beside her in the shrubs and quivered with fear if someone had been shooting at them. She couldn't quite bring herself to think of her arrogant, over-bearing father as weak, but he fell short somehow when compared to the man beside her.

"I didn't mean to be so rough when we were crawling through the bushes," he said huskily. "I know I hurt you a couple of times. I don't have a light touch when I get scared, I'm afraid."

"Oh, Mac...you didn't hurt me."

"Then why does the end of your nose look like I smacked you? Seems to me I remember shoving your face in the dirt."

The rasp of his fingers against her skin sent a shiver over her. With a feeling akin to horror, she recognized her body's reaction, and it had nothing to do with nearly dying or needing comfort. Perhaps fear and sensuality were like hate and love, divided only by a thin line. She had read about a syndrome—couldn't remember the clinical term—where people became infatuated with one another in dangerous situations. Was that what was happening? Terror playing havoc with her hormones?

She tried to break eye contact with him and was powerless to do so. What if he read her feelings? He was reaching out to her as a friend, nothing more. His fingertips stilled on the curve of her neck. Almost imperceptibly, his face drew closer. Then his expression became quizzical, uncertain, and he withdrew as though the touch of her burned him. Throwing open his door, he exited the car in a rush.

She pushed her own door open and climbed out. He threw her another look over the top of the car, then turned to gaze at the house. He stood with his back to her, head tipped back, arms akimbo. His hair shone like burnished gold. She walked around the front of the car, her face averted, her cheeks scalding hot. What must he think?

"Mallory?"

She ignored him and climbed the steps. The only explanation for her behavior was that she was losing her mind. She had only known him for a day. Keith was gravely ill. Em's life was in danger. And he had been the one to pull away?

"Mallory, for Pete's sake—" He was right behind her.

She reached into her purse for the house key. The moment she pushed it at the lock, the door swung in. Fear flashed through her. When Mac saw that the door was ajar, he seized her by the arm and spun her away, pushing her against the house as he stepped sideways. He slipped his hand under his jacket and pulled out his gun.

He moved back to peer through the now yawning doorway. "Don't move," he whispered to her. "I'm going in. If anything happens, run to the nearest neighbor's."

She wanted to tell him to stay with her on the porch where he'd be safe, but he had already moved beyond her reach, disappearing across the threshold. She held her breath and listened. The sound of her own pulse seemed deafening. Seconds dragged by, and stretched into minutes. Her fear mounted. Where was he? She imagined someone leaping out and hitting him over the head, pictured him lying unconscious someplace inside while she stood here, letting him bleed to death or something…like Darren.

When she could bear the waiting no longer, she inched out from the wall and peeked into the silent entry. She couldn't just stand there. She *was* a nurse, after all. *Nothing.* Emboldened, she crept inside, her skin aquiver as she moved the length of the hall and angled frightened glances into the rooms as she passed. The house had been ripped apart, paintings pulled off the walls, lamps overturned, furniture slashed, books thrown from the shelves. Where was Mac? The kitchen was a disaster, drawers dumped, food spilled, flour everywhere.

Mallory couldn't believe so much damage had been done during their brief absence. Forgetting to be silent, she spun and ran back into the entry hall. As she came abreast of the den, someone stepped out the doorway directly into her path. She screamed as she plowed into a broad chest. Strong hands grasped her shoulders.

"I thought I told you to stay put?"

Her knees almost buckled. "Oh, Mac, you scared me to death."

"Good," he growled. "Next time, do what I tell you."

"I was afraid you might be hurt."

His grip grew so tense she could feel him trembling. From the look on his face, she had the feeling he wanted to shake her. "You do what I tell you, *exactly* what I tell you, is that clear?"

As recently as yesterday afternoon, an order issued to her with such undiluted arrogance would have galled her. However, as short a time as had passed since, she had come to know Mac quite well. He was angry, all right, not so much over what she had done, but because she might have been hurt doing it. Knowing that, she was able to bite back her retort. She disliked playing the role of helpless female, but she supposed he was justified in thinking of her as one. Deadly skirmishes weren't her area of expertise.

Apparently satisfied that he had drilled his point home, he sighed and planted his hands on his hips. "The house has been ransacked."

She had already ascertained that much but it didn't seem wise to say so.

"They went through everything, even the pillows and your talcum powder. The lids are off the toilet tanks. Every place where something could have been hidden has been checked."

"Do you think they found it?"

"Not from the looks of this house. They even tore up Keith's jackets." He raked a hand through his hair. "This has got me worried. Somebody wants that key awful darned bad. Which leads us back to the original question. Why are those ledgers so important? Could someone not want Lucetti getting them? Do they want them for themselves? Who is Steven Miles? Could it be him behind this? Two of those guys must have come here while the third was at the law firm trying to blow us away.''

"I've never heard of an accountant named Miles.''

He groaned with frustration and threw up his hands. "We don't have time for this. I wish I could have reached Shelby. At least he could do some legwork, ask questions.''

"I think we ought to search here again. Plan B, remember? Take apart the light fixtures, the bedposts, everything. They might have missed something we won't.'' She was afraid he might disagree. "It's a big house. They couldn't have looked everywhere.''

"Where do you think we should start?''

"You take Keith's bedroom. I'll take his study. We'll spread out from there.''

"Maybe not. We might find it by then, you know.'' He flashed her a grin and touched her chin gently with his fist.

SUNLIGHT GLINTED off the cream-colored paint of the car's hood and momentarily blinded George Paisley. He squinted to see the traffic light. "Well, what's our next move?''

On the passenger side, Paul Fields slanted a questioning glance at Dennis in the back seat. "You're the brains, Godbey. What next?''

Dennis gazed out his window. "We're back at square one.''

"Eliminating her isn't going to be as easy as you guys thought, though.'' George glanced sideways at Fields. "Mac Phearson is a problem. What did you dig up on him?''

"Mostly just bad news.'' Fields shuffled through some papers on his lap. "Several brushes with the law as a kid, all misdemeanors. Lied about his age and joined the Marines at fifteen. Rated an Expert Marksman when he finished boot camp in San Diego. Came home from Vietnam with honors, would you believe? Just what we needed, a real live hero. Single. Got out of the service, became a security guard. Lost his only brother at twenty-five. Took to some serious drinking.'' He glanced up. ''This isn't documented, but I went by the firm where he first started doing P.I. work and a lady there told me that Keith Christiani hauled him out of the gutter, dried him out and helped him get his life back together. Later, he footed the bill for some classes in law, vouched for his good character and got him on at her firm as an investigator. He opened his own agency eight years ago.''

''I wonder if he can be bought off?'' Dennis mused.

''Have you gotten a load of the Christiani woman? Come on.'' Fields chuckled. ''And he's in to his eyebrows, even without that. Probably feels beholden to the old man. Heroes can't be bought. They're too damned dumb.''

''Hey, it'd be worth a try,'' Geroge argued. ''Money talks. With a healthy bribe, he could buy a dozen pretty broads if that's one of his weak spots. And we wouldn't have to kill his little friend. The kid would be the only casualty, and that's not on our conscience.''

''Does he have any experience with explosives?'' Dennis asked.

''None in his military profile. Why?''

Dennis just grinned.

THREE HOURS LATER, Mallory had her arm elbow deep in a Cheerios box, feeling for small, foreign objects in the cereal. Mac was sweeping up the last of the flour. When he finished, he dusted off his hands and emptied the dustpan into the trash. ''I can't think of one place we haven't looked. I even went through his other car out in the garage. It's just not here.''

She set the box on the counter with a thump and, from sheer habit more than anything, grabbed a cloth to wipe the counter. *No key.* She had to face it, think of somewhere else to look. A vision of Em's face crept into her mind, and she blocked out the picture, knowing it would only make her frantic. She had to be calm, make every second count. ''I was so sure we'd find it.''

Her voice rang with such discouragement that Mac turned

to look at her—really look. Her hair hung in tangled, unruly waves around her small face. Her previously flawless ivory skin was now marred with scratches and bruises. Her smart blue suit, fresh that morning, was dirty. Bits of bark were snagged in the fabric. There were circles under her eyes, she was pale, and she looked exhausted. Alarmed, he went back upstairs to the front bathroom where he had seen a bottle of disinfectant and a package of cotton balls. Mallory was poking around inside a refrigerator container of applesauce when he returned. *That* was getting desperate.

"Time for first aid," he said in a deliberately light tone.

She frowned. "I can clean myself up. I *am* qualified to do that much, at least."

"You can't see all of the cuts that well. Come on, sit down. Afterward, we'll go check the clothes and belongings Keith has with him at the hospital."

As she sat by the table, he strode toward her, holding the disinfectant bottle up so she could see it. "Does this stuff sting?"

"No, I keep it on hand for Em."

Her mouth trembled slightly at the mention of her daughter, but she quickly suppressed it, controlling the emotion that was undermining her. He put the bottle and cotton on the table and leaned over her to examine the deep gouge on her collarbone.

"Tip your head back."

She obliged and met his gaze with those beautiful brown eyes of hers. A completely irrational response swept through him. *Careful.* He couldn't understand the feelings erupting within him—this almost compulsive urge to gather her into his arms. When this was over, the last guy on earth she'd want to spend time with would be him. And the feeling ought to be mutual. As he separated the edges of the wound, he tried not to notice how silken her skin felt. What *was* his problem, anyway? *Randy, remember Randy.*

"Ouch!" She pulled away and threw him an accusing glance.

Mac realized he hadn't been paying enough attention to what

he had been doing. He apologized and uncapped the bottle of disinfectant and saturated a cotton ball. Leaning over her again, he dabbed gently at the cut. She kept her head tipped back to afford him a clear view, her face only inches from his, the sweet steaminess of her breath feathering on his cheek. His guts tightened.

"Undo the blazer so we can see what else we've got."

She started to do as he asked, then hesitated. Mac met her gaze head-on. He had to get those cuts cleaned. No telling what chemicals might have been on those shrubs and the bark dust. Weed killers, insecticides. He hated to think about it. She could medicate most of the abrasions herself, but he'd seen a couple of deep-looking cuts that she couldn't get at unless she was a contortionist.

She unbuttoned the second button and her jacket fell open. He hunkered next to her and peeled back her ruined blouse. Keeping his gaze on the lacerations, he tried to ignore the fact that her small breasts were right at eye level. What was he, a Class A creep? She was numb with exhaustion and worry. What she needed was tenderness and caring from a friend. Only a heartless heel would let his eyes stray. Especially when she probably felt desperate to stay on his good side. Her daughter's life hung in the balance. And if he allowed her to see how she was affecting him, she'd not only feel uneasy around him but also trapped, afraid to reject him because she needed him. The woman had enough problems.

Mac had to accept the fact that, like it or not, he was a Class A creep. Whenever she wasn't watching him, his eyes were drawn to the embroidered pink rosebud on her bra. Right above it was her cleavage and a wealth of creamy skin. The cups of the bra were a tease of filmy white over nipples the same delicate pink as the rosebud. How had he gotten himself into a situation like this? His hands began to shake. He tried to think about Randy—a sure cure for what ailed him—but Randy had been dead fourteen years and Mallory Christiani was here, just inches away.

To even think about making love to her was contemptible.

Subconsciously was he seeking some sort of sick revenge? Randy had been used, then thrown aside. Did he want to use Mallory? Was that why he felt this sharp yearning to hold her? It was a possibility he couldn't ignore. He kept telling himself he just felt sorry for her, that his protective side was rearing its head, but that didn't hold water. The ache low in his belly wasn't in any way chivalrous.

He shoved the bottle of disinfectant into her hand and stood so fast he felt dizzy. He had done some things he wasn't too proud of in his lifetime, but using emotional blackmail on a vulnerable woman wasn't going to be added to the list. "You can get the others by yourself. I think I'll clean up a bit before we go to the hospital."

Mallory straightened in the chair, clearly startled by his abrupt withdrawal. Mac ignored her and strode away, loosening his tie with a vicious jerk, tempted to strangle himself with it.

MALLORY WASN'T SURE what it was that she had done to make Mac angry with her, but there was no question that he was. Ever since… She tried to remember and decided it had begun in the kitchen when he was cleaning her cuts. Ever since then, he had been as cold as a blast of arctic air, scarcely speaking, keeping his distance, his expression unreadable. During the drive to the hospital, he had ignored her presence in the car.

Now that they were inside the hospital and approaching the ICU, the temperature still hadn't reached thawing level. Mallory walked along beside him, aware of every brush of his sleeve against hers, every sharp rap of his heels. She grew more than a little irritated. The long strides he was taking forced her to a near run just to keep pace. In an attempt to dress as much in character as possible, so as not to upset Keith, she was wearing high heels and a brown suit. The narrow skirt and heels didn't lend themselves well to a foot race. She didn't mind someone becoming angry with her, but it would be nice to be told why. Fat chance of that when Mac would hardly talk to her—as if either of them needed added tension. Just being back at the hospital was enough. For all they knew, there could be a man with a gun lurking behind one of the closed doors...or stalking them.

When they reached ICU, Mac requested admittance over the intercom and was promptly denied it. Mallory would have to go in alone.

"Try to question him," he instructed her before she went in. "I'm sure he can't speak yet, but if he can even manage a blink upon command, you could set up a yes or no signal."

The moment Mallory stepped inside, the attending nurse cautioned her not to upset Keith. The doctor had been keeping him sedated because he seemed agitated. Mallory hated herself for what she was about to do. She had no choice, though. Em's life was at stake. If Keith was able to communicate in any way, she had to question him. Her only comfort was knowing that Keith would have had it no other way. Em was everything to him.

Keith's eyes widened when he saw her and promptly filled with stark fear. This time, she knew why the sight of her upset him so badly. She took his cold hand in hers and told him, in as steady a voice as she could, that he mustn't worry. "Mac told me everything, Dad. He's been wonderful. He's taking care of it."

Keith's eyes drifted closed. He was clearly exhausted. Mallory's stomach twisted with guilt. "Dad, can you blink your eyes for me?" His eyelids fluttered crazily. "No, I mean just once."

Again his eyelids fluttered. Not one blink, but a dozen.

Mallory gave his hand a squeeze and tried not to reveal how disappointed she was. She glanced at the monitor. Did she dare press him? "Dad, can you move any of your fingers?"

Keith's body strained as he tried to comply. Mallory forced a smile. What movements he could manage were uncontrolled. In a few days, he might improve, but she didn't have a few days. Again she checked the monitor. His heartbeat was accelerated. She was upsetting him...endangering him. And for what reason? Unless she could think of a way to communicate with him, there was little use in continuing. Because of her medical training, she knew how easily he could have a second, possibly more severe stroke.

There was no point in telling him Em had been kidnapped, not if he couldn't communicate. Better that he believe Mac had somehow taken care of everything. Not so hard to believe if you knew Mac. "I, um, can't stay, Dad. I wish I could, but something has come up. I'll try to come back tomorrow when I have more time." She prayed he didn't wonder why she wasn't haunting the hospital, that he didn't realize something had happened. Bending to kiss his cheek, she whispered, "I love you so much. You remember that, okay?"

A tremor ran the length of his body. Mallory left his bed and walked to his locker. Her hands shook as she lifted the latch. Hopefully he wouldn't become alarmed when she began searching his clothes. She ran her hands into all his pockets first, praying with each thrust of her fingertips that she would find the key, fighting back disappointment when she didn't. She felt the lining of his jacket. Again nothing.

Panic rose in her throat. It was a quarter after five. In the morning, Lucetti would call. She turned and looked at Keith, holding herself rigid to stop herself from pouring her heart out to him. Her eyes burned with unshed tears as she shut the locker door and leaned her back against it. He looked as though he was sleeping. She hoped he was. Hurrying by his bed, she gained the door and shoved out into the hall, one palm pressed to her waist.

Mac stood with his shoulder propped against the opposite wall. He straightened and took a step forward when she came out. Their eyes met, and his mouth tightened. "Nothing?"

She shook her head and blinked frantically, dashing a hand across her cheek. "I'm going to have to get his wallet from the hospital safe. I figure you might need his ID later when you go to the bank to try to get into his deposit box."

"Good thinking." He took hold of her elbow and guided her gently along the hall. His strides were shorter now to accommodate hers. She knew he must feel her trembling. He let go of her elbow and encircled her shoulders with an arm, pulling her snugly to his side. "Hey…it was a long shot, right?"

"Yes, but what are we going to do now?"

"Keep looking. We'll ask for more time." He hit the elevator control. "Don't panic. Lucetti wants that package. He has nothing to gain by being unreasonable."

The walk through the hospital and the ordeal of retrieving Keith's wallet passed in a blur. Once inside the car, Mallory handed the wallet to Mac. He quickly removed the pieces of identification from it that he thought he might need and transferred them to his own billfold. Then he leaned his head back and closed his eyes, his hands braced against the steering wheel. She knew he was trying to think of someplace else they might search. At least he could still think. Mallory's mind felt like congealed gelatin. She closed her eyes, too. How could she feel tired? Or think of sleeping? There wasn't time to rest, to eat, to do anything.

"She loves Pop-Tarts," Mallory blurted out. "On Saturday mornings we cuddle under her Pooh bag and watch cartoons. Sometimes, Keith even joins us."

A lump rose in Mac's throat. "Maybe she'll be home by Saturday."

He heard Mallory make a strange noise, but when he glanced over at her, she looked composed, her head back, eyes still closed. "You like Pop-Tarts? There's room for three under the Pooh bag. It's kind of fun, actually. Some of the cartoons aren't bad."

"Now that sounds like a date I wouldn't want to miss. Not often I get to cuddle with two beautiful women under a Pooh bag. What *is* a Pooh bag, by the way?"

"A Winnie the Pooh sleeping bag. You've seen them."

Mac hadn't. He had no nieces or nephews, so he wasn't familiar with things like Pooh bags. "I like Pop-Tarts."

He heard the strange little noise again and tensed, not sure what to say. If only she didn't fight showing her emotions. He wanted to throttle her mother. He sighed and reached to start the car. He no sooner turned the key in the ignition than she sat bolt upright, eyes wide with excitement.

"His shoes! I didn't check his shoes."

At this point, Mac's mental clock was ticking like a time bomb. He was willing to look anywhere. If they didn't find the key soon, Lucetti might make good on his threat and kill Em. When Mallory leaped from the car, he wasn't far behind her. She broke into a run, crossing the parking lot at dangerous speed for a woman wearing heels. He loped along in her wake.

Just as she reached the automatic doors, a deafening explosion rocked the parking lot. The ensuing blast of air knocked Mallory off her feet and she staggered against the building. Mac whirled. Orange flame shot into the air above his Volvo. The doors hung at crazy angles. The glass was all blown out. *A bomb.* Reaction set in immediately. His legs felt as limp as hot rubber and his stomach heaved. If they had remained in the car a few seconds longer, they would both be dead. Someone had wired the doors or starter with a timer.

No one had been injured, but the fire was bound to set off a chain reaction of explosions in nearby cars, and their luck wouldn't hold forever. Spinning on his heel, he grabbed Mallory's hand and together they dashed into the lobby. "Call the police and the fire department!" he roared at the woman behind the information desk. "There's been an explosion. Hurry! Other cars are gonna blow!"

Chapter Nine

Mac's hand was gripping hers firmly as he dashed through the lobby, hauling her in his wake. Veering down an intersecting hall, they raced by doorways so swiftly that everything seemed a blur. Up ahead, Mallory saw a sign with arrows pointing to the Emergency Room. Mac turned the opposite way, toward an exit.

"Where are we going?" she asked as they paused outside.

"Anyplace. If the guys who put that bomb in my car aren't still around, the cops soon will be." As if on cue, sirens wailed in the distance. "The minute they find out that's my Volvo, they're going to want to question me."

Before Mallory could catch her breath, he struck off again at a dead run, this time dodging through the emergency parking area to an adjoining business lot. He didn't stop until he spied a public phone booth that was not easily visible from the street. Throwing the door open, he stuffed Mallory inside and wedged his way in behind her. The space was so confined that his elbow poked her as he dug in his pocket for change. Through the thick glass, she could barely hear the sirens.

He dropped a coin into the slot and grabbed the phone book to find a cab company number. He was breathing as hard as she was. He had to gulp and swallow before he could speak to the dispatcher and arrange for a taxi.

After hanging up, he shoved his hand back into his pocket and then fed a second quarter into the slot. "Keep an eye out for me," he ordered as he dialed another number. "I'm going to try that friend of mine again."

As she checked the area around them, tremors shook her legs. This wasn't a bad dream she was having. She wasn't going to wake up and make it all go away by telling Keith about it over breakfast. It felt as if a balloon were being inflated to bursting point inside her chest. *Panic.* Even though she recognized it for what it was, she still had difficulty staving it off. *My baby. Terrible men who blow up cars have my baby.* The words echoed in her mind, a funereal litany. Men like that wouldn't hesitate to kill a child.

Steady. Don't think. Not about Em, not about anything. She scanned the parking area again, craning her neck to see around a stand of shrubs that blocked her view. A woman with a toddler on her hip came out of an insurance office. A man pulled his car up near the phone booth and studied a street map.

Mac listened intently as the call he'd made went through. No one seemed to be answering. Then he gave her a thumbs-up signal and started talking. "Hey, Shelb, you're finally home. Can we talk?" He shot one quick look at the parking lot, then glanced at Mallory to make certain she was still standing guard for them. She heard the sound of male laughter coming over the wire.

"Shelby, this is no social call. I'm sorry I didn't call before this, but I was afraid our lines were tapped and every time I've tried to reach you from a phone booth I couldn't get you." Mac listened a moment. "Shelb, I don't—you took it off the hook?—no, I don't—" He held up a hand. "Shelb, really— this is *serious*—would you quit clowning?" He cocked his head, listening again, and began to look mollified. "First off, how long's it been since you saw Corrine?" He sighed. "Yeah—no, me neither. Okay, forget that idea, I guess. I need you to do a little street work for me. Find out what you can on a guy named Steven Miles. An accountant, connected somehow to Pete Lucetti."

Mallory heard snatches of the other man's voice coming over the line, the most pronounced word being *Lucetti*. Mac nodded his head every few seconds. When at last he got another opportunity to speak, he explained their predicament, leaving nothing out. The intermittent voice on the other end of the line grew louder.

"Yeah, yeah, I know that, Shelby. But sometimes trouble comes knocking, you know? While you're at it, dig up anything you can on a newer model cream-colored sedan. A Buick, Washington plates. If I remember right, the first letters were LUD. I had it written down, but my car just got blown up. We want to know who the guys are that use it. There are three of them, businessmen types, wear suits. Slick operators."

Shelby's voice had risen to such a level now that even Mallory could make out what he was saying. "You *did* say Mallory Christiani? Maiden name Steele? You done lost your mind?"

"No, not yet, and I don't intend to if I can keep from getting my brains blown out. You be sure to watch your back, okay?" Mac's scowl deepened even more as he listened to his friend's reply. "No lectures, Shelb, just check around for me. Did you write that info down? I'll call you late tonight to see what you've got, okay?"

He snapped his fingers with sudden inspiration. "Say, you might try Teddy down at the gun shop. Have him call around to his competitors. At least one of them packs a modified Uzi with a clip. And today one of them took some shots at us with a seven mag—my guess is a Winchester—mounted with a scope. They have to visit an indoor practice range on a regular basis unless they go outside the city. There can't be many guys packing that kind of weaponry and driving around in a cream-colored Buick. Tell Teddy I need anything he can dig up on them."

More yelling ensued from Shelby's end, but Mallory couldn't be certain of what he was saying because Mac was running interference with a number of *uh-huhs* and *yeahs*.

"She's standing right here listening," Mac cautioned. When his friend didn't take the hint, he said, "Shelby, you're yelling loud enough to be heard in Tallahassee! Do you mind?"

After a moment's dead silence, Shelby resumed yelling.

"That's because I'm upset. I *yell* when I'm upset. You're my best friend. What am I s'posed to do, keep my mouth shut? Let little Miss High 'n' Mighty take care of her own problems. She's got plenty of bucks. She can *buy* her way out of trouble."

Mac tipped his head back and stared at the ceiling of the booth. "Shelby, I'm counting on you to come through for me. I'd go myself, but I've got Mallory with me and it would be too risky to take her down there after everything that's happened."

"Lucetti? You're talkin' *way* outa my league. And even if you weren't, why would I risk my neck for the likes of her?"

"Yeah, but when a kid's involved, it's a different ball game, right? I knew you'd see it my way."

"That's blackmail, Mac. Don't go puttin' no guilt trips on me about no kid, man."

Mac grinned. "Big brown eyes and freckles. She's got a stuffed dog named Ragsdale."

"That's dirty pool. That's not even *playin'* fair."

"It's times like this, Shelb, that I know the true meaning of friendship."

"Yeah! It's a real pain in the neck."

A loud clunk came over the receiver. As Mac hung up, he met Mallory's startled gaze and said, "Shelby...he's really a nice guy. You just have to get to know him."

Mallory couldn't help feeling alarmed. How did Shelby know her maiden name? And why did he seem to harbor such dislike for her? "Mac, what was that all about?"

"Nothing." He flashed her a smile. "Nothing I want to get into, anyway. Don't worry. He squawks a lot, but he comes through. I trust him with my life."

The question was, could she and Em?

They left the booth and stood behind a bushy evergreen so no one would see them while they waited for the cab. The wailing of sirens grew increasingly loud. They could smell rubber burning. The Volvo's tires? The thought made her sick. A police car careened around the corner and sped past. Seconds later, two fire trucks went barreling by. Mac drew her closer to the tree. She noticed he kept looking over his shoulder to scan the parking lot. A cold feeling crept up her neck. Even now, they weren't safe. She began to sneak glances over her shoulder, too. Black smoke roiled above the hospital parking area.

The minutes crawled by. Her feet began to hurt, and the prickly fir needles made her back and legs itch. Her thoughts drifted to Mac's conversation with his friend Shelby. Did Shelby know her? Was Mac hiding something from her? Should she question him about what she had overheard? Glancing up at him, she decided to keep her mouth shut. Mac was her only hope of saving Em. Antagonizing him would be stupid. If there *was* something he was holding back from her, he'd tell her when he was ready.

At last, the cab came. As Mac opened the back door for her and she slid onto the seat, she tried to read his expression.

Mac climbed in after Mallory and slammed the door. He leaned forward to give her address to the cabbie. As he sat back, he felt her watching him. He was going to scalp Shelby for mouthing off. She had enough to worry about. For an instant, he considered telling her the truth, that he was Randy's half brother, but the words caught in his throat. The old hurts ran too deep for him to glibly tell her about them and pretend they were water under the bridge. They weren't. Never could be.

"What's goin' on there at the hospital?" the cabbie asked.

"I'm not sure," Mac said. "We heard an explosion of some kind. I wasn't about to get close enough to see what it was."

"Smart thinking. One thing's good. If anyone got hurt, they chose a great place." With a loud guffaw at his own joke, the driver merged the cab with traffic. "Lots of doctors handy," he elaborated when neither of them laughed. When that still didn't get a chuckle, the man settled down to drive in silence. Mallory simply didn't have a laugh in her. All she could think of was Em.

They were halfway home before Mac realized that he was holding Mallory's hand. He didn't know if he had initiated the contact or she had. It didn't really matter. Some things just felt right, and her hand in his was one of them. He didn't want to analyze that right now or think about the implications. Shelby's question rang in his head. *You done lost your mind?* Mac was afraid maybe he had.

MAC WAS SILENT all during the drive home. Mallory knew there must be risks involved in returning to her house. At first she wondered if that was why Mac was so quiet. But by the time they stepped into the entry and closed the door behind them, she was convinced that he was just still angry at her. There was an empty look in his eyes, a grim set to his lips. He backed her into a corner and pressed a staying hand to her shoulder.

"Stay put," he ordered, his tone brooking no argument.

She stood there in the cool semidarkness and watched him creep up to the doorways along the hall one by one, gun in hand. Each time he exploded into a room she flinched and held her breath until he emerged unhurt. When he finished the first floor and went upstairs to check the bedrooms, she really began to sweat. She hated feeling so helpless. As much as she detested guns, right now she wished she knew how to use one, just so she could help.

If there was one thing she couldn't stomach, it was feeling useless. If she came out of this alive, she was going to learn to shoot a handgun and take lessons in the martial arts. The next time something like this happened—heaven forbid that it should—she'd be better equipped to handle it. Better equipped to protect Em.

When Mac came back downstairs, she led the way into the kitchen and located an unopened container of Folger's in the cupboard over the stove. She lifted her chin and swallowed down a wave of self-disgust. Her daughter was being held for ransom and her big contribution to finding her was to make coffee? After opening the can, she stepped to the sink to fill the reservoir of the coffee maker. Menial though the chore was, she knew caffeine would do them both good. They couldn't keep going on sheer willpower. She imagined Mac was as exhausted as she. He was sitting at the table, long legs stretched in front of him, arms folded across his broad chest. She filled the filter cup with grounds, inserted it into the coffee maker and turned around. Something was on his mind; she sensed it.

"I know you too well. Something's wrong. What is it?"

It seemed a silly thing to say. *I know you too well.* She scarcely knew him at all by normal standards. Yet somehow, inexplicably, she felt that she knew him better than she had ever known anyone. She knew all the important things, at any rate. That he was kind, that he had more courage than anyone she had ever known, that he cared about little girls he had never met, that he noticed things like freckles on noses and remembered a stuffed dog's name was Ragsdale.

He sighed and said, "I'm just wondering, at this point, if you don't want to cry uncle and go to the police for protection. The guys after us are getting into some pretty serious stuff."

Fear mushroomed inside her. Had he already decided they couldn't save Em? "Are you saying you want to give up?"

"No, I'm just giving you the option. You could be killed, you know."

"Better me than Em!"

He smiled. "Just checking. Some people would be reevaluating things at this point. Be wondering if it was worth the risk."

Mallory couldn't imagine doing that. She loved her daughter so much that no risk was too great. No matter how nasty this situation grew, Mallory would keep fighting.

"You know that friend I was talking to—Shelby?" Mac asked.

"Yes, what about him?"

"I'm going to take you over to spend the night at his place."

"Why would I want to go there? If I leave the house, who will be here to take Lucetti's call?"

"I don't want to leave you here alone. They know where you live and there are places I have to go before morning. I don't need any extra baggage slowing me down."

Extra baggage? That wasn't very complimentary. Mallory caught her lip between her teeth and bit down hard. As much as she hated to admit it, she knew she *was* a burden to him. Had been from the start. He knew it, she knew it. She had no business letting her ego get in the way. Em's safety was the only consideration.

"Would you stop that before you make a sore?" His gaze was fastened on her mouth. "You're constantly gnawing that lip."

She immediately stopped. "It's better than grinding my teeth like you do. My lip will mend. Molar enamel won't."

He tightened his jaws and ground his teeth. When he realized he was doing exactly what she had just accused him of, he rolled his eyes and tried to stop. Perverse though it was, she was pleased when she saw his jaw begin to ripple again.

"I guess it's not a good time for either of us to swear off a bad habit," he admitted. "It just worries me, that's all, the way you go after that lip. It's going to be hamburger by the time this is over."

Her mouth was the least of her worries, Mallory thought. The gurgle of the coffee maker was the only sound in the room for several seconds. At last he ended the silence with another heavy sigh and glanced at his watch. "I've been doing some thinking, Mallory. We only have a few hours left. The key would have been found if it was in Keith's shoe, and whoever undressed him would have put it with the other valuables. I'm fresh out of ideas where else to look for the key. There's not much point in my sitting here doing nothing when I could be working the streets. We may not be able to deliver that package to Lucetti, after all. And if we can't, there's only one other way to rescue Em."

"What's that?"

"I have to find her. To do that, I have to find Lucetti."

"But you said he'd give us more time. You said you couldn't find him, that no one could, that—"

"I *know* what I said. But what if he won't give us more time? It wouldn't be a smart move on his part to refuse, but neither was kidnapping Em before he knew we had the things he wanted. Getting information on him won't be easy. But if I hit the streets and grease enough palms, I should be able to get some leads. Between Shelby and me, we should come up with something. I have a few—" he paused and cleared his throat again "—a few *friends*, old connections. One of them, a gal named Corrine, could probably give me something on Lucetti if I can find her."

"But—" she lifted her hands "—why can't I help?"

"It's not your kind of neighborhood. Look…I've done it a hundred times. I don't need you along."

"Maybe I need to go. Did you think of that? It's my daughter we're talking about. I can't just sit someplace—in some stranger's house—doing nothing." It was on the tip of her tongue to add that she didn't feel welcome at Shelby's, but she swallowed the words back; how she felt about *that* wasn't important. She'd do it in a minute if she thought it would help Em. "How would you feel? I'd go crazy. I want to help, Mac. Even if I can't do much, I'll feel better trying."

"No!" An angry glitter crept into his gaze. "Mallory Christiani combing the streets? It'd be like parking a Rolls-Royce in a junkyard and expecting no one to notice. And don't forget, someone's trying to kill you. You shouldn't be going anyplace where you stand out."

"I've got slacks and stuff to wear."

"Slacks? You think that'll make you—" He broke off. "I'll be questioning prostitutes. You just don't have the look."

"Meaning?" Mallory glanced down at herself. "I don't have the right equipment or what?"

Mac certainly hadn't meant to infer that she was sexless. Far from it. If she stood on Aurora Avenue to advertise her wares, she'd draw passing cars like a tollbooth on an expressway. Twice today, she had nearly been killed. To knowingly put her at risk again would be insane.

He clenched his teeth. He was having trouble dealing with this fierce feeling of protectiveness she brought out in him.

Talk about acting like a jerk; he deserved an award. How could he have been so cruel? Was it necessary to hurt her? *Yes.*

Ordinarily taking her into downtown Seattle wouldn't have been a concern. It was rough, but not *that* rough. But with killers after them? That was a different story. He understood her need to be actively involved in trying to save her daughter. He knew how miserable she would be sitting at Shelby's. But miserable or not, at least she wouldn't get hurt there.

"You aren't going," he said in a reasonable tone.

"How do you know we won't be followed to Shelby's? The minute you leave, I could find myself facing three men with guns. Mac, please, I won't get in the way. I could stay in the car."

"Won't be any car. Yours is still at the hospital, remember? And mine no longer exists. I'll be taking a cab, then walking."

"But that would leave you stranded. We can take Keith's BMW. The one in the garage."

He studied her pale face with a sinking feeling in his guts. She was right about a lot of things. He didn't want to be stuck downtown without a car. And someone might follow them to Shelby's. It was so obvious a possibility that it scared him to think he had overlooked it. Was he so exhausted that his brain was no longer functioning? If he left her, he might return to find her dead. At least he could watch out for her if she was with him. Or make arrangements for someone else to. It would make his job much more difficult, worrying about her every second while he was dealing for information, but the more he thought about it the better it seemed than the possible alternatives.

"Oh, all right. But no slacks. Don't you have some jeans?"

"Um...some designer types. Would those do?"

Mac hated to think what Mallory's idea of designer jeans were. "Go get them on. And go heavy on the makeup. You don't want to stand out any more than you have to."

He rose from the chair and stepped over to the bar.

"Who are you phoning? I thought the lines might be bugged?"

"If I take you along, I won't be able to stay with you every second. I'm calling in some recruits. I'll watch what I say."

AN HOUR AND A HALF LATER, Mallory stepped across the threshold into Mac's downtown Seattle apartment, where they had stopped so he could change into what he called street clothes. As he shoved the door open for her it pushed aside the heap of mail that his landlord had been sticking through his mail slot this past week. She sidestepped the scattered envelopes and cast a curious glance around. The mail-littered entranceway stretched into an equally untidy living room. She remembered all the junk in his Volvo and realized neatness was not one of Mac's strong suits. Neither was interior decorating. She had never seen such a hodgepodge. Nothing matched, not even the two end tables.

He scooped a pair of running shoes off the floor, grabbed some sweatpants and several newspapers off the brown recliner, then smiled. "Excuse the mess." He dumped everything on the sofa, looking a little embarrassed. "Have a seat."

Mallory eased herself into the recliner and watched him disappear through a doorway. Drawers thunked. She could hear him stripping off his clothes. His change jangled as he tossed his slacks—probably onto the bed or a chair. Her gaze trailed around the living room. Lived in, but not really dirty. The furniture didn't reside under layers of dust, so he apparently cleaned, or had it done, on a regular basis.

Restless, she rose from the chair and wandered around the room. Along one wall, he had a bookcase. Law books, a dated preparation course for a general equivalency diploma, several blockbuster novels—the lusty variety—a book that promised perfect spelling with an investment of ten minutes a day, a dog-eared Bible, and books on investigation. A pile of gun manuals rested on the bottom shelf with three large and very expensive volumes on the works of great painters. She trailed her fingertips down the spine of the GED preparation book. *You spew big words like a walking dictionary.* The accusation came back to haunt her. Had Mac been deprived of a high-school education?

She wandered over to the component stereo system and portable television, which were housed in an entertainment center along the opposite wall. As she scanned the albums and tapes to see what kind of music he enjoyed—mostly outdated rock and roll—her attention was snagged by a flash of metal. Midway up on a right-hand shelf, a photo of a lovely, gray-haired woman smiled down at Mallory from a gold filigree frame. Moving closer, Mallory wondered if this was a likeness of Mac's mother. Looking into the woman's clear gray eyes, she guessed it must be and found herself envying Mac for having been raised by someone so plump and huggable looking. A real "mom" type who probably still wore an apron when she made pies, the kind who would probably say "I love you" at least once daily. Mallory's gaze shifted to another photo, a candid shot of a much younger Mac standing with his arm around a slightly built boy with platinum-blond hair and blue eyes.

Randy.

Mallory's heart felt as though it stopped beating. Randy Watts? Her late husband's best friend in college? She stared at the picture, at the two youthful faces, one startlingly similar to the other when you saw them so close together. Mac's face, even in his early years, had been rugged and masculine, but his mouth and chin resembled Randy's. Their noses had even been alike before Mac's had been broken so many times. *Brothers.* The truth hit her hard, right between the eyes.

She remembered now that Randy had told Darren he had an older half brother, an ex-Marine. Whirling away from the irrefutable evidence, Mallory clamped a hand over her mouth. All the snide remarks Mac had made to her since yesterday came back to taunt her. No wonder. She had once been Bettina Rawlins's best friend. Bettina had killed Randy Watts as surely as if she had held a gun to his head and pulled the trigger. Mallory and Darren had seen it coming, but they had been helpless to stop it.

Oh, no, please… She turned to look at the picture once more. It was terrible of her, but as much as she regretted what had happened to Randy, her foremost feeling now was desperation. She needed Mac. So did Em. If he abandoned them, what would she do? What should she say to him when he returned from the bedroom? *I didn't know you were Randy's brother. My, it's big of you, helping me like this.*

She dragged her hand from her mouth and pressed it to her waist. Mac had known who she was from the first. Looking back, she felt sure of that. For some reason, he had chosen not to talk about Randy. Maybe it was cowardly, but she wouldn't risk alienating him by forcing the issue. Not *now*.

She could hear him rummaging in his bedroom. At any moment, he would come out. She couldn't be standing here looking like she had just seen a ghost. He would guess why. She looked around for something constructive to do so he wouldn't think she'd been snooping. She stepped into the kitchen and found where he kept his empty paper bags. Returning to the living room with one, she began gathering his mail, stuffing it into the sack.

When Mac reappeared, she was just finishing. Face flaming, she turned to look at him. "I, um, thought I'd pick it up for you, take it along. Maybe you can go through it later."

He had undergone a transformation in the other room. Gone were the respectable jacket and slacks, replaced by tight, faded blue jeans and a red sport shirt that revealed a sexy V of tanned, muscular chest. At his throat was a heavy, gold chain. The outfit was capped off with a black leather jacket, the collar tipped up around his neck. Showing below the frayed cuffs were thick leather wristbands, peppered with brass brads. Even she had seen enough television to know the wristbands were to protect the forearms in a knife fight. They were wicked looking, so uncharacteristic of the Mac she knew that they made her shiver.

His blond hair was tousled, curling across his forehead in lazy waves, slicked back on the sides. He looked like someone she wouldn't want to meet in a dark alley, hard and ruthless.

For an instant, she almost felt like laughing. But the way he stood, one lean hip slung outward, shoulders hunched, doused her amusement. That tough-guy air wasn't something he'd acquired by practicing in front of a mirror. For an instant, an icy tendril of alarm coiled in the pit of her belly. Which was ridiculous. This was the man who had held her in his arms last night.

She folded down the top of the sack with tense fingers, acutely aware of Randy's picture smiling down at her only a few feet away. Mac's attention dropped to her hands. She prayed he wouldn't see how they were trembling. "Ready?" he asked softly.

"I—" She licked her lips. "Sure. I'm ready if you are."

He studied her for a long moment. Then he glanced over his shoulder at the entertainment center. When he looked back at her, there was a question in his eyes. She averted her face and prayed he wouldn't choose to confront her now. She had no idea what to say. *I'm sorry?* That seemed pitifully inadequate. *I had nothing to do with it?* That wasn't entirely true. Both she and Darren had known how Bettina operated, that to her Randy was nothing but a passing fancy. A poor kid, someone she never would have dared take home. The Rawlinses had planned for their daughter to marry a local senator's son. Randy wouldn't have even been in the running. Darren had tried to warn him, but Randy had believed Bettina's coquettish lies, that she loved him and would one day defy her father to marry him. No, Mallory couldn't honestly claim she was blameless. She could have done something more. What, she wasn't sure, but there must have been something. Wringing Bettina's neck, for starters.

Mac didn't glance toward Randy's picture again, but she still had the feeling he knew why she was suddenly so nervous.

"Before we leave, let's go through a few ground rules," he told her in a low voice. "Number one, in case there's trouble, I want you to promise you'll do exactly what I tell you."

She nodded in agreement.

"Number two, don't call attention to me by looking surprised or asking questions. We'll be hitting the waterfront area, Aurora Avenue and the intersecting streets. If that's a dead end, maybe the airport. As I'm sure you know, those areas draw lowlifes this time of night. To get information, I have to be part chameleon.''

Again she nodded.

He ran a hand over his eyes. His weary sigh was the only indication he gave of how unutterably tired he was. "When we get near there, we'll have to leave the car a few blocks away and strike out on foot. That expensive BMW would be a red flag to anyone who saw it. And since it's registered in Keith's name, I don't dare leave you sitting in it for fear those three guys might recognize it.'' He settled his cloudy-gray eyes on her. "There'll be times when I'll have to leave you. Some of my contacts are reluctant enough about talking to me when I'm alone. I'll be leaving you with those friends I called earlier. They'll meet us downtown.'' He hesitated and gave her a long study. "They aren't exactly the kind of kids you're accustomed to. They may even seem a little intimidating to you. But I trust them. Because you're a friend of mine, you can, too. When you're with them, you listen to Danno, the oldest boy, just like you do to me. If something should go wrong, Danno knows his way around.''

Mallory forgot all about Randy's picture. "A boy?''

"He's nineteen. A very old nineteen when it comes to that neighborhood.''

"Mac, I'm thirty-four years old. Born and raised in the Seattle area. I *am* capable of taking care of myself. I have been in rough areas before, you know.''

"Oh, I'm sure you have. But have you ever gone down there looking for trouble? There's a big difference.'' His eyes searched hers. "Put your pride in the back seat a second. Somebody's trying to kill you. We've already decided that it's somebody connected to Lucetti. We're going down into the roughest part of town to ask questions. About Lucetti. About Miles. And about the three guys who have been after us. At the best of times, hanging around in those places isn't the wisest way to spend an evening. Tonight, it could be downright deadly if the wrong people see us or get wind of why we're there.''

Put like that, Mallory was beginning to see his point.

''Shelby's apartment is still an option for you if you'd rather not go. If you are going, though, then Danno gives the orders and you stick to him like he's covered with super glue.''

Mallory could see that Mac meant it. And he had her over a barrel. The realization rankled.

Stepping closer to her, he touched her hair, his expression softening. ''I know it's hard on you, being kept out of the thick of things when you want to be helping. But you have to remember there's a very important third party involved in this. If something happens to you, she's sunk. Danno knows how to blend in down there, who he can trust, who's trouble and who isn't. This way if anyone comes looking for us, I won't have to worry about your being seen.''

Mallory suspected that he would be protective of her no matter what, that he was using Em as a smoke screen, but regardless, he had a point. She couldn't afford to risk herself until Em was safe. ''All right, Mac,'' she at last conceded. ''You win. Danno's the boss.''

He lowered his hand and hooked his thumb in his hip pocket. ''I just don't want anything to happen to you.''

''If something happens to me, it'll be my own fault for having insisted on going, not yours.'' A flutter of panic blocked her throat. This conversation was dangerous. It could flow so easily into a discussion of blame about Randy's death and they didn't have time for that. She tucked the bag of mail under her arm and turned toward the door. ''Besides, it's not my welfare I'm worried about. Finding Em and getting her home safely is the important thing…the only important thing.''

Chapter Ten

Mallory had never ventured into this part of Seattle after dark. Respectable people avoided the area once dusk fell. Even driving through here with the car doors unlocked could be risky. The sidewalks weren't as crowded as she had expected, but because the people seemed intimidating to her, she felt as though she was walking through a solid wall of humanity, bums, drug pushers, runaways, streetwalkers. There was no light in their faces, no hope. Life was a struggle to survive and if you got in their way, they would walk over you.

When Mac stepped into a grimy tavern to buy a pack of cigarettes, his hissed order "stick tight" was one she hastened to obey. Some of the men standing under the flashing neon sign outside of the establishment were staring at her as though she was an all-you-can-eat special. She didn't know if it was her appearance that appealed—she found that hard to believe—or if she looked as though she might have money.

"Hey, Bro," Mac said to the barkeep. "I'm lookin' for Corrine. She been around?"

"I ain't seen nothin'," the man snarled, his brown eyes gleaming with hostility as they fastened on Mallory.

Mac tossed his quarter of change into the air, palmed it and slapped it on the bar. "Tell her I'm lookin' for her."

"I'll tell her if I see her, Mac." The bartender, who seemed to know Mac well, took the quarter and tossed it into a jar of coins, muttering something under his breath that cast serious doubts upon both Mac's generosity and his legitimacy.

"Guilty on both counts," Mac called over his shoulder.

The bartender guffawed and rubbed his sizable paunch. Walking past the occupied bar stools, Mallory noticed that the men and women patronizing the establishment looked at her as if she was a cockroach in the center of a banquet table. Were these the kind of people that Emily was being held by? People who whiled away their lives staring at rows of bottles?

Mallory doubled her hands into fists and dug her nails into her palms, picturing her daughter's guileless brown eyes.

"I didn't think you smoked," she said to Mac as they emerged from the bar. *I can't think about Em. I have to keep my perspective, stay calm.* Tears burned in her eyes, and she blinked rapidly to keep them from falling.

"Chameleon, remember? I don't inhale." He dipped his head toward his cupped palms to light the cigarette. As he straightened, a purple-haired youth dressed in skintight black leather veered in Mallory's direction. Mallory's face flamed when he directed an insolent look at her breasts. Mac draped one arm over her shoulders, his face settling in harsh lines. Snuffing the match with his fingers, he met the kid's gaze. It was an unspoken challenge. The younger man turned sharply away.

Glancing down at her, Mac said, "I'll say this for him, he's got good taste."

Mallory tried to smile and failed. The vision of Em's face still floated in the back of her mind. "Do you think she's down here? With men like these?"

Mac placed his hand on her hair and threaded his fingers to her scalp, his touch warm and soothing as he traced circles above her ear. "I don't know, Mallory. We just have to pray that whoever has her is a decent person. There *are* some down here, you know. A lot of them."

"I've never told her about the really ugly things that can happen to little girls. The closest I ever came was warning her not to talk to strangers. I didn't prepare her for anything like this.''

''She'll be okay, Mallory. Think positive, hmm?'' His eyes met hers and, imagination or no, it seemed to her that some of his strength flowed into her. He placed the cigarette in his mouth to free his other hand, then smoothed the wetness from her eyelashes. His eyes narrowed against the trailing smoke, and the lines that bracketed his mouth deepened as his lips tightened on the filter. Dropping his arm back to her shoulders, he drew her close. Glancing around them, he said, ''Not getting fresh, just don't want anyone deciding you look lonesome.''

When they first began to walk, her hip bumped against his thigh, but they quickly fell into a rhythm. She slipped an arm around his waist. ''Not getting fresh,'' she said. ''Just don't want to *look* lonesome.''

He chuckled.

A drunk staggered toward them. Mac swerved to avoid a collision, but not in time. The man bumped her shoulder and would have sent her reeling if not for Mac's steadying arm. She swallowed, her throat parchment dry. She looped her shaky fingers under Mac's wide belt and moved even closer to him. Being an unattached female down here was clearly not wise. Mac struck off down the sidewalk again. His hand curled warmly around her upper arm, his fingers making light circles on her sleeve. That absentminded caress was the only sign he gave that he was even aware of her. When she looked up at him, she noticed that his face had assumed the harsh and unreadable expression she had seen before, the cigarette dangling from the corner of his mouth as if it were a permanent fixture.

A young girl sidled up to them. She jutted out a hip, her denim-clad leg brushing Mac's as she flashed him a smile. ''Hey, honey, ditch Goldilocks and I'll show you a good time.''

Mac's arm tightened around Mallory as he sidestepped the girl and continued walking.

Shock coursed through Mallory. ''She's not that much older than Emily. Thirteen, fourteen, maybe?''

''They grow up fast down here. And as much as you might

want to, as hard as you might try, you can't rescue all of them.''

From his tone, Mallory knew he had learned that lesson the hard way. The longer she knew this man, the more she liked him. *Liked?* She pressed closer to the lean hardness of his body. No, what she felt for Mac had already gone far beyond mere liking. The feeling had sort of snuck up on her. She wasn't quite ready to pin a name on it. Her practical side, which was and always had been dominant, told her she hadn't known him long enough to feel anything for him. Was it gratitude? Desperation? Those were possibilities she couldn't ignore. Mac was her one and only hope when it came to saving Emily. Mallory sighed. What did it matter? The feeling was there, nonetheless, waiting to be faced, a one-way street to heartache. Even if Mac could forgive the fact that she had been Bettina's friend, he was never likely to forget it. Randy *had* been his brother, after all.

His gaze shifted back and forth, taking in every person, checking every dark doorway. ''The boys should be down this way someplace. As soon as we meet them, I need to find Corrine.''

''Who is she?''

''An old school chum. She's worked the streets for over twenty years. Started at about the same age as the girl back there. Has her own stable now. I hope she still runs a string down here. From what I've heard, the big money is made out by the airport.''

''A stable?'' The question no sooner left her lips than she knew what he meant. Em was so much in her thoughts that Mallory's brain seemed to be functioning at half capacity.

Mac took a drag on the cigarette and squinted as smoke drifted from the corner of his mouth uninhaled and got into his eyes. ''Corrine's got more connections than the governor. If anyone knows who works for Lucetti, it's her. The problem will be finding her. She doesn't work herself anymore, just manages her girls. And she doesn't go for rough stuff. If someone wants to quit or move on to greener pastures, she doesn't get nasty. Lucetti, unfortunately, doesn't deal that way. She hates his guts, which is why I figure we can count on her for information.''

Mallory bit her lip. They were going to comb the streets looking for a woman who supported herself managing prostitutes? For a moment, she felt appalled. Then she shoved the feeling aside. She didn't care who Corrine was or what she did for a living, not if she could help them find Emily.

''Hey, Coach!'' someone yelled.

Mac stopped walking and pivoted on his heel. His change of direction was so sudden that Mallory lost her hold on his belt and fell out of step, dislodging his arm from around her. Four teenage boys converged on them. Mallory, who was following closely on Mac's heels, took one glance at the youths and faltered. They looked as rough as dirt roads after a torrential winter rain. Mac greeted them with a ritualistic bumping of elbows and clapping of palms. Then, as if he missed the weight of her hand at his waist, he turned to look for her.

Feeling intimidated, just as he had predicted she might, Mallory was hesitant to join them. Mac held out a hand to her. When she walked over to him, he put his arm around her. She groped for a hold on his belt, acutely aware that she was being looked over by four pairs of impenetrable eyes, two sets of blue, one of green and one as black as obsidian.

The boy with the black eyes appeared to be the oldest, a tall young man of Indian or Spanish descent with shoulder-length ebony hair. He regarded her with an almost contemptuous curiosity, his youthful and extremely handsome face cast in light, and then in shadow by the bar's neon sign that flashed on and off above him. A thin scar angled across his right cheek. From a knife fight, possibly? A length of chain dangled from the hip pocket of his tattered blue jeans, and the handle of what she guessed was a switchblade protruded from his waistband. Unlike Mac's, his wristbands were adorned with sharp little spikes.

With a snort of anger, Mac plucked the boy's knife from his waistband and hefted it in his hand. ''What's this, Danno? You know what will happen if you guys are caught packing blades. You don't run the streets anymore.''

"You said it might be dangerous. We came prepared.''

Mac held out his hand. "No way. Hand them over.'' He snapped his fingers at the other boys.

"Coach!'' Danno cried. "Do you know how much those switchblades cost me? We walked ten blocks one way to get them.''

"Next time, you won't buy them, then, will you? When I said it might get dangerous, I didn't mean it as a call to arms. I just thought I should level with you. Besides, the danger will most likely be to me. You can't violate your probation. You know better. Come on.''

With sullen glowers, all four boys handed over their knives. Mac tossed them into a nearby trash receptacle. When he returned, he inclined his head toward her.

"Danno, I'd like you to meet Mallory Christiani.''

Danno shifted his unreadable black eyes to her. After a tension-laden moment, he extended his hand. Just as hesitantly, she placed uncertain fingers across his palm. His grasp was loose and noncommittal but warm. She tried to smile with stiff lips, then forced herself to meet his gaze. With a shock, she realized he was afraid, afraid of being rejected. The realization made her heart catch. He was too young to be so bitter and suspicious. Mallory's smile relaxed and spread across her mouth. "I'm pleased to meet you, Danno.''

The obsidian glassiness left his eyes, revealing a vulnerability that disarmed her. His mouth tipped into a crooked grin. Glancing at Mac he said, "Hey, Coach, she's *choice*.''

The next boy, Mark, was a scruffy redhead with freckles, which made him seem a tad less ominous. Mallory shook hands with him and suffered through being referred to as *sweet*, another term she knew was popular with teenagers. Then she was introduced to Eric and Toby, blue-eyed with shaggy brown hair, on the shy side of fifteen. Toby pumped her arm up and down with so much enthusiasm that her shoulder felt as if it might become dislocated.

"Mark and Danno are college boys this year," Mac informed her. The pride in his voice made the boys stand taller.

Danno smiled and arched his bushy black eyebrows. "So what's up, Coach?"

"I've got to do a little street work tonight. When I have to leave Mallory, I need you guys to watch over her."

Danno threw Mallory a curious look. "She in trouble?"

Mac quickly briefed him. "I want you out from under the lights, staying low. Think you can handle it? I don't want her getting hurt, and you're the only friends I can completely trust to watch out for her. I won't color it. These creeps on our tails mean business. My Volvo got blown to smithereens this afternoon. We've been shot at. Just being in the same vicinity with us could be bad for the health."

"If there's anything we're good at, it's gotta be blending in." Danno grinned and slid his dark gaze toward Mallory again. She was beginning to suspect he had practiced that crooked smile for hours, perfecting the lazy, careless twist of his lips so it had just the right effect. The way he stood somehow reminded her of Mac, his hands shoved into his pockets, his shoulders slouched, one hip angled outward. "I'm real sorry about your little girl. All of us are."

Not trusting herself to speak, Mallory merely nodded. She fell into step beside Mac as he struck off down the sidewalk, the four boys flanking them. She noticed that oncoming pedestrians, rather than walk through their number, preferred to spill into the street and brave the traffic, which was considerable. The first time it happened, she wondered why. Then she remembered who she was walking with. If she had met these four boys on a sidewalk, she would have taken her chances in the street, too. And now that she came to think of it, Mac didn't exactly look like the kid next door.

Within the safe circle of his arm, Mallory absorbed the sights and sounds around her. Though it was night, the city seemed bright and glaring to her. She found herself searching every face and wondering if that person knew where Em was. Pain swelled within her. A few hours, that was all they had left.

Every step they took measured off a second, the seconds accumulated into minutes, minutes into hours, taking them closer and closer to deadline.

"Try not to think about it," Mac whispered.

Taken off guard, Mallory threw her head up and stared at him, wondering how he had known. "It's hard not to."

"Think about the welcome-home party we'll throw for her. I have a friend who's a clown."

"Seriously?"

"Yeah, me!" Toby interrupted.

Mac smiled. "What's her favorite cake?"

"Chocolate." Leaning her shoulder against his side, Mallory took a deep breath. Visions of Em at home drifted through her mind, and the frantic feeling inside her slowly subsided. She was lucky to have Mac on her side, she thought. So lucky.

As they walked, the boys relaxed enough in her presence to talk among themselves, including Mac in their teasing banter. Mallory deduced from their conversation that they were on Mac's baseball team, which he had begun coaching several years ago, volunteering his time to an organization for underprivileged, delinquent boys who were thought to be still redeemable. Now she understood why Mac had been so hesitant to discuss the area of Seattle he had grown up in. She also discovered why Mac's end tables didn't match. He was paying for Danno's and Mark's tuition at the University of Washington. Little wonder he drove an old clunker Volvo.

Danno's major was going to be law. Mallory had trouble picturing him in a suit, sitting behind a desk like Keith's. Mark proudly announced he planned to be an accountant. Just when Mallory was beginning to be impressed, Mac winked at her and said Mark already had a job lined up keeping books for the local fence. Mark roared with laughter, then skipped back, doing the elbow bumping thing with Danno.

Watching them, Mallory could see why Mac would fork out thousands of dollars for their education. They were just kids like any others, no matter how they came across when you first met them. Had Mac been a Mark or Danno once? She suspected he had. Glancing at the surrounding throngs of humanity, she could even see why all five of them worked so hard at looking mean. Down here, the weak weren't going to inherit much of anything. A kick in the teeth, maybe.

That thought brought Mallory full circle, back to worrying about Emily. On the upper floors of some of the taller buildings, there were low-rent apartments, their grimy windows mirrored by the lights below. Was Em up there someplace? Was she gazing down, even now, hungry and afraid? Could she see them? Mallory's steps faltered but Mac hauled her relentlessly forward.

They walked several blocks, until they reached a cluster of even taller buildings with graffiti on the exteriors. As they wove in and out of the throngs of people, Mac became watchful, his eyes scanning the women who advertised their wares curbside to passing men in swank cars. Every half block or so, he left Mallory in a shadowed doorway with the boys while he approached one of the girls, slipping her money as he asked her questions. Each time, he came back looking discouraged.

They finally came upon a young woman who whispered something when Mac slipped her some money. Mac thanked her and returned to them. "Pay dirt," he said, satisfaction gleaming in his eyes. "Hey, Danno, do you know of a new—" Breaking off, Mac threw a glance at Mallory. "A new *house* around here?"

"Over two blocks. Why?"

"Corrine's set up there."

Danno's grin vanished. "The redhead?"

Mac nodded. "Lead the way. We'll follow."

Danno clearly found this to be an unacceptable turn of events, but he finally shrugged and struck off down the sidewalk. A few minutes later, he pulled up and glared at Mac over his shoulder. "This is it."

Once more, Mac left Mallory standing on the sidewalk with four grim-faced boys. He went inside a large, run-down house. A quarter of an hour later, he emerged from the building, reclaimed Mallory and lifted an eyebrow at a glaring Danno. "I have to go back downtown and find a fellow called Chapin."

Danno planted his hands on his hips and jutted out his chin. "What's up, Coach? You flipped or what? First we come here. Now we're going to find Chapin? He's a pim—"

"I *know* what he is," Mac cut in. "We don't need it spelled out."

Danno stood there, head cocked to one side, questions shining in his eyes. "You're always preaching to us about avoiding trouble and now you—"

"Danno, trust me," Mac said, reaching out to grip his shoulder reassuringly. "I wouldn't talk to him if I didn't have to."

By the time they had walked clear back downtown, exhaustion was beginning to take its toll. Mallory had had little sleep for days, and it was starting to show.

Mac approached a young woman dressed all in red. Money changed hands and with a slight nod, she indicated a man up the block.

"Thanks." Whirling, Mac walked back to them, giving Danno a thumbs-up. "If something goes wrong, Danno, take her straight to Shelby." Mac's eyes locked with Mallory's. "You remember our deal? Stick to Danno. He'll take care of you."

Mallory grabbed his jacket sleeve. "What do you mean, if something goes wrong?"

He tried to pry her fingers loose and flashed her an unconvincing grin.

Panic flooded her. Until this moment, she hadn't realized just how dangerous this might become for him. It wasn't his fight. "No! Mac, wait. If it's that dangerous, let me go."

Mac cradled her face between his hands. "Mallory, I didn't mean to scare you. I've done this a hundred times."

"But never to get information about someone like Lucetti. This is just as much out of your league as it is for Shelby, isn't it?" It seemed to her that his hands pressed harder against her cheeks. "Answer me! You could be killed, couldn't you? For asking questions about him? I—I don't want you hurt. Em's *my* daughter. It should be my risk. Keith wouldn't expect you to do this.'' His face started to swim, and she realized she was looking at him through tears. She struggled to keep her voice firm. ''Let *me* do it. All you'd have to do is point him out and I'd—''

He was looking down at her as if he had never really seen her before. ''You really mean that, don't you?''

''Well, of cour—''

Her words were smothered midstream by his fingers on her lips. His eyes seemed to look down into hers and see forever. Then he released her. Stepping back, he pried her hand from his sleeve. ''If I get hurt, it'll be my own fault for having insisted on going,'' he said softly, echoing what she had said earlier when he had been afraid to bring her along. ''Besides, I intend to come back. I have an important date to keep, remember? Watching cartoons and eating Pop-Tarts with two beautiful ladies. Now do like you promised me, Mallory, and stay with Danno.''

With that, he slipped away through the crowd, leaving her with the boys. She watched his bobbing blond head. About a quarter block north of them, he approached a man wearing black slacks and a vest over a leopard-patterned silk shirt. Mallory glanced at her companions. They were all four staring at her.

Danno motioned for her to follow him back to the darkened doorway. She fell in beside him. ''If something happens to him, I—'' She gulped and made a helpless gesture with her hands.

''Nothin'll happen. The coach is too slippery.'' He drew her deeper into the shadows. ''You watch. He'll be back before you know it.''

Eric and Toby stood guard, one on each side of the doorway. Mark joined Danno and Mallory in the darkness and reached inside his jacket for a pack of cigarettes. He lit up and took a quick succession of drags, keeping an eye out for Mac.

''The coach will snatch you baldheaded if he catches you,'' Danno warned him. ''You're on your honor to quit.''

''I'm tryin','' Mark snarled. ''Give me a break.'' When the

cigarette was about half gone, his gaze fastened on something beyond the crowd. He quickly tossed the cigarette. "Whoa, Danno, look sharp. We got trouble."

Danno stepped from the shadows to see. Mallory followed. Standing on tiptoe, she saw Mac grab the man in the leopard-patterned shirt by the front of his vest, lift him off his feet, and slam him against the cement wall of the building.

Danno stiffened. "Uh-oh, he's got company comin'."

Mallory's stomach dropped. The people who had gathered around Mac fell back to let a flamboyantly dressed man get through. She saw metal shimmer. Mac threw the man in leopard print onto the sidewalk and whirled, leaping back just in time to avoid a flashing arc as the newcomer swung a knife at him.

"Whoa…" Danno started forward, then turned to look at Mallory. Their eyes met in silent communication. She nodded encouragingly. Grabbing Eric by the sleeve, Danno shoved the younger boy toward her. "Eric, Toby, you guys make like her shadow. The coach needs help."

Eric did a nervous little jig on the sidewalk, jumping to see what was happening. Toby, who was even shorter, grabbed his friend's shoulders and bounced around behind him, his chin lifted. "Oh, man. They got blades! I *knew* we were gonna need ours. The coach is such a priss sometimes."

Mallory craned her neck. Danno and Mark were running at breakneck speed, turning sideways and shoving their way through the throngs, their long hair flying behind them. Mac was now surrounded by three men, the man in leopard print and two others. Jumping into the air, Mac delivered a kick to one man's chest. As he landed, he did a backswing and caught another guy with a stunning blow to the side of his head. The third man slashed with his knife and connected with Mac's side. Mallory clamped a hand over her mouth. Before she realized it, she was running along the sidewalk, Eric and Toby right beside her.

She saw Danno break through the crowd that had gathered to watch the fight. He leaped into the fray, whipping his chain from his jeans as he landed beside Mac. The chain seemed to come alive in Danno's hand, snaking through the air to pluck the knife from one man's fingers. The weapon no sooner clattered onto the cement than Danno spun and whacked another man in the temple. Mac took advantage of the confusion and let fly with another kick to one fellow's chest. After delivering that blow, he followed up with a fist to the man's unguarded midriff. Mark hurtled through the crowd at that point, evening up the odds. The confrontation was over in short order. The two men who had attacked Mac from behind disappeared among the spectators, leaving the man in the leopard-skin patterned shirt alone.

Mac grabbed the man's vest again and shoved him against the building, planting his fist in his midsection. The man grunted under the force of the blow and expelled his air in a gush. "Now start talkin', mister," Mac hissed. Drawing his gun from under his jacket, he pressed its nose against the man's ribs.

Danno and Mark flanked Mac and stood guard to make sure no one interfered. Danno wrapped his length of chain around his arm, prepared to use it as a weapon again if anyone stepped forward. Mallory elbowed her way through the crowd, then stopped, caught up in the breathless tension. A chill slithered over her skin as she glanced at the faces around her. There was a sick eagerness in the air, so thick she could have scooped it with a spoon. They *wanted* Mac to kill the man, were hoping he would. Especially the prostitutes. From the hatred gleaming in their eyes, Mallory suspected they would like to rip Chapin apart. She couldn't blame them. Looking at him, Mallory felt the same primal thirst for revenge. Chapin might not have been directly involved in Emily's abduction, but he was still an associate of Lucetti's. That gave her cause enough to hate him.

Chapin started to shake. "Miles is dead, Bro. That's all I know."

"How did Lucetti figure into it?"

The man rolled his eyes toward the gun. His larynx bobbed

and he cried, ''He'll have me killed if I say. Give me a break, man, please.''

''Talk!'' Mac gave him a threatening shove with the gun.

''Lucetti had three of his goons waste him. Miles was gonna double-cross him. That's all I know. I swear it.''

''How was Miles gonna cross him?''

''I—Lucetti killed somebody, some professional fellow. Miles found out about the killing! I don't know all the details. All I know is Lucetti got wind that Miles had gone sour on him.''

''And how did Miles fit into the organization?''

''I—I think he kept the books. Yeah, that was it. He kept the books. The head accountant.''

''Where can I find Lucetti?''

''I don't know.''

''You'd better tell me, friend, or I'll blow a hole in you the size of a baseball diamond.''

''I—I don't know. I'd tell you if I knew. I would. I never see Lucetti, just the guy under him. I swear it.''

''And who is that?''

''Andrews, Jake Andrews. You can find him at Longacres on the weekends. He likes to bet on the horses. Otherwise, I don't know. That's where I always meet him.''

''Okay. What about the three men who wasted Miles? What were their names?''

''I—I don't know. One was a guy named Fields, I think. They work together—on the financial end—collecting I think. I'm not sure, man. I'm not lyin'. I'm just not sure.''

Apparently satisfied, Mac released his grip on the man's vest. The boys backed off and continued to check out the crowd. Mac ran his hand down over his eyes, blinked, then gave his head a shake as if to clear it. He spotted Mallory then and moved toward her, Danno and Mark closing in behind him. The moment he reached her, Mac seized her arm.

''We have to get out of here,'' he growled, pulling her forward into a run.

Mallory knew that Mac was afraid the other two men had

gone for help. As they sprinted up the sidewalk, the boys fell in around them. The pounding of their feet on the cement seemed deafening as they took the corner and headed east.

"Mac, are you cut?" she asked breathlessly.

"Just my jacket. *Miles.* I knew I recognized that name!"

"What d'you mean?" she panted.

"Dead, he's dead. I read about it in the paper right before I left town. They found his body in an alley. Beaten to death."

Jerking her half off her feet, Mac took a sudden left turn down a dark alley. When Mallory saw the looming swath of blackness ahead, she nearly balked. If the streets were dangerous, a dark alley like this was suicidal. Then she remembered who she was running with and decided they were probably at home in dark alleys.

They spilled out at the other end of the alley onto a street that intersected with the block they had just fled. Cutting through traffic, ignoring the many screeching brakes, they picked up the alley again on the other side. Mallory lost all sense of direction. Mac was circling, backtracking to throw pursuers off their trail. It seemed to her they ran for hours. She reached the point of exhaustion and passed beyond it into blessed numbness. She couldn't feel her legs, couldn't tell if her sides were still aching. But she was keeping up.

When Mac drew up beside the white BMW, she fell across the front fender and labored for air. It was some comfort that Danno looked like a blob of jelly beside her, his mouth gaping as he fought to breathe. Mark leaned against the building and slid down it to sit on the sidewalk. Holding his belly with one arm, he groaned and started coughing.

"That's what cigarettes do for you," Mac said with a growl as he unlocked the passenger door of the car. "Come on, pile in. I want to get out of here."

Mallory skirted the open door on quivery legs, so weak she felt as though she might collapse before she made it onto the seat. Danno boosted her in by placing a hand on her back. He slid in beside her and sank low, throwing his head back and gulping for air. The other three boys climbed in back. After

Mac got in, he gave everyone a quick once-over, then cranked the engine. "Everybody in one piece?"

"Yeah," Danno assured him. "Fine, Coach."

"Good, that means I can wring all your necks. I thought I told you to stick with Mallory?" He swerved the car out onto the street. "What did you think you were doing, Danno? You could've been killed. Or what if the cops had come? Assault with a deadly weapon? I asked you not to carry chains anymore."

"Sorry, Coach. We'll trash them, I promise." He took several deep breaths and swallowed. "Tomorrow. We'll do it tomorrow. Right, Mark? I'm sorry."

"Sorry? Sorry wouldn't comfort your mother much if you ended up hurt! That wasn't a game out there. Those guys were trying to kill me. And what about Mallory? How would you have felt if you'd gone back and found her with her throat slit?"

Eric leaned forward to peer over the seat. "Coach, Danno didn't leave the broad alone. I stayed with her."

Mac reached back and smacked Eric's forehead with the heel of his hand. It was more an affectionate thump than a reprimand. "Apologize, idiot. You don't call women broads."

"Why not? I've heard you—"

"Er-rr-ic! Just apologize, please."

"Sorry."

Mallory closed her eyes. "Apology accepted." Glancing at Mac, she said, "And it was my fault Danno left me. I could have stopped him."

"I'll wring *your* neck, too, then. If I get into a spot, I don't want the *diaper* brigade coming to help." Glaring into the rearview mirror, he said, "I'm trying to get you guys straightened out, not killed. A serious offense for any of you and it's going on your permanent records. End of career. Is that what you want, Mark?"

"I'm nineteen," Danno protested. "That's not exactly the diaper brigade. You were fighting in Vietnam when you were younger than me."

"Just old enough to go to trial as an adult, that's what you are. No more juvenile hall and a slap on the wrist for you, Danno. You do realize that an attorney can't be a convicted felon? You keep your nose clean, understand?"

"I have! I've been so straight, my back aches!" Danno jack-knifed forward so he could see around Mallory. "You were in trouble. What was I supposed to do? Let them cut you to pieces? You wouldn't have deserted me, law or no law."

Mac took a right turn and pulled the car up next to a curb. Mallory peered out the window at a two-story Victorian row house that had been converted into apartments. Many of the windows were patched with cardboard. Trash was strewn across the porch and small yard. Dim lights shone through tattered curtains.

"Danno, I'm counting on you to keep these yahoos off the streets tonight. Got it? Those guys might recognize you."

"Consider it done," Danno replied sullenly.

"Coach…" Mark's voice sounded strangely off-key. "Coach, I think maybe I'm bleeding."

Even in the dim light, Mallory saw the color wash from Mac's face. He twisted in the seat. "You're what?"

Mallory had seen Mac scared a number of times, but never had she seen such stark terror in his expression. He loved these boys as much as he would his own. She could feel his body going taut. Struggling for room to turn around and battling a suddenly writhing ball of frightened boys, Mallory at last managed to get on her knees so she could look over the seat. "Open your door, Danno," she said crisply as she reached for Mark's uplifted arm. "I can't see anything in the dark. Mac, give me some room."

The cool authority in Mallory's voice brought Mac's head around. The dome light flickered on. A little amazed, Mac did as she said and scooted aside, watching as she gently slipped Mark's jacket off his shoulder and freed his arm from the sleeve. "Don't look so scared, Mark," she said with a grin. "If it was serious, you would be pumped dry by now." She turned his arm to examine a long slash that ran from his elbow toward his wrist. Placing a thumb on each side, she pulled at the edges of the wound. "It'll hurt like the devil, but it's not going to need stitches. Hardly more than a scratch. You were lucky."

Mac realized he was shaking. The calm in Mallory's voice soothed him like a balm. Passing a hand over his eyes, he let out a breath of pent-up air. Some of Mark's color was returning. The boy grinned. "Yeah, I figured it was nothing."

Danno laughed. "Which explains why he's green. Admit it, Mark, you thought you'd got it bad."

"Well…" Mark's voice rang with anger. "I couldn't feel anything. When it doesn't hurt, it's usually real deep."

Mallory gave his shoulder a pat. "I think you were just too scared to feel it. Have you had a recent tetanus shot? Good." Turning toward Danno, she said, "I want you to disinfect it—"

"Not with merthiolate, either," Mark cut in.

"—and wrap it with clean gauze," Mallory went on. "By morning, it won't need a bandage."

"It's not *that* teeny a cut," Mark cried. "Whatcha think you are, a doctor or something?"

"A nurse. Used to be, at any rate. Not a very good one, I admit, but I do know enough to recognize a life-threatening wound." Mallory gave him a reassuring smile. "Trust me, Mark. It's superficial. Your jacket got the worst of it."

Mac's attention snagged on what she had said. She was a nurse, but not a very good one? There was an underlying bitterness in her voice. From where he sat, watching her in action, he would have said she was top-notch. Even before she had known how serious the injury was, she had reacted with calmness and decisiveness. Which was better than he had done. She was a natural, able to instill trust in others, take control.

"I'll take care of him," Danno teased. "Once I finish with it, he'll *think* it's life threatening."

The boys piled out and slammed the car doors, plunging the interior back into shadow. Mac lowered his window and reached out to collar Mark as he walked past. Drawing him toward the car, he ruffled the boy's hair. "Thanks, my friend."

After giving him a light punch on the chin, he plucked the cigarettes out of Mark's shirt pocket. "I'll be in touch."

"Coach, don't you know how much those are a pack now?"

"Yeah, too expensive for a college kid. So quit, huh? And the next time I see you, that chain better not be in your pants. Clear? I'm serious, Mark. No weapons, period, no matter what. I have too big an investment in you."

"Yeah, yeah."

Mac leaned his head out the window. "Hey, Danno! Come here a minute."

Mallory sat down and leaned across the seat to roll down the window so the boy wouldn't have to open the door. Danno braced his hands on the top of the car and bent at the waist to bring his face on a level with theirs. "Yo?"

"I owe you one," Mac told him huskily. "If you hadn't come along when you did, I wouldn't be here. If I came across as ungrateful, I didn't mean to. You saved my bacon. Thanks."

"What goes around, comes around. It's called a payback, Coach. I'm sorry I left your lady. It just seemed like the thing to do at the moment, you know?" Even in the dark, Danno's teeth gleamed as his mouth slanted into the lazy grin. Extending his hand to Mallory, he said, "I hope I see more of you."

"I'd like that." Mallory was faintly surprised to realize that she actually meant it. She gave Danno's hand a friendly squeeze, then dug in her purse for her business-card case. "Hold on a sec." She found a pen and scribbled notes on the backs of two cards, signing off with her initials. Handing them to Danno, she said, "There's one for you and one for Mark. Go to that address and tell them I sent you. You can both get on-the-job training there with fairly good pay. After school, summers. When you get your degrees, get in touch with me through Mac. I know a couple of influential people who may be interested in promising young graduates."

"No lie? Hey, that'd be radical. Why would you want to do that?" He tipped one card toward the streetlight so he could read the print. "Attorneys at Law? Hey, it's right downtown. Me and Mark can walk there. You sure they'll hire us?"

"Guarantee it." Mallory snapped her purse closed. "As for why? It's called a payback, Danno. Thank you for all your help tonight."

With a chuckle, Danno threw his chain on the seat beside her. "She *is* choice, Coach. Don't let her get away."

Mac bumped the horn as he pulled out into traffic. Craning her neck, Mallory watched the boys until the car rounded a corner and she could no longer see them. Turning back to Mac, she sighed. "Quite some baseball team you've got there."

"They're especially good with bats."

She wished she could manage a smile, but it simply wasn't in her. Leaning her head back, she closed her eyes. "Now what?"

"Now we can relax until Lucetti calls in the morning. I have enough information on him to hang his—" he cleared his throat "—to hang him. Because of that he'll have to give us the extra time we need. At least if he doesn't want the wrong people to hear he wasted Miles and that other guy. Which I'm sure he doesn't. Knowing his penchant for keeping his trail swept clean, he wouldn't like the heat it would generate. Even if the cops couldn't find him, they'd sure make a massive effort to." Her shoulder was touching his. He glanced down at her. "Hey, you okay? You're skaking."

Mallory tried to smile. She wasn't at all okay. Mac's line of reasoning seemed sound, but that was all it was, a line of reasoning. He didn't have an insight into the future. He couldn't predict Lucetti's next move with any certainty. She knew he meant to comfort her, but a new kind of terror had her in its grasp. If Chapin was the kind of man who had Emily, was her daughter still alive?

Chapter Eleven

Before they went home, Mac stopped at a pay phone to call Shelby. Thus far, his friend had learned nothing about the identities of the three men chasing them. Teddy, the gunsmith, had come up with zilch. If the men did business anywhere on a steady basis, it was outside Seattle. Shelby's luck had been no better. A friend of his had run a tracer on the car, and the only real lead he got on a cream-colored Buick with similar tags turned out to be a vehicle that had been reported stolen. The three would-be killers were clearly professionals, far too clever to do their misdeeds in a car that could be traced to them. And Shelby had gotten no information on Miles out on the streets. He did agree to keep trying with the information they'd just gotten.

Mallory's house seemed eerily silent when they went inside. And the overturned and dismantled furniture left by the searchers was a grim reminder of the danger they and Emily were in. Mallory tossed Mac's sack of mail on the table in the breakfast nook and, driven by hunger she could no longer ignore, stepped to the refrigerator. She needed her strength.

She withdrew a container of yogurt. "Want something?" Mallory asked.

"Two of those for me," Mac replied, pointing to Mallory's yogurt.

They ate standing, backs to the counter, their gazes locked on nothing, eyes glazed with exhaustion. Mallory was trying desperately to be optimistic. Mac had to be right. Lucetti *would* give them more time. She either had to believe in that or lose her mind.

When the containers of yogurt were scooped clean, they gravitated upstairs to reassemble Mallory's bed. It would accommodate two bodies. Both of them were too tired to wade through the shambles in another bedroom to fix a second bed, and Mac seemed inclined to sleep near her. She supposed he was uneasy because of the attempts on their lives that day. She could understand that and appreciate it. She needed to stay alive until Em was home safe. But it seemed an unnecessary precaution; every window and door had a safety latch. Then she remembered Lucetti's men had already gotten into the house, and how easily Mac had broken in. Maybe it was a sensible precaution.

Mac stripped off his jacket, holster, shirt and wristbands, discarding them in a pile on the rug. Then he toppled onto the bed on his back. Slanting an arm across his eyes, he yawned and groaned. Mallory stared at him, convinced the breadth of his shoulders took up more than half the space. Her gaze lowered to his bronzed chest and her throat tightened. She had never seen male flesh contoured into so many rock-hard bulges and ridges.

"I'm so tired, I'm dead," he murmured on the crest of a sigh.

He looked amazingly vital to Mallory. Suddenly she needed a little distance. "I'm going to wash off and put on my nightclothes. That is, if you don't mind. I have a flannel gown that's—"

"Honey, you can come back in nothing and I won't notice," he cut in gently. "Just do whatever you have to and come to bed so you can get some rest. There's nothing more we can do tonight."

Closeted in the bathroom, Mallory washed her face, applied night cream, brushed her teeth and wriggled out of her clothes. The clean flannel gown felt like heaven. She supposed she should sleep dressed since there was a man in her bed, but she was too sore. She had chosen her primmest gown. Stepping back into the bedroom, she felt suddenly shy and doused the light. As she moved toward the bed, a rumbling sound made her leap. She peered through the darkness. There it came again. Mac was snoring. The sound was comforting, made her feel less alone. She lay down, trying not to wiggle the mattress, and hugged her side to keep space between them.

Mac muttered something and rolled toward her, slinging a heavy arm across her waist. He pulled her close and nuzzled his face into her hair. Just when she was about to protest, he let loose with another rumbling snore that fluttered the hair at her nape. The stiffness left Mallory's body. If this was a sly pass, he was a master and his embrace was comforting.

She leaned back against the broad, cushioned wall of his chest. It had been so long since a man had held her that she had forgotten how good it felt. Surely it couldn't hurt...just for a while. He was asleep, after all. And—as she often told Em—everyone needed a hug now and again, even mommies. His arm was heavy, but not too heavy, the bone and sinew overlaid with a thick layer of muscle and smooth flesh. Wonderfully warm. Lying close to him made her feel confident that everything would indeed be okay. If needing that kind of reassurance was wrong, if it was weak of her, then it would be her secret. In just a few minutes, she would pull away. He would never know. She closed her eyes, absorbing his heat, finding solace, however meager, for this little while. Her last thoughts were of Emily as she plummeted into a black void of exhaustion.

Some time later—Mallory had no idea how long—she awoke with a start, her heart slamming as she clawed her way up from a nightmare. She had been standing on a city sidewalk, looking up at the grimy window of an apartment. Emily's face was on the other side of the glass. Creeping up behind her was a horrible man with a switchblade, his mouth twisted in an evil grin. Running frantically back and forth in front of the building, Mallory sought a door. Above her, she heard Emily screaming. There was no way inside the building, no way to reach her.

She was going to be killed, and Mallory couldn't save her.... Drenched in sweat, Mallory had jerked awake, her hands clawing the mattress.

For several moments, the dream still held her in its clutches, so real she could hear Em crying, "Mommy, Mommy, save me, save me!" Not wishing to wake Mac, Mallory slipped out of the bed. The residual horror of the nightmare drove her into the hall. She went to Em's room and flipped on the light. After staring at the mess for several minutes, she began putting Em's clothes back into her drawers. When that was done, she dragged the mattress into place and remade the bed. One chore led to another, and before she knew it, she was putting the whole room back together, feverish in her need to have everything as it had been before.

She worked until she was limp with exhaustion. Then she found Ragsdale. The little dog had been gutted, his stuffing tossed all over the floor. A cry tore from her throat and she began to shake. She fled the room, hugging the destroyed toy to her breast. She walked aimlessly through the house, stumbling sometimes on out-of-place cushions and lamps. Tears flowed down her cheeks and soaked Ragsdale's floppy ears. When her sobs became so ragged that they sapped her remaining strength, she sank to her knees and leaned against the dining-room wall. She had no idea how long she cried, only that she at last cried herself empty. No more tears, no more anything. Just a great aching hole where her heart had once been.

That was how Mac found her. He had missed her in his sleep and jerked awake to go find her. In the moonlight, she looked like a little girl, huddled on the floor in a trailing nightgown, hair tousled into a silken cloud. Dropping to one knee beside her, he touched Ragsdale and felt the wet fur.

"Mallory, sweetheart, what're you doing down here?"

"Just thinking."

"Thinking? You've got to get some sleep."

"I did. I slept. They tore Ragsdale apart, Mac."

He glanced down at the dog's flattened torso. There was a peculiar, hollow sound to her voice. He knew that she was somehow equating the destroyed dog with her daughter, imagining Em destroyed as well. Mac settled for touching her hair, but what he really wanted was to gather her into his arms and soothe away her pain. If only he could. "Can you think in bed where you won't get chilled?"

"I didn't want to wake you." She turned her face toward him, "That Chapin man—he was a horrible person, wasn't he? Em may be dead, Mac. I have to face that."

He sighed. She had seen an ugliness tonight she had never glimpsed before. He wished there was something he could say to ease her mind, but there was nothing. The bald truth was, she was right. Em might be dead. And if she wasn't yet, she might be soon.

Gathering her into his arms, Mac rose to his feet, amazed that she weighed so little. As he shifted her so he could maneuver the stairs, Ragsdale's wet ears flopped against his bare chest. He felt her drop the dog onto her lap. The next instant, she looped her slender arms around his neck and pressed her face into the hollow of his throat, clinging to him as though he were a lifeline. She smelled like night cream and flannel, a sweet, clean scent that was far more arousing to him than expensive perfume. Some knight in shining armor he was, he thought with disgust.

When he crested the landing, he turned left down the hall to her room. When he lowered her onto the bed, she still held on to him. Warning bells rang in his head. He stretched out beside her. She pressed close, flattening her small breasts against his ribs, fitting her pelvis to the slope of his denim-clad hip. Her hair fanned across his chest like warm silk. He felt her lips, velvety against the hollow of his shoulder, her breath a mist of sweetness. He could feel her trembling.

"Mac…" Her voice drifted to him no louder than a whisper. "Would you—" She pressed even closer, clinging, almost frantic. "Would you love me?"

Mac wasn't sure where his stomach went, but from the feel of things, it was somewhere under the bed. His arm stiffened around her. It seemed to him that her small body turned molten, impressing itself into his skin like a searing brand. Would he love her? As if it would be some gigantic favor? He wanted her with aching intensity.

"You'd be sorry later."

"I don't care about later. Make the hurting stop. Make me stop thinking. Hold me. Oh, please, Mac, hold me."

Her voice broke on the last word. Mac's every instinct told him to go for it. Only a heel would turn a lady down when she said please, right? Wrong. Only a heel would take her up on it. For a long while, he lay there, battling with his hormones. At last she relaxed and nuzzled her cheek into his shoulder. It ignited his every nerve ending. He rolled toward her so he could come up on one elbow above her. Placing a hand on the curve of her narrow waist, he lowered his head and feathered kisses across her forehead, ignoring the inviting curve of her tear-swollen mouth.

"You're not yourself right now, Mallory. You're frightened and exhausted and vulnerable. Ask me when Em's safe and sound, and I'll take you up on it, fast." As if she would. This was a once in a lifetime chance and, idiot that he was, he was passing it up.

She said nothing. He imagined that she was lying there feeling humiliated, and he wanted to kick himself. Truth was, he wasn't well practiced in turning down gorgeous women. First off, not many had asked. Secondly, he was no monk. Mallory, however, seemed different. Too sweet, too vulnerable, too precious to him. Her hipbone fit into his palm as if she had been molded especially for him. One of his knees had slipped between her thighs, stretching the flannel taut between their juncture so he could feel the white-hot softness of her. The fire in his loins intensified. Without realizing it, he trailed his mouth to her cheek, to the corner of her mouth. He felt his willpower slipping, imagined plunging into the honeyed slickness of her, imagined touching every satiny inch of her skin.

"Unless you're sure," he amended, hating himself for being so completely conscienceless. "Do you promise not to hate me later?"

No answer.

"Mallory?"

He brushed his lips across hers. Her silken mouth was slack. His twisted into a reluctant grin. She had fallen into an exhausted sleep. He groaned and rolled off her, doing a face plant on the mattress. His body found no solace there. Nearly an hour later, he was still awake, his hands curled into loose fists. *Mac, would you love me?* The question replayed in his head a hundred—no, a thousand—times. When at last the ache of need released its hold on him, he was glad his answer had been no. Only desperation could have driven her to such a request. He had to find her child. It wasn't just a favor to Keith anymore, something he was involved in because he felt obligated. It was something more personal. *Mac, would you love me?* Heaven help him, yes. It went against everything he had believed in for fourteen years, but yes....

LUCETTI CALLED at eight fifty-nine the next morning, which was a vast improvement on the waiting game they had endured the previous day. They had discussed strategy, so this time Mac answered the phone. Mac was afraid Lucetti might get nasty, and they thought Mac would be better able to withstand his threats. In an icy tone, he explained that Mallory had not yet been able to find the key.

"I told you twenty-four hours," Lucetti snarled.

Mac cocked his head. In the background, he could hear a church bell ringing out the hour. No horns, only an occasional hum of tires. Wherever Lucetti was, it was an extremely quiet neighborhood. "We did our best to come through. A key is hard to find. We've had some complications, namely some men trying to kill us at every turn. And they aren't in any way connected to me, I can guarantee that. Three men, wearing suits—"

"You're lying, Mac Phearson! I have my men shadowing you every minute of the day. If there had been an attempt on your lives, I would have been informed of it."

"Then it must be *your* men doing it. At least check out my

story. Put a tail on them or something. We can't find a key while dodging bullets and car bombs.''

"You're stalling. My men don't act without orders. That's how I operate and they know it.''

"We need more time. Two extra days, at least.''

"Forget it. Eight hours, Mac Phearson, then it's funeral time. You don't seem to understand. I'm holding the trump card, the kid.''

Mac had hoped to avoid admitting that he and Mallory knew about Miles's murder, but Em's life was at stake and it was the only bargaining chip he had. "You hold *most* of the trump,'' he replied. "If you're a pinochle player, however, you know that's not enough. To shoot the moon, you need them all.''

"Meaning?''

"I went slumming in downtown Seattle last night.'' Mac could only hope that by hinting around, he could imply that he knew a great deal more than he actually did. "Does the murder of Steven Miles jog any memories? And the death of a certain professional? If the wrong people get wind of that, things could become very uncomfortable for you.''

The silence on the other end of the line stretched into infinity. "Leak it to the cops and the kid's dead.''

Mac swallowed down an upsurge of anger. "I have no intention of leaking anything. We need more time. And to borrow your phrase, I'm playing my trump. Cooperation's the name of this game. Now do we get some leeway here, or not?''

"Another forty-eight hours. And that's it. If you don't come through by then, Mrs. Christiani will be the one who receives a package. A small one, to start. Would her daughter's little finger motivate her, do you think?''

Mac heard a whimper erupt from Mallory. Sweat popped out on his face. He wanted to shove the phone down Lucetti's throat. "Put the child on the phone. I stress this. If I don't talk to her, if I'm not completely satisfied that she's not only alive but in good spirits, I phone the cops. In short, you'd better treat that little girl like she's made of glass. Got it?''

"I'll call back."

The line went abruptly dead. Mac hung up and turned to look at Mallory. She stood near him, her face blanched pasty white, her eyes gigantic. She looked like she'd topple if he touched a finger to her forehead. Mac closed the distance between them and enfolded her in his arms even though he had sworn off any further physical contact with her. Four o'clock that morning seemed like a lifetime ago. She felt so small and insubstantial. He tightened his embrace, hunched his shoulders around her and buried his face in her hair.

"It's okay. Just threats. He won't really do it."

"H-her finger? Oh, Mac…" Her voice trailed off into a wail. She clutched his shirt so hard that he felt her nails dig into his skin. "What am I going to do?"

"Mallory, it's all right. Shh. Don't let him do this to you."

Unable to think of anything else to say, Mac simply held her, stroking her hair, swaying with her from side to side, keeping his arms cinched tight as if he could pour his strength into her. When the phone rang, he lowered her onto a chair.

"You want to talk to her?"

She covered her face with trembling hands and gave her head a vehement shake. "In a minute. I don't want to f-frighten her."

Mac stepped to the phone, lifted the receiver and said hello. A brief silence ensued. Then Em's hesitant voice came over the wire. "Where's my mommy? Do I have the wrong house?"

That voice reached right down inside Mac and wrapped itself around his heart. He closed his eyes and smiled. "This must be Em. I'm Mac, your mommy's friend."

Another silence. "A boyfriend?" she asked, clearly amazed.

Mac's smile widened. "Sort of."

"Do you have hair?"

That question took him aback for a moment. "Um—yeah, I have hair."

"Oh, good. Gerald didn't. I didn't want a new daddy who didn't have hair so Mommy stopped bringing him. Gramps said he was stuffy, anyway."

Good for Keith. "How are you, Emily? Are the people there treating you nice?"

"Yeah, but I still wish Gramps would get well so I could come home. The lady where I'm at brings me movies and ice cream, but it's not fun like it is with Mommy. I don't have my Pooh bag and I miss Ragsdale."

The child evidently still believed she was staying away from home because her grandfather was still in the hospital. "Your mommy's been really busy," Mac replied. "She couldn't get away to bring you Ragsdale."

"Is my Gramps real sick?"

"He's a little better, but still very weak."

"Can I say hi to my mommy, please?"

Mac glanced toward Mallory. She was so white, she looked as though she might faint, but she stood and came to take the phone. In a tremulous voice, she said, "Hi, princess. How's my favorite girl?"

"Fine. Do I get to see you today?"

Mallory closed her eyes. "Not today, darling, but soon."

"Tomorrow, then?" Em whispered something and the line crackled. "I have to go, Mommy. Would you bring me quarters when you come so I can talk a long time? I love you. Don't forget Ragsdale, okay? Bye."

"I love you, too, Em." Mallory tightened her grip on the phone. Mac heard more rustling noises coming over the wire. The next moment, Lucetti's voice rasped over the speaker. "Forty-eight hours, same place, same time of morning." Lucetti punctuated the order with a click of the phone. Mac sighed and cast a concerned glance at Mallory as she dropped the receiver into its cradle. She was still shaking.

"I want to try questioning Keith again," she said. "There m-must be a way to set up some s-sort of signal. There has to be. I'll call his physician and get special permission for you to enter the ICU."

"Are you sure you want to take that risk? If he realizes Em's been kidnapped, it might make him worse."

She nodded. "If something happens to her, he'll n-never forgive me for not at least trying."

Mac wasn't as concerned about Keith's feelings as he was about Mallory's. If questioning the older man caused a second stroke, she would spend the rest of her life blaming herself for it. On the other hand, if they didn't question Keith, and Emily was killed... Mac shuddered. Just talking to the child for a few minutes, he had completely lost his heart to her. And if he felt that strong a pull, what must Mallory be feeling?

THE MOMENT THEY STEPPED into the ICU, Keith's eyes filled with apprehension. Mallory caught her lower lip between her teeth and approached the bed. As before, Keith's hand felt cold when she grasped it. Was it her imagination, or was he thinner? The network of bones in his hand felt fragile. Mallory tried to smile and failed miserably. Keith's mouth drew down at one corner and he moaned, glancing pleadingly at Mac.

"Dad," Mallory began hesitantly. "I, um, want you to stay calm, okay? I have something to tell you—bad news, I'm afraid." She hesitated to let that sink in. "Em's been kidnapped."

Keith shrank into the mattress like a deflated doll, his eyes falling closed.

"She's safe. We spoke to her just a few minutes ago. They're giving her ice cream and showing her movies. She sounded fine." Mallory took a deep breath. "In exchange for her return, Lucetti is demanding a package. He believes it's in your safe-deposit box at the bank. We, um, are having some difficulty finding the box key."

Keith's eyes flew open. He looked imploringly at Mac. Leaning forward, Mac grasped his shoulder. "You can count on me, Keith. I'll get her home, safe and sound."

Mallory took another deep, bracing breath. "We're hoping to set up some kind of signal with you so that you can give us some hints as to where the key might be."

Keith kept his gaze glued to Mac and moaned. The sound was so pitiful that Mallory flinched.

"Anyway, I came up with an idea. I know that you can't control your eyelids enough to blink just once. We tried that last night. But if you could only blink when you mean yes and try your best not to let your eyelids close when your answer is no, maybe we can ask you enough questions to find the key. Do you think you could do that?"

Keith blinked in rapid succession. Mallory threw Mac a joyful glance. "Oh, Dad, that's great."

Mac drew up a chair and sat down. Mallory lifted Keith's hand to enfold it in hers. "Dad, it's crucial that you stay calm through this. We don't want to hurt you, you know. So before we start, I want to assure you that Emily will be fine. Mac dug up some dirt on Lucetti, so he doesn't harm her. If he does, he knows we'll have him arrested. So there's no reason to feel frightened for her, okay?"

Keith's eyelids fluttered and Mac smiled encouragement to Mallory. "Okay," she said, "if you get tired, just keep your eyes closed and we'll let you rest. First question. Is the package in your safe-deposit box?"

Keith blinked furiously.

"Okay, so all we have to do is find the key." Mallory glanced at Mac. "Is the key at the house?"

No blinking.

"Not at the house. Okay. Is it at your office?"

No.

"Is it in your car?"

No.

"Is it in Bellevue?"

No blinking. Mallory began to squirm. This yes and no questioning could only go so far. *Please, God.*

"Is it in Seattle?"

Keith's eyes went crazy and he moaned.

"Now, Dad, stay calm," she reminded him. "Don't become frustrated. Remember that every answer you give us eliminates a wild-goose chase and brings us one step closer to finding the key. Think of it positively, even if you can't tell us everything you'd like." A frown drew her brows together. "Is it in another safe-deposit box in Seattle?"

No.

"In a locker at the bus depot?"

No.

"At the airport?"

No.

Keith was breathing heavily now, his air rasping as it went down his throat. Mallory glanced at the monitor. His pulse had accelerated. "Mac, it's about time for him to rest," she warned.

Mac rose from his chair to place a staying hand on her shoulder, his gaze intent on Keith's. "Just one more question. Did you give it to a friend?"

Keith's eyelids fluttered wildly and his bottom lip twisted in a grotesque grin as he tried desperately to say something.

"Okay—okay, relax, Keith," Mac said soothingly. "It's with a friend. That's something for us to go on. The rest is elementary. We'll just get on the horn and start calling people. Did you tell this friend not to give the key to anyone?"

No.

"That's great," Mac said enthusiastically. "Now all we have to do is find the friend. There can't be that many people you trust that much."

Keith looked so tormented that Mallory wished they hadn't come. "Dad, you have to stay calm."

The ICU nurse came bustling in just then. Her blue eyes shot daggers at Mac as she came around the end of the bed. "He's going to have to rest now. I'll have to ask you to leave."

Mac leaned over Keith. "Trust me. I'll find it. We'll try to get word to you as soon as we have news. Meanwhile, remember one thing. When I needed you, you were there. This is my chance to pay you back. I'll come through for you. You've got my word on it. So don't worry, okay? Concentrate on getting well."

AS THEY EXITED the hospital, Mallory glanced up and spied tears glistening in Mac's eyes. To her surprise, he made no effort to conceal them. When one escaped and trailed down his cheek, he wiped it away, throwing her a rueful smile.

"I love that old man," he muttered. "It kills me, seeing him like that. I hated upsetting him. Makes me feel like I ran the knife in deeper and gave it a twist."

"I know what you mean," she said in a tight voice.

"No. I don't think anyone can." He lifted one shoulder in a shrug. "He's—" He shook his head. "To me, he's the father I never had."

"What was the favor he did for you?"

He shoved his hands deep into his slacks pockets. "Put my life back together for me. Have you ever been completely alone?"

Mallory hadn't been, but she understood now what he meant, better than he knew. If not for Mac, she would have been alone since Em's abduction. Alone and desperate.

"So alone that there's no hope, no way out? I—" He took a ragged breath. "Someone I loved got killed. My brother. We'd had an argument. I was working to put him through school. He was throwing four years of my life away, his grades going to hell, his attitude disintegrating. I had put up with all I was going to. He left in a rage. Got drunk. Killed himself in a car. I blamed myself. Couldn't forget the ugly things I had said. I felt like I had driven him to it."

Randy. Mallory averted her face.

"I started drinking. I know that sounds weak, but I was young, confused—I think I wanted to die, too. I'd sit by his grave, me and my whiskey bottle, and stare at his name until I got so blasted I couldn't read it anymore. When my poor mother was at her wit's end, she called Keith Christiani. He found me. Took me to a hotel. Threw me in a cold shower. And made me so miserable I sobered up in self-defense. It took him a while, but he finally made me see that I wasn't to blame, that I couldn't have stopped what happened, even if I'd seen it coming."

"He's a wonderful man," **Mallory** whispered. "A loving man."

Mac sighed, a shaky, wet sound. "I never knew my biological father. Maybe it sounds corny, but Keith's the only person besides my mother who ever believed in me. Because he had been so fond of my brother and knew I had worked to put him through school, he saw something worthwhile in me that I had never been able to see. He stuck his neck out for me, not once but a dozen times. When I didn't have confidence, he had enough for both of us. If not for him, I'd be— You said once that I didn't owe him my life? I do, Mallory, I really do."

She at last found the courage to face him. "Add another person to that list."

"What list?"

"Of people who believe in you." She felt tears welling in her own eyes. "Make that two people. I have a feeling Em will want to be on it one day."

When they reached the BMW, Mac checked the car over for explosives. When he found nothing, he waved Mallory in on her side, then climbed behind the wheel and cranked the engine. He didn't seem to want to talk about Keith anymore. She didn't, either. It could lead too easily into a discussion of Randy.

"Well, now where to?" he asked. "Your head seems to be operating better than mine, today. You choose."

"His office."

"But he said it wasn't there."

"Yes, but Trudy is. If anyone would know who Keith would have given something that important to, it'd be Trudy."

"WHY MAC, of course," was Trudy's immediate response after she had pummeled them with questions about the gunfire yesterday. "Of all his friends, it would be Mac he'd call if he were in trouble. What kind of trouble was he in? I knew he was upset, but I didn't know why."

Mac ignored the question. "I was out of town. Who else, Trudy? Think hard. It's extremely important."

Trudy hesitated. "Well, he has dozens of friends, all of them loyal, I'm sure. Keith inspires that in people."

"Dozens?" Mac said faintly. "Do you have a list?"

"I can give you his Rolodex."

Mallory's heart sank. It would take the remainder of the day to call all the people in a Rolodex. "Would you, Trudy?"

Trudy disappeared into Keith's office and reappeared a moment later with the Rolodex, which she handed to Mac. Her green eyes filled with concern as she peered at Mallory over the tinted lenses of her glasses. "There's something terribly wrong, isn't there? Something's happened? Something other than Keith's stroke."

"I—I can't say," Mallory told her gently. "Just pray for us, Trudy. We need all the help we can get."

THEY DID THE PHONE CALLING in shifts. Late in the afternoon, while Mallory took her turn dialing and interrogating people, Mac cleaned up the kitchen, then foraged in the freezer and quick-thawed some sirloin for dinner. She wasn't sure how she was going to manage to eat. But she knew she must. To help Em, she needed to keep her strength up. That meant eating nutritious food and resting whenever an opportunity presented itself. It also meant she must have faith that everything would turn out all right. Otherwise, swallowing food would be an impossibility. And so would closing her eyes.

In less than an hour, Mac insisted she take a break from telephoning and eat the meal he'd prepared. She finished her conversation with a man from Seattle named Harry Reisling who claimed to be an old service buddy of Keith's. No, he hadn't seen Keith in months. No, he didn't have a key belonging to Keith. He was extremely sorry to hear that his friend had suffered a stroke. Mallory rang off with a promise that she would give her father-in-law Harry's best.

To her surprise, she was ravenously hungry and managed to make quite a dent in the food Mac had heaped on her plate. When she couldn't swallow another morsel, Mallory settled back in her chair and toyed with the handle of her coffee cup. Mac propped his elbows on the table and rested his chin on his fists. "Now," he said in a low voice, "how about a long, hot shower and an early night. You didn't get much rest last night.''

Despite the fact that she had only just lectured herself on the importance of getting rest, Mallory found it difficult to follow through. Em was out there somewhere. Her life was in danger. She glanced at the Rolodex. ''I'm not finished.''

''I'll finish. We have an entire day left.'' Not a lot of time, he thought, but he wasn't about to say so. ''You can afford to rest and recoup your strength.''

As tired as she was, Mallory hated to leave him with all the work. ''Only if I clean up the kitchen first.''

''A deal. I hate dishes.''

They finished their coffee in silence, the first real lull they'd had all day. Mallory avoided looking at him, afraid of what she might read in his eyes. Had she really asked him to make love to her last night? Or had she dreamed it? It was a question that had plagued her all day. An unanswerable question because her memories of it were so jumbled and vague. She remembered feeling frantic, clinging to him, wanting him to make the pain go away. And then…nothing. Had she fallen asleep in his arms? What had he said? When she had awakened beside him this morning, both of them were still clothed. Clearly Mac had declined her offer if she had made one.

Rising from the table, she gathered the plates and scraped the food off them into the disposal. Mac stationed himself on the other side of the counter and began phoning the *S* section in the Rolodex, hitting every Seattle address. He had finished and begun the *T* section by the time she wiped the last trace of their meal from the counters and table.

Folding the dishcloth and laying it across the sink divider, Mallory waited for him to end a conversation, then said, ''I'll take Em's room. You'll be more comfortable in the larger bed.''

His gray eyes lifted. Mallory glanced uneasily away, unable to meet his gaze. Heat flamed to her cheeks.

''You sure? I hate to run you out of your own room.''

"Her bed is perfectly comfortable. And I'll feel closer to her in there. Really, I don't mind."

Escaping the kitchen, Mallory took the stairs at a near run. After gathering her night things, she showered in the main bath just in case Mac finished up the Rolodex and wanted a shower himself. The hot water felt wonderfully soothing on her bruised body. After soaping down and shampooing her hair, she stood under the spray for several minutes, making her mind completely blank. No thoughts of Em. Of Keith. Of his many friends in Seattle. Of anything. She had to relax if she intended to sleep. And she *needed* sleep. Exhaustion was weighing on her, making her feel rubbery all over.

After blowing her hair dry, she tugged on her gown, straightened up the bathroom and went across the hall to Em's room. The bed felt like a mother's arms as she stretched out between the sheets and pulled the pink down comforter to her chin. Now if only she could sleep. A picture flashed in her head of Em's finger lying inside a small box and she rolled onto her stomach to bury her face. The tears that she had held at bay all day flooded from her eyes, accompanied by muffled sobs. She cried until she was empty and numb again, then just lay there, her eyes squeezed closed, her hands knotted into fists.

It wouldn't happen, she promised herself. She and Mac were going to find the key. They had to. If they didn't, Mallory didn't want to live. That was her last thought. Like a blown bulb, her lights went out. Blackness swooped over her.

RUFFLES AND LACE and Mallory Christiani…a heady combination. Mac leaned a shoulder against the bedpost and studied the sleeping woman before him, his mouth curved into a wry smile. He toyed with his tie, rasping his fingertips across the silk, imagining silken skin instead. *Mac, would you love me?* An ache of longing had centered itself in his chest last night and hadn't eased up all day. Not a sexual longing, just need, raw and elemental and completely baffling. He wanted inside her skin, to drown in the sensation of simply holding her. Dangerous feelings. Not even thoughts of Randy seemed to douse the fire.

She had been crying. Even in the shadows, he could see the puffy blueness of her eyelids, the swollen vulnerability of her lips, the streaks on her cheeks. All day long, she had held it in. He wished she hadn't, that she could let herself go, but at the same time, he had to admire her grit.

Mac sighed and turned away. The last of the Rolodex file hadn't turned up the possessor of the key. No key, no kid. Simple as that. He strode to Mallory's room and flung open the door. As he stepped across the threshold, memories of the previous night washed over him. He approached the bed and stared down at the destroyed toy dog. Good old Ragsdale. Ripped apart. Just like Mac would be if he didn't get a handle on his emotions. His and Mallory's worlds were so far apart. When this was over, he'd go his way, she'd go hers. He would probably see her only rarely, from a distance, just as before. Which was as it should be.

He glanced at the beautiful bedroom. It had taken a great deal of money to decorate it. More money than he had to spare in a year, probably. Even if Mallory fell in love with him, which was hoping for the moon, she'd soon grow unhappy when she found out he couldn't afford the life-style she was used to. Not for her. Not for her daughter. There'd be no fancy canopy beds. No Mercedes. No tailored suits. No salons.

He flopped onto his back and closed his eyes, determined to banish foolish thoughts about Mallory and any kind of future with her from his mind. He was just a poor kid from Seattle. That was all he had ever been, all he would ever be. He'd best remember it and keep his mind on the job.

Chapter Twelve

Two-thirty. Mallory stared at the luminous dials on Em's Snoopy alarm clock, wondering what had disturbed her. She had been asleep for several hours. Too long, from the feel of things. She was wide-awake, her mind clamoring with thoughts of Em and the elusive key. In some nether region of her mind, she heard a continuous whisper, *time is running out, time is running out.* It filled her with panic.

Throwing her legs over the edge of the bed, she sat up and stretched. Some of the soreness had left her body. She reached for her robe with trembling hands, donned it and left the bedroom. Up the hall, she could hear the uneven sputter of Mac's breathing. The sound beckoned, and for a moment, she thought about sneaking in to be near him. He soothed her, somehow. But after last night, if he woke up and caught her, he'd think she was throwing herself at him. A man, especially a childless man, would never understand the hysteria that nipped constantly at her heels. Only a mother could know how she felt, how her body ached to hold her daughter. She turned in the opposite direction and headed for the stair landing.

She didn't turn on lights for fear of waking Mac. A cup of herb tea sounded good, but there was no point in him losing sleep while she had one. She would wait and turn on lights when she reached the kitchen. The layout of the house was so familiar to her, she could walk it blind, anyway.

The front half of the entry reached two stories high to the

skylight in the vaulted ceiling. Moonlight illuminated the hall, throwing everything into eerie shadow. Her pink robe looked blue. The tile felt cold on her bare feet and made her wish she had worn her slippers. She stepped into the kitchen and reached for the light switch. Just as her fingers touched the plastic, she heard a sound out on the patio that made her hesitate. Not overly alarmed because she knew the sliding doors had safety locks, she tiptoed to the adjoining dining room. As she approached the glass doors to peer outside, she saw the silhouette of a man standing beside the patio umbrella table. From his sudden stillness, she guessed he had spotted her.

For a moment, Mallory stood frozen in her tracks and stared. Then she saw the man lift his hand, saw moonlight glint off blue-black metal. Orange flame licked the air. *Tatta-tat-tat.* The glass in the doors erupted toward her. She threw up her arm and staggered backward, using the hutch as a shield, horrified as the night and the room around her shattered into a million exploding fragments.

Tatta-tat-tat. Tatta-tat-tat. Mallory's ears rang as the guttural burping of the gun surrounded her. Instinctively she dropped to the floor, slamming the air out of her lungs upon impact. The carpet beneath her was peppered with glass fragments. Bits of flying plaster splattered her face, sharp and stinging. Above her, bullets found the ornate, gilt-framed mirror. Its moon-silvered surface erupted and rained shimmering shards, their musical tinkling filling her ears as they pelted her body. She tried to move. Couldn't. She tried to scream. No sound would come out. All she could do was stare. At the man. At the glinting gun. He was stepping through the door frame—into the room with her.

Panting, Mallory scrambled on her belly into the kitchen. As she clawed for purchase on the tiles, she heard footsteps behind her. Her heart slammed like a kettledrum. *The breakfast nook. I have to reach the breakfast nook.* Upstairs, she heard a thump. Tearing her nails as she fought for handholds on the smooth floor, she reached the table and crawled beneath it, praying the moonlight wasn't so bright she could be seen.

Tatta-tat-tat. Tatta-tat-tat. The kitchen burst into a grotesque symphony of sound. Bullets thudded into the oak cupboards, rang out against pots, *kerplunked* on tile. She heard a sudden gush of water cascading onto the floor. A water pipe? The faucet? Throwing a glance toward the day room, she wondered if she could make it across the floor without being seen. Mac, where was Mac? Another burst of gunfire. Zigzagging streaks of blue light flared in the kitchen. In the explosions of illumination, she saw that the automatic coffee maker's cord had been severed close to its base. Still plugged into the wall socket, the cord was live, dancing and whipping like a snake, spurting tongues of electricity. She no sooner ascertained the source of light than she realized the man entering the kitchen might be able to see her.

"Mallory!" Mac roared.

His footsteps thumped above her and came down the long upstairs hall. A moment later, the stairs creaked. Terror paralyzed her throat. If Mac ran into the kitchen, he would be killed. If she dared call out to warn him, she would be. Footsteps, running. Closer, closer. The man in the kitchen pressed his back to the cupboards, his gun raised.

"Mac, no!" she screamed. "The kitchen, he's in the kitchen!"

Splat—Splat—Splat. The table did a tap dance around her. Slugs from the Uzi buried themselves in the wood above her head. Mac's sack of mail fell to the tile. Diving, Mallory rolled across the floor to the archway that opened into the day room, every nerve in her body raw with expectancy as she anticipated a bullet. She thudded over the step-down and scrambled for cover behind the sofa.

Silence swooped over her, broken only by the spurting hisses of electricity frying water. Blue-white light flashed as she peeked over the cushions. Mac, where was he? She held her breath, listening, glancing first toward the kitchen, then toward the door that opened into the entry hall. Had he heard her?

"Mac! He's in the kitchen!" she screamed again.

A shadow moved in the entry. Mallory peered out and saw

Mac, gun uplifted before him, easing along the hallway wall. She threw an anxious glance toward the blue-white bursts of light. She thought she detected a stealthy footstep in the kitchen. Another. She dug her fingers into the sofa upholstery and held her breath.

"Ar-rr-gh!"

The cry ripped through the semidarkness, shrill agony tearing up from a masculine throat. Coldness washed over her. She stared at the intruder's silhouette, thrown upon the breakfast room wall by moonlight and electric blue. Jerking, twisting. A grotesque dance of death. A ceaseless spatting of bullets rent the air as the intruder's finger convulsed on the Uzi's trigger.

"Mac?"

"Stay down!" he growled from somewhere nearby.

She couldn't drag her eyes from the silhouette. A sickening smell drifted to her. Bile rose in her throat along with an upsurge of horror. She felt Mac crawling up beside her. He, too, stared at the breakfast room wall, his face taut in the play of blue-white light, his muscles twitching each time the other man's gun spat bullets.

"Electrocuted, he's being electrocuted," she cried. "The coffee maker cord. A pipe broke." Disbelief mushroomed inside her. "M-Mac? He'll die if we don't do something."

His only reply was to grab her arm and jerk her to her feet. Dragging her in his wake, he sprinted across the day room, out into the hall, his destination the front door. Throwing it open, he leaped out onto the porch and hunkered down to avoid being seen. Mallory followed his example. They jumped off the end of the porch into the shrubs. She didn't even feel the branches scratching her legs, she was so scared. Off across the lawn. Through the shrubs that divided their yard from the neighbors. They zigzagged back and forth, keeping close to the ground. Porch lights along the street were coming on.

"Other men," he panted. "Back at the house. Keep low."

This isn't happening. Mallory kept thinking that as Mac hauled her relentlessly through one yard, then another. His pace never let up, not even when they hit pea gravel in their bare feet. At the end of the cul-de-sac, they took to the sidewalk. One block, two. He turned right. They ran another block. Another. Mallory feared she might collapse. The only sound in her head was the laboring rasp of her own breathing. She fell back slightly. Mac's arm was stretched out behind him to keep a hold on her hand. She forced her legs to keep pumping. Another block. Another. Her lungs began to whine.

At last, Mac drew up beside a black Cadillac. Relief washed through Mallory when Mac tried the door and it wasn't locked. He threw his gun on the seat and bent to locate the ignition wires under the dash. Within seconds, the engine sputtered, kicked over and roared to life. "Let's go!" he cried.

Mallory leaped in on the passenger side, slammed her door and put on her seat belt. Glancing over at Mac, she clamped a hand to her chest and gulped for air. He ran his palms over her, feeling for blood. "You okay?"

"Fine."

He jerked the shift into drive and peeled the tires in a U-turn, throwing her sideways in the seat. As the car sped down the street, she leaned her head against the rest and struggled for air, her mouth slack, eyes closed, body slick with sweat. They were safe—at least for now. It didn't matter that they were in a stolen car. It didn't matter that there was a dead man in her kitchen. It didn't matter that her house was shot apart, bullets embedded everywhere. They were safe.… She didn't know how she would ever explain this to the police, and for the moment, she didn't have the energy to worry about it.

MAC DROVE NORTH to a seedy motel on Highway 99 on the outskirts of Everett. Mallory sat in the stolen car while he rousted the motel manager out of his bed and rented a room. At any moment, she expected him to come back to the car and say he had been turned away, but evidently run-down motels with white paint and hot-pink trim weren't all that particular about their patrons. Shirtless and barefoot, Mac looked none too respectable, nice car or not. Thank goodness he hadn't emptied his pants pockets earlier tonight before crawling into bed. He had his charge cards with him.

"Room eleven, my lucky number," he said as he climbed back into the Caddy. His voice sounded oddly tight. He pulled into a parking space only a short distance from the office and cut the car engine. Picking up his gun, he wedged it under his waistband. "I'm afraid this isn't the Ritz. The big advertised feature is a vibrating bed."

Mallory hugged her robe to her breasts and climbed from the car, glancing nervously around the dark parking lot before she closed the door. The manager peered out the lobby window at her and shook his gray head, clearly bewildered. She supposed it wasn't often that women arrived here in their night-clothes. It was putting the cart before the horse, she had to admit. Just so long as he didn't think they looked so suspicious that he called the police. That was all that mattered.

Horrid wasn't the word to describe their room, but close. The hot-pink walls had faded and gathered grime until they were more gray than pink. The pink chenille bedspread was missing sections of fringe. The scarlet rug was worn bare in places. Mac jerked the bedding back. "Sheets are fresh." He stepped into the bathroom and flipped on the fan-light. A loud rattle began in the ceiling. He quickly hit the switch again to turn it off. "Clean towels and a sanitary guard on the toilet. I guess it'll do until daylight. Sorry, Mallory, but places like this don't ask questions or call in to check license plates."

With that, he put his gun on the dresser and sank into a frayed red easy chair, propping his elbows on his knees and burying his face in his hands. Mallory stared at him. He was shaking. She had seen him walk away from a switchblade fight and an exploding car without any outward sign of fear. Had he been shot and not told her? She scanned him for any trace of blood.

"Mac?" She took a halting step toward him. "Mac, you aren't hurt?" He didn't answer. She ran to him and began searching frantically for a wound. "Mac?"

With no warning, he snaked an arm around her waist, fell

back in the chair and swept her onto his lap. A strange sound erupted from his chest as his arms tightened their hold. His body trembled violently. He buried his face in the curve of her neck and clung to her. She felt wetness trickle past the collar of her gown and realized, with a shock, that he was crying.

"I—I thought they'd killed you," he croaked. "I woke up to the gunfire, and I thought they'd killed you."

"Oh, Mac…I'm all right." She ran her hands into his hair and closed her eyes. "I'm fine. Nothing happened."

For an endless time, he clung to her. Then he rubbed his cheeks dry on her robe and whispered, "I've never felt this way before. Not about anyone."

She knew he was referring to the crazy, irrational attachment they were developing for each other. How long had she known him now? She tried to count the days, but they stretched into eternity in her mind. Mac had always been there, always would be.

"Mallory…?"

There was a weak note of warning in his voice. He loosened his hold on her and moved back to capture her face between his hands. His eyes searched hers, aching with confusion and need. For a moment, she thought he might kiss her. But at the last second, he cursed under his breath and averted his face.

"This is insane," he said with ragged intensity. His hands dropped to his lap and he gave her a little nudge to move her. The moment she stood, he sprang from the chair, took a step and sprawled on the bed, rolling onto his back. He grabbed the pillow lying above his head and plopped it down in the middle of the mattress. "I don't know about you, but I'm getting some sleep before I do something we'll both regret. And, please, no cracks about a pillow not being enough to keep me away from you. It's better than nothing."

With that, he turned onto his side, his broad back to the pillow, his head resting on his folded arm. For a moment, Mallory stared at the pitifully inadequate barrier he had erected, then she stepped to the door and touched the light switch. The room was plunged into an eerie blackness that was soon streaked by muted pink rays of light that shone through the red drapes. The silence dripped tension, suffocating and electrical. She pressed her back to the wall.

"Come lie down," he whispered. "You can't stand there all night."

Mallory peeled off her robe, slung it on the floor and circled him to climb into the bed, careful to stay on her side. The pillow was soft against her hip as she stretched out on her back. His breathing was tense and measured. She found herself wishing he would fall asleep and begin to snore. It was a comfortable sound, and she had grown accustomed to hearing it.

For what seemed like forever, she lay there, rigid and uncertain. She had already slept several hours and, tired as she was from running, it wasn't a drowsy tired, just bone-deep weariness. Than, at last, he started snoring and her eyelids grew heavy. She slipped into slumber without realizing it. At first she dreamed of men chasing them with guns.

Then the scene changed abruptly, and Mallory found herself in a room filled with small white gift boxes, lids decorated with shimmering ribbons. For some reason, the sight of them struck terror into her. She didn't want to open them, didn't want to see what they held, but there were so many on the floor that she couldn't take a step without bumping one. Her skin began to prickle with panic. A scream slid up the back of her throat. She whirled to run and overturned a box. A fluff of tissue paper spilled out and began to unfurl. Within its folds was a child's hand. Mallory stared down at it. *Emily.* She began to whimper. All the boxes began to tip sideways. She knew what they held. She heard Darren's voice pleading with her. *Do something. Don't just stand there and let us die. Not again. Save us.* Cruel laughter began to echo off the walls....

Mac jerked awake, his muscles knotted, every nerve ending alert. He wasn't sure what had disturbed him. Then he heard it, a strangled whimpering sound. Rolling over, he rose on an elbow. In the shafts of pink light, he could see Mallory thrashing in her sleep. He grasped her shoulder to waken her. Her flannel gown was sopped with sweat. "Mallory? Sweetheart, wake up."

She woke up, all right, swinging at him and screaming, the sounds shrill and piercing. Acutely aware of how thin the walls probably were, Mac clamped a hand over her mouth and scrambled over the pillow lying between them. He felt her teeth sinking into his palm. He used his body to pin her thrashing limbs.

"Mallory—honey, it's me, it's only me. It's a nightmare, just a nightmare."

Her teeth worried the leather skin that padded his knuckles. Her breath whined through her nose. Her eyes were huge above his hand, still glazed with terror. Then, with a muffled sob, she went limp and began to cry, an awful, tearing sound. His stomach knotted. He drew his hand from her mouth and enfolded her in his arms, pulling her close and slinging his leg over hers.

"Boxes," she sobbed. "Everywhere. He did it, Mac, he did it. Her hand…he sent her home to me in pieces."

Nausea rolled through him in waves. "Oh, Mallory…."

The violent shaking of her body reminded him of that first night when he had found her rocking Ragsdale. Only this time, he didn't have to ask her to come to him. She was wrapped around him like a sarong. He could feel her heart slamming, her skin pulsating and growing hot as her blood sluiced through her veins. Her slender arms were cinched around his neck, rigid in their hold, her face pressed against his shoulder.

Mac feathered kisses from her temple to her brow and whispered softly, not sure what he was saying, responding instinctively to her need. Running his hands over her, he kneaded her tortured muscles, forcing out the kinks, his one thought being to comfort her. *Damn Lucetti for doing this to her.*

He wasn't sure when his motives changed. Desire flared inside him with a suddenness that blinded him, red and searing. His own heart accelerated its beat to match hers. He wanted her, had to have her. It wasn't a thought or even a decision, just an instinctive taking that erupted from a dark, conscienceless place within him.

As overwhelming as the impulse was, Mac would have stopped if Mallory had seemed hesitant. But when he kissed her, she sobbed into his mouth and pressed closer, the urgency in her body matching his own. He had imagined loving her...sweetly, gently, languorously, coaxing her not to be shy. This was nothing like that. It was hunger that left no room for gentle coaxing, too elemental to be sweet.

In the nether regions of his mind, he was vaguely aware that he was peeling off her gown as though it were the skin on a succulent fruit and he was a starving man. As the flannel hem skidded up her torso, he followed in its wake with his mouth, devouring the taste of her skin, nibbling with his lips, then with his teeth, his senses electrified by her cries as he grazed each of her ribs. Like a moth drawn to flame, he found her breast, drawing its sensitive peak into his mouth to lave it with wet heat. She whimpered and arched her body up to him, her muscles quivering and jerking with each relentless pull. Little warning bells went off inside his head. She was a small woman with skin as soft as velvet. He didn't want to hurt her. But the moment he started to surface to a more reasoning plane of consciousness, she moaned and clung, dragging him back down with her into a kaleidoscopic world where sensation ruled.

Mallory. She was rose petals and honey, berry froth and cream, an elusive, silken temptress who entwined herself in a pink mist around him. Or was it the pink shimmering shafts of light that angled across the bed? When he slitted his eyes, he saw only her, felt only her. A delectable confection that melted against him. Beautiful, precious, unattainable Mallory.

With feverish urgency, he trailed his hungry lips down her belly to her navel and the satiny skin below, his tongue finding the tiny white ridges left there by her pregnancy with Em. Oddly enough, each mark made her all the more beautiful to him. When he started to move lower to find the throbbing sweetness of her womanhood, he felt her stiffen, heard her call his name in a tremulous whisper.

He murmured a husky protest, but forced himself to stop. He could tell by the way she had said his name that she was shocked right down to her prim little manicured toenails. Trailing kisses back up her body, he once again found her mouth, claiming it with masterful thrusts of his tongue that soon made her forget her momentary shyness. When he felt her melting against him, he slid his hand to the juncture of her thighs, found her moistness and contented himself with gently stroking her. The first sweep of his fingers made her gasp. He felt her lashes brush his cheek as her eyes flew open. Perplexed, he deepened their kiss. She grabbed his wrist and tried to pull his hand away. It was his turn to feel shocked. Maybe wealthy fellows didn't make love the same way poor boys did.

Freeing her mouth, he feathered kisses to her ear, keeping his hand insinuated between her thighs. "Trust me, Mallory."

"I—" Her breath caught and she shuddered. "I'm sorry."

He drew back slightly to see her. "Sorry?"

"It's been—since Darren—no one else—ever." Her eyes widened and her facial muscles tightened as his fingers found with unerring accuracy the supersensitive flesh they had been seeking.

He couldn't resist kissing the quivering corners of her mouth even though part of him wanted nothing more than to watch her small face while he explored her sensitive flesh and made her passions peak. "Don't hold back. Trust me." He felt her legs relaxing, parting ever so slightly. Her hips instinctively lifted toward his hand and he watched as her pupils dilated and her lashes drifted halfway closed. A tremor ran the length of her, slight but unmistakable. He read her expressions and knew the exact moment when she felt herself slipping over the edge. "Ah, Mallory, let go, let it happen."

A whimper worked its way up her throat and her eyes drifted completely closed. With arms that were suddenly aquiver, she hugged his neck and arched toward his hand with mindless abandon, a cry tearing up from her throat as he brought her to climax. Afterward, he cradled her shuddering form against him, pressing kisses to her closed eyelids. When at last the aftershocks left her body, he peeled off his slacks and rose over her.

She showed no hesitation as he entered her. She was honey and silk and fire, all rolled into one small perfectly shaped woman who clung to him and met him thrust for thrust. So sweet. He couldn't believe how good she felt, how good she made *him* feel.

When he had spent himself, Mac didn't want to release her. It was over, yet it wasn't. He realized as he gathered her close in his arms that with Mallory it would never be over, never be something he could walk away from and forget the moment his tie was straightened. He doubted that he'd ever get all of her that he wanted.

A smile curved his mouth. He buried his face in her hair and inhaled the sweet smell of her. When had her scent become so familiar and so dear to him? *Mallory.* How had he let himself fall for her like this? Was he out of his mind? Had Randy's death taught him nothing? He closed his eyes and drew her closer. Later, he'd worry about it later....

Time drifted by like mist on a windless night. Mallory had no idea how long she lay there in Mac's arms. He was long since asleep, his arms locked tightly around her, his face buried in her hair, clinging to her as if to assure himself, even in slumber, that she was there and safe. She pressed closer to him. He had been her one and only constant since this had begun. Warm, solid, her only security. She stared into the shadows, afraid to close her eyes. The nightmare she was living was terrifying enough. She couldn't bear to face it in her sleep, where she was completely helpless against it.

COME DAYLIGHT, the room looked even dingier than it had last night. Mac woke slowly, deliciously aware of the silken body he held clamped in his arms, of the soft curve of buttock pressed against his awakening manhood. He had a small breast cupped in one hand. Desire shot through him like an electrical charge. Instinctively he started to disentangle himself, then hesitated. Sudden movement would wake Mallory, and she needed rest.

He closed his eyes on a wave of guilt. What had he been

thinking last night? That was exactly the problem. He hadn't been thinking, period. He had woken up out of a sound sleep and done what came naturally, the devil take tomorrow. She wasn't the kind of woman to have sex with just anyone. And what could he offer her? He had seen the look on her face the night before last when she had first seen him in his street clothes. Shock, apprehension, uncertainty as to what to expect from him. And later, on the streets, she had been completely out of her element.

She was the daughter of an ex-congressman. She had grown up eating her cereal out of a crystal bowl. She thought poor meant driving a Caddy instead of a Mercedes. Mac could show her what *poor* really was. He had lived poverty, breathed it, clawed his way up from it. They had nothing in common, nothing. If they ever once got into a deep conversation, she would immediately realize how little education he had. And it would tear him apart to lose her once he let himself start to love her.

Once he let himself? What a joke that was. He was already in over his head and floundering. Gently he disengaged himself from her sweet softness and slid from the bed, dragging on his slacks. She murmured something and rolled over, reaching for him. He stared over his shoulder at the bruise on her face, at the cut on her collarbone. *Fragile.* If he had even a grain of decency, he'd end this now. For her sake. And for his own.

"Mac?"

"I'm here." His throat tightened as her thick lashes lifted and her deep brown eyes sought his. How could he be brusque with her? Or hold her at arm's length? She needed someone to lean on, someone to hold her, comfort her and care. And like it or not, he was the only someone available. With a silent groan, he sat down and enfolded her hand in his. "I'm here, honey."

She clung to his fingers. "I thought you'd left."

"I won't leave. You know that." His problem was that he liked being there for her all too well.

She started to sit up, then remembered she was naked. Her cheeks flushed a delicate pink as she scrambled for the sheet and covered herself. Momentary confusion played upon her face. He could almost read her thoughts as she slowly cataloged the room around her and remembered exactly what had transpired between them a few hours before. Guilt roiled within him. He should have maintained control. Her blush deepened to crimson as her gaze slid to his back. Slowly her eyes climbed the ladder of his ribs to meet his gaze. There was a question in the look. *Are you sorry?*

He jerked his hand from hers, stood and buckled his belt. Damned right, he was sorry. To distract her and himself, he strode to the window and glanced out, pretending he thought there might be someone out there. He didn't, but any ruse that worked wasn't beneath him. "You know, I just can't figure it out. We've both agreed that it can't be Lucetti trying to kill you. But if it's not Lucetti, who?"

Relief washed over him as he turned from the window. She was not only distracted, but deep in thought if her frown was any indication. He wasn't ready to deal with what was happening between them. How could he verbalize feelings he couldn't yet understand himself? He needed time—time to sort things out, time to come to grips with his involvement with her, time to rationalize it all into something he could deal with. If they discussed it now, his uncertainty would only hurt her. And he couldn't bear the thought of that.

"They're smart, I'll say that for them," he went on. "Amateurs wouldn't let up, but these guys back off, let us relax a little, then hit when we least expect it. I tell you, they work like Lucetti does. That bomb in my car was made by an expert or it would have demolished half a block. It was also timed in hopes that we'd leave the congested parking lot before it went off. Less risk of bystanders getting hurt that way. Those fellows have been around and know exactly what they're doing, no guesswork. If I didn't know better, I'd swear they were following Lucetti's orders."

"Which makes no sense."

"No, none at all. Which convinces me we were right all along, that they're Lucetti's men, acting on their own."

"They don't want me giving him that package." Mallory leaned back against the headboard. "And what's the best way to make sure I don't?" She snapped her fingers. "Waste me. It makes sense. Unless he finds that key on his own, which is unlikely, Lucetti doesn't have a prayer of getting into that deposit box without me."

Mac nearly smiled at how quickly she had picked up on the lingo she had heard downtown. He was willing to bet that until the night before last, the only "waste" Mallory had known about was the kind that went down her garbage disposal. "It's something in that package that they don't want Lucetti to see. But what?"

"Ledgers equal embezzlement," she said with certainty. "What else could it be? Embezzlement or proof somehow that they had cheated him."

Mac dropped into the red chair, his mind racing. After a moment, he shook his head. "To embezzle, they'd have to be bookkeepers. No way. Bookkeepers aren't that friendly with guns and explosives." He lifted an eyebrow. "Maybe they aren't bookkeepers. What if they're collectors? Like Chapin said?"

"Collectors?"

"Yeah, the money boys." Mac's eyes began to gleam with excitement. "Mallory, you're a genius. They've been skimming! Miles's ledgers must implicate them somehow." Leaping up, he began to pace. "If Lucetti sees the books and discovers his collectors have betrayed him, they're as good as dead. Perfect motivation! No wonder they're trying to rub you out. It's you or them."

"What a comforting thought," she said in a faint voice.

He flashed her a grin. "Hey, so far, we've outsmarted them."

"Correction. *You* have."

"Well, I'd say luck has bailed us out more times than not. And it's your luck as much as mine. Those guys are good at what they do, damned good." He settled back in the chair.

She managed a wry smile. "You can't say it's all been luck,

Mac. Your driving skills saved us the first time, your quick thinking, the second. If not for you, I'd be wearing a toe tag by now.''

That grim thought brought silence swooping over them for a moment.

"So…" He lifted his hands. "What next, Einstein? Any ideas?" He leaned forward and draped his arms on his knees. "So far, I haven't got any leads on Lucetti unless I want to wait till the weekend and go to the racetrack to find Andrews. But we don't have time for that. We don't have an ID as yet on the three thugs, just the one possible name Shelby's checking out. And no clue what friend it was that Keith gave the key to. I'm fresh out of ideas.''

"You know what's weird?" Mallory said. "Lucetti doesn't *know* what friend Keith gave it to. He wanted those ledgers so badly, he admitted he'd had Keith followed—to be sure he mailed the package. And he was having *me* followed too, after all, or he wouldn't have known where Em was. You'd think he'd know everywhere Keith went, everyone he came in contact with.''

Mac shook his head. "You're forgetting the mail.''

"True. I don't suppose Lucetti could have monitored all the mail that left the law firm, even if he tried." Mallory stared at Mac, the germ of an idea taking root. The mail? She remembered a plot twist in a mystery novel she had read some time ago. *Evidence found on a typewriter ribbon.* "Mac?" she squeaked. "Oh, good grief! Why didn't we think of it?''

She leaped from the bed and fumbled for her nightgown. Mac stared at her. "Come again?''

"The typewriter. Don't you see? If Keith sent the key to someone, he would have typed an accompanying letter. If he was being secretive, he wouldn't have had Trudy do it. We can get the name off his ribbon. He uses a film cartridge on the typewriter. And a film ribbon is one-strike. You simply reverse your ribbon, find the section of film you want and transcribe the letters in the proper order to see what was written.''

"Why would he bother to type a letter? It would be quicker to do it longhand."

"Keith's handwriting is awful, he never writes by hand."

Mac rose slowly from the chair. His mind whirled as he tried to remember whether or not the typewriter, like everything else in Keith's office, had been torn apart. "Don't get too excited. That ribbon could have been tossed when Trudy cleaned up the mess in his office."

She threw him a glare as she shoved her arms into the sleeves of her robe. "Don't even *think* that way."

Chapter Thirteen

It was over two hours before Mac and Mallory could get to Keith's firm. First, they had to be decently attired. When they drove by Mallory's to get clothes, they saw that the doors and windows of the house had been sealed with tape, the yard cordoned off. Evidently the police had been called by neighbors who reported the shooting, and the electrocuted body of the intruder had been discovered. Mac and Mallory didn't dare enter the house. As it was, they needed to ditch the stolen Cadillac as quickly as they could before the police made a connection between the missing car and the shooting incident.

They were left with no choice but to stop someplace and buy Mallory clothing. After going to Mac's apartment so he could dress, they drove to Bellevue Square. Mac took a list of Mallory's sizes and went inside to buy her a new set of clothes and shoes. She had to dress in the rest room of an Exxon station across the street.

"Not bad," Mac commented when she emerged from the ladies room and climbed back into the Cadillac. "Jeans and sneakers do something for you. Or maybe it's the other way around, you do something for jeans and sneakers."

She brushed her hair with her fingers, flashing him a smile. "It's just your great taste."

Giving her another once-over, Mac had to agree. The pale blue knit top he had chosen hugged her sleek lines like a second skin. *Choice,* as Danno would say. The question was, could

Mac afford her? She didn't seem to mind blue jeans and ten-
nies, but he wasn't offering them to her as a steady diet, either.
Not that he wouldn't buy her nice clothing if dressing her ever
became his responsibility. He simply couldn't compete with her
father. Never would be able to, for that matter.

"Well, this is where we leave the Caddy." Mac pulled out
his wallet and cast a gloomy glance at his quickly dwindling
money supply. "I wish we could leave them something to com-
pensate for all the trouble we've caused them."

Mallory took off her diamond solitaire earrings and stuck
them in an old registration envelope she found in the glove
box. Laying the offering on the seat, she threw Mac a smile.
"No great sentimental value. A gift from my father."

"Mallory, diamonds from your father? If they didn't mean
a lot, you wouldn't be wearing them."

She threw open her door. "The only reason I wear them is
that he has a fit if I don't."

He climbed out on his side and shut his door, eyeing her
over the shiny black roof. "Fifteen hundred dollars of ice?"

"Ice—exactly—not love or a hug."

The fleeting sadness that touched her face made Mac's heart
catch. She skirted the car, walking with a new jauntiness in the
comfortable sneakers. His gaze dropped to the swing of her
hips. She definitely added new dimensions to denim. Dropping
an arm around her shoulders, he gave her that hug her father
had failed to give her as he fell into step with her. As they
crossed the parking lot, he was achingly aware that he wanted
to do a whole lot more than just hug her. And he wanted a
whole lot longer than a day in which to do it.

They walked to the law firm, which was several blocks away.
Mallory looked so different in her new outfit that Mac didn't
think anyone was likely to recognize her. Trudy proved him
right when they entered the firm's lobby. She cast a vague
glance at Mallory, zeroed in on Mac, and then did a double
take.

"Mallory?"

"It's my new look. Uh, Trudy, can we slip into Keith's office for a moment? There's something I need to check on."

"Certainly, help yourself. I know Keith wouldn't mind."

Mallory spun toward the office. Mac, much to his consternation, found that he couldn't take his eyes off her jeans as he fell in behind her. Though he lectured himself that this was no time to be thinking about making love to her, another part of him kept arguing that it might very well be the *only* time he ever could.

Mallory whooped with delight when she found the IBM still had a ribbon cartridge inside it. She flipped the lock lever and pulled the cartridge free from its base. After carrying it to Keith's desk, she bent over it and began turning the right-hand knob counterclockwise until a fair amount of black ribbon was unwound. She gave a section of it a close study and smiled.

"We're in luck, Mac. Grab a pad and pen. I'll call off the letters."

He hovered beside her, pen at the ready. The first string of letters she called off were part of a dated memo. No luck there. She skipped a section of tape. "*O—N*—an apostrophe, I think—*T—C—A—L—L—T—H—E—P—O—L*..." She heaved a disgusted sigh. "Is it making any sense at all yet?"

"Keep reading," he ordered in a tense voice.

"*I—C—E—U—N—T—I—L*—" She leaned over to see what he had written thus far and her eyes widened. "Don't call the police? Oh, Mac! This is it—part of the letter he sent with the key." Her hands began to shake as she bent back over the tape. "I *knew* it!"

"Calm down! You'll tear the film."

She closed her eyes for an instant and took a deep breath. "Right. I have to stay calm. Okay. Ready?"

He grunted, hardly able to contain himself as he jotted letters down and tried to make sense of them.

"*D—O—N*—another apostrophe, maybe a comma—*T—T—R—U—S—T—A—N—Y—O—N—E*—another itsy mark, an apostrophe or period—a period, I think—*I—A—M—C—O—*

U—N—T—I—N—G—O—N—Y—O—U—a period—*K—E—I—T—H.*"

"Stop a sec." Mac frowned and went back over the last string of letters. "Don't trust anyone! I'm counting—yeah—I'm counting on you. Then he signed off. The rest, Mallory. The address should be coming up. Hurry, sweetheart."

"Um…" She squinted at the film and slowly began calling off letters again, unable to make words from them because she was too intent on deciphering the indistinct type. "*B—U—D—M—A—C—P—H—*"

Mac threw the pen down and grabbed her by the arm, nearly jerking her off her feet. As he hauled her with him across the room, he cried, "How could I be so stupid! He mailed it! That's why he looked at me that way!"

"What did it say?"

"He mailed it to *me*! Trudy was right. If he was in a jam, I'd be the one he'd call! I wasn't in town, so he mailed it to me. *I've* got the key, Mallory. I've had it the whole damned time and just didn't know it."

Trudy's eyes widened when they burst into the lobby. Mac dropped Mallory's arm and ran to the older woman's desk. "Trudy, I need to borrow your car."

"My car?" She leaned sideways to grab her purse off the shelf and get her keys. As she handed them to Mac, she said, "Why do you need my car?"

"Mine was blown up." Mac snagged the keys, blew her a kiss and grabbed Mallory's arm again. "Thanks, Trudy. You're an angel. Take a cab if I don't bring it back before you get off work. I'll pick up your tab later."

"But—blown up? Oh, my, what on earth is—"

They never heard the rest of what Trudy was going to say. Mac slammed the door behind them and took off down the hall at a run, hauling Mallory in his wake. When they reached the parking lot, he staggered to a stop. "Which car does she drive, anyway?"

"That Honda." The words were no sooner out than Mac

was off and running again, towing her along. "If he mailed it to y—"

"He did. Trust me." He parted company with her at the fender of the car, ran around to the driver's side, unlocked the door and leaped in. For a moment, Mallory thought he might drive off without her, but he remembered her and unlocked her side. She climbed in and threw him a worried look. He didn't even notice, just kept talking nonstop. "We drive to my place, get my mail. Go to the bank, get the package. Spend the night at a motel. Wait for Lucetti's call in the morning at your place. It'll be a little risky getting inside your house. Might have to go before daylight so no one sees us and calls the cops, but—"

"Mac!"

He at last focused on her. "What?"

"The mail. *Your* mail?"

"What about it?"

"I gathered it up in that sack. It's *inside* my house. At least I hope it is. What if the police took it?"

For a moment, he stared at her. Then he swore—not under his breath this time—and began to pound his fists on the steering wheel. Mallory watched anxiously. At last, he leaned his head against the rest and closed his eyes, his teeth clenched.

"I—" She licked her lips. "I guess I really messed up. Oh, Mac, why didn't I *look* at the mail when I was gathering it."

"You were upset. It's not your fault. I didn't take time to *read* it. I can't believe I was so dense."

"Mac, we've scarcely had time to eat."

"But I've had it all this time! We've been running around like a couple of fools—" He broke off and groaned. "I hope the cops didn't take that sack as evidence. If they did, how will we ever get that key?"

THERE WAS NO SACK OF MAIL in the breakfast nook. Mac searched the kitchen, the day room, then the entire downstairs, dreading the moment when he'd have to tell Mallory. Either the killers had taken it, or the police had. Either way, they were in big trouble. He crept upstairs to grab Mallory's purse in case she needed it later, then left the house and snuck through the backyard, cutting across an adjoining property to reach Mallory where she waited in the Honda over on the next block. They hadn't been able to park nearby, for fear someone would spot them.

"Well?" she demanded when he climbed into the car. "Did you get it?"

He shook his head. "Don't panic, though. If the cops took it, we might still be in business."

"How so?"

"Remember that first night up at Lake Tuck? I told you one of my best buddies worked for the department? Well, I think he'll get me the key if I level with him."

"But the grapevine. You said we didn't dare tell any police."

"Not to have them do an investigation. Several policemen would have known about it then, and one of them could have leaked it to the wrong fellow. This is different. Scotty won't tell anyone."

"You're sure?"

He locked gazes with her. "Mallory, let's put it this way. We don't have any other options. I have to call him."

FIFTEEN MINUTES LATER, Mac was on hold, waiting to be put through to his friend, Scotty Herman, a King County detective. The moment Scotty heard Mac's voice, he began yelling so loudly that the sound reverberated inside the phone booth.

"What in hell are you up to, Mac? Do you know how disconcerting it is to be investigating a case and suddenly find out a friend is somehow involved? First the Volvo. Then a fried goon. Then a stolen car? We found your prints, you know."

Mac waited for Scotty to wind down, then explained the situation. "I'm counting on you to keep your lip zipped on this. You don't dare tell anyone. The kid could end up dead."

"Mac, you ever heard the cardinal rule? Call your local police? Who do you think you are, Superman? And now you want me to—" He broke off, cleared his throat and continued in a whisper. "You want me to steal evidence gathered from a homicide scene? Have you lost your mind? They itemize that stuff. I could lose my job."

"Just one little envelope, the one from Keith. Come on, Scotty. You can fix it so no one realizes anything's missing."

"You're asking me to put my career on the line."

"It's a kid's *life* on the line. Will you do it?"

Long silence. "Yeah, yeah, I'll do it. I'll meet you in two hours at the Denny's on 116th. We're even after this one, though. Consider me paid up in full."

"Scotty, I've never kept score. Two hours? I still have to get some fake ID made so I can get into Christiani's safe-deposit box sometime today."

"I didn't hear that." Scotty groaned. "Mac, breaking the law is one thing, but do you have to outline your itinerary to me before you go do it?"

"So throw me in jail. What should I do, let him kill her? What would *you* do, Scotty. I wanna hear this."

"Oh, shut up. Two hours, take it or leave it. I gotta go through channels, you know."

SCOTTY WAS A TALL, dark-haired man in a gray suit and a perfectly awful blue-gray tie with turquoise polka dots. Mac met him at the entrance of Denny's. Scotty seemed none too thrilled about standing around with Mac, so he passed the envelope with all speed, lifted a hand to acknowledge Mallory, who had stayed in the car, and left as quickly as he had come.

Mac hurried back to the car, ripped open the envelope, and whooped triumphantly when the key fell out in his hand. Mallory felt tears welling in her eyes and had to look away for a moment. Mac would have none of that. He placed a hand behind her head and pulled her toward him. "Home free, Mallory. We've got it."

She clung to him.

"Tomorrow, honey, and she'll be home. I'll set up the exchange with Lucetti when he calls in the morning." Bending his head, he kissed the tears from her cheeks. "What do you say we call the hospital and have the nurse tell Keith the good news, hmm? We'll have to watch what we say, but we should be able to get the message across. Then we'll run over to Seattle.''

''Why do we need to go to Seattle?''

''I'll need authentic looking ID when I go to the bank. I know a guy downtown who can take Keith's identification, put my picture on it, alter the dates with transfer lettering, laminate it, and no one will ever know it isn't mine.''

Mallory's stomach clenched. She had completely forgotten that Mac would have to forge Keith's signature to get into the box. ''Oh, Mac, what if it doesn't work?''

He caught her face between his hands and pressed a kiss on the tip of her nose. ''Have I let you down yet?''

''No.''

''Then trust me. I'll get that package if I have to rob the place.''

He said it in a teasing tone, but when Mallory glanced over at him, there was a determined glint in his eye that made her wonder. She believed he would do it if it came to that, risk his whole future for a little girl he had never met. Her little girl. She stared straight ahead as he backed the Honda out of the parking space. Memories of last night drifted through her mind. She regretted nothing. She had fallen head over heels in love with this man. Sneaking another look at him, she decided that most women would. Big, rugged and handsome, with a heart like a marshmallow, that was Mac. One in a million.

MAC'S HANDWRITING was *worse* than Keith's—if that was possible. Mallory stared at his last attempt at duplicating Keith's signature, then cast a worried frown at the bank. ''Mac, I'm afraid this won't work.''

He held up his bandaged right hand. It looked as though it had been wrapped by a professional, which of course it should, since Mallory had done it. ''A guy can't be expected to write too well when his hand is bunged up. Relax, Mallory. They don't know the life history of every customer. For the next ten minutes, I *am* Keith Christiani.''

''If you get someone who knows him, you're sunk.''

Mac jabbed a thumb skyward. ''*He* has to take care of that part. Where's your faith? I'll be back before you know it.''

Five minutes dragged by. Mallory tried not to look at her watch, but she couldn't help it. *Ten minutes.* How long could it take to open a safe-deposit box? Panic tightened her throat. She wasn't worried about Mac getting into trouble. She not only knew the best defense attorneys in the state, but she could also afford their fees. But Em... If Mac couldn't get that package, Mallory would have to get a court order to have the box opened. To do that, she would have to tell the authorities why. And if she did that Lucetti would kill her daughter.

Just when she was about to go inside to see what on earth was taking so long, Mac rounded the corner and came striding down the sidewalk toward the car. Tucked under one arm, he carried a large manila envelope. He was grinning from ear to ear, his eyes dancing with triumphant laughter.

Chapter Fourteen

Once they were certain they hadn't been followed from the bank, they went back to the same motel they had stayed in last night. They both sat on the bed, the ledgers and several of Steven Miles's letters spread before them. Mallory, sitting cross-legged, propped her elbows on her knees and covered her face with her hands. "This is a nightmare. Darren was murdered? It wasn't an accident?"

Her voice shook so badly that Mac put a hand on her shoulder to steady her. He knew how frightened she must feel. She'd just found out her daughter was being held by the same man who had slain her husband. "We knew Lucetti was slime. This just proves it."

"Worse than slime, a monster." Her eyes sought his, aching with questions. "Darren was a good person. Why kill him? And why inject him with an anticoagulant? All this time, I thought that—" She shook her head. "Why, Mac?"

"He knew too much. As for the anticoagulant, they probably wanted to be sure the wound would be fatal. It sounds like Lucetti's MO. No loose ends. He has a reputation for it."

A sick knot settled in Mac's stomach. He was as floored by the contents of the package as Mallory. Pete Lucetti didn't really exist? The identity was a front for a prominent Seattle businessman named John Carmichael? The man was almost legend, the owner of two perfectly respectable and highly successful corporations. He had even run for mayor, and indications were that he'd win the next election. The more Mac read, the more it all made sense. Small wonder the cops could never nail Lucetti. He was a fanatic about never leaving evidence because Carmichael had too much to lose if any of his criminal activities were ever traced back to him. Mac remembered thinking that Lucetti's speech patterns were odd for a Seattle lowlife. He also remembered the lack of noise on the phone when Carmichael had called. The clues to Lucetti's true identity had been there all the time, but he had failed to see them.

"Keith was trying to make sure Darren's murderer was sent to prison. That's what got us into this whole mess, revenge?"

"You can't blame Keith, Mallory. Rather than turn the evidence over to Darren's killer, he tried to outsmart him. I'm sure he must have thought he could protect you. Things got out of hand. He had the stroke. It wasn't how he planned it."

She sighed and looked down at the letters Steven Miles had written. "Talk about a domino effect. Two girls come into Seattle, start working Carmichael's turf without paying him a percentage, and my little girl ends up paying for it."

"It's not quite that simple. It started with the two prostitutes, all right, but then it mushroomed, and finally involved Keith. Em is peripheral. Remember when I told you my friend, Corrine, was a decent sort, that she hated Lucetti? The reason is that he plays so dirty. Girls don't work his turf without giving him a cut—a big one. They end up with only a fraction of what they earn. If they complain, he has them roughed up. If they try to run out on him, he gets rougher. Once they go to work for him, there is no escape."

"And meanwhile he gets rich?"

"Exactly. And if they defy him like these two girls did?" He made a slashing motion across his throat. "Angela and Vicki and several other girls were skimming. Carmichael chose Vicki to take the fall."

"And Angela decided to avenge her by putting Carmichael in prison? She must have realized he would suspect she was gathering evidence against him and have her killed."

"Without a doubt. Carmichael runs a tight organization. He

wouldn't have someone killed, then fail to monitor the movements of the victim's best friend. Angela knew that. He *did* overlook one thing, though. The dead girl and his accountant, Miles, had been having an affair.''

"And Miles was in love with her?''

"He risked everything to avenge her murder.''

Mallory closed her eyes for a moment, her head swimming. It was like reading a disjointed, convoluted mystery novel. She desperately needed to put it all in order. Right now, only one thing seemed clear, that Em was being held by a killer. The rest seemed like a nightmare of craziness.

Aloud, she went through it one more time. "So…two prostitutes named Vicki and Angela came into Seattle and were coerced into working for Lucetti—whom we now know is actually John Carmichael. Vicki became disillusioned and despite warnings from Angela and her lover, Steven Miles, she began holding out on Carmichael. Carmichael discovered she was cheating him and had her killed. Angela couldn't bear for Vicki's murder to go unpunished, even though she knew she could end up dead herself, and began compiling evidence to put Carmichael away.''

"Right. And after about a year, when she had enough to send Carmichael up, she confided her plan to Steven Miles, gave him duplicates of the evidence, just in case something happened to her, and called your husband, the do-gooder lawyer, to see if he would help her. She would have been afraid of going to the police, remember, because she'd found out two men on the force had been bought.''

Tears gathered in Mallory's eyes. "And of course, Darren agreed to take the evidence to the right people.''

"So Angela arranged to bring it to him the next day.''

"Only she was murdered before she could?''

"Probably within hours. I'm sure Darren didn't realize his own life was in danger.''

"After Angela's call, Carmichael knew Darren might know who Pete Lucetti really was, so Darren had to be silenced. Within forty-eight hours, Darren was dead, his death made to look like an accident.'' Mallory sighed shakily. "So Miles was left holding the bag.''

Mac nodded. "And plenty scared. Three people were dead. He assessed the situation and decided to wait to make his move until Carmichael's guard was down. Miles was an accountant—a man who spent most of his waking moments recording stuff. For years, he had been the head accountant for Carmichael, laundering his ill-gotten gains, so to speak, by making it all look legal on paper. After Vicki and Angela were killed, he decided to start a second set of records, a truthful set, documenting every criminal activity Carmichael's organization was involved in.''

"An exposé.''

"Exactly. The stuff Angela had dug up on Carmichael was probably child's play by comparison. If Miles was going to blow the whistle, he decided to go foghorn-style, tattling on everybody involved, the cops on the take, the pimps, the working girls, the bookies, everybody. When he got done, there would be no organization left.''

"What a boon for Seattle that would have been.''

Mac nodded. "While he waited, building up his evidence, he formed an alliance with—'' Mac tapped a finger on one of the ledgers "—Paisley, Fields and Godbey, the murderous trio who've been chasing us—they skimmed the money, he doctored the books so Carmichael couldn't tell. The profits were divided four ways.''

"And Miles slowly transferred his share to foreign banks?'' Mallory asked.

"With enough money, a man can begin a new life anywhere. While Carmichael rotted in prison, Miles wanted to be lounging on a sunny beach someplace.''

"But he needed someone he could trust to deliver the package to the D.A.''

"And who better than Keith Christiani?'' Mac looked resigned. "Keith was knowledgeable about the law, knew which authorities to contact, and he would be well motivated to want

Carmichael behind bars once he received evidence Darren had been murdered.''

"So Miles sent Keith a copy of the exposé accompanied by lengthy letters of explanation, asking him to help get the package to the D.A.'s office.''

"My guess is that Miles called Keith to be certain he had received the evidence in the mail.''

Mallory licked her lips. "Which was probably his mistake. Carmichael, typically paranoid, must have become suspicious of Miles for some reason and had his phone tapped.''

"And Miles was killed. Then, of course, the threats against Keith started. He was told to return the package to Carmichael, or else.''

"But instead Keith tried to trick him?''

"Carmichael said Keith mailed him a dummy package and must have put the real one in his safe-deposit box. He probably planned to get you and Em out of town before Carmichael received the package, and have me deliver the key to the district attorney after you were safe. Then something went haywire. He called me and was leaving me a message when he collapsed. The rest, we know.''

Mallory shoved the papers away as if the sight of them sickened her. Dropping her forehead to rest against her palm, she whispered, "One thing doesn't make sense. Those three men, how did they know that Miles had exposed their skimming activities?''

A grim smile curved his mouth. "Remember when I was questioning Chapin down in Seattle the other night? He said Carmichael had sicced three goons on Miles, one named Fields?''

Mallory leafed quickly through the papers. "Fields! One of the men who had skimmed with Miles!''

"Exactly. This is only conjecture, but my guess is that after hearing that telltale phone conversation between Keith and Miles, Carmichael sent his not-so-trustworthy employees to eliminate Miles and get the ledgers. They probably caught Miles by surprise, and saw his copy of the exposé. When they realized exactly what was in it, they knew they would wind up dead if Carmichael ever saw it.''

"So they destroyed the set Miles had and started trying to get their hands on the set Carmichael had told them Miles had sent to Keith?''

"And so began the frantic search for the safe-deposit box key. When they couldn't find it, they had one other option.''

"To take me out of the picture? So the entire time Carmichael has been trying to make me cough up the evidence, those three have been trying to keep me from it?''

"Exactly. They're probably terrified. Carmichael doesn't slap hands. They were racing against time. They needed you out of the way. I'm sure Keith would have been next. Eventually someone would have been awarded the contents of the safe-deposit box. Once that person had the package, they would have stolen it.''

"And killed anyone who got in their way.''

"Their lives are on the line, Mallory. These fellows have killed for less.''

Mallory groaned. "Poor Keith. It must have been awful for him when he realized he wasn't going to be able to pull things off.'' Her voice rang hollow. "His only hope was to reach you. He must have thought you were due back that day.''

"I *was* due back that day. Something came up, and I came home a day late, which was why I went directly to the baseball field after I landed at Sea-Tac.'' Mac sighed. "No wonder poor Keith had the stroke. He was under incredible pressure.''

"Not to mention the shock it must have been to learn Darren had been murdered. I wish he had confided in me. But I guess he thought the less I knew, the safer I was.'' Mallory lifted her head. Her mouth trembled. "I still can't believe Darren was murdered. He was a gun collector, you know, antique weapons.'' She made a feeble little gesture with her hands. "It looked as if he had been cleaning one of the weapons and it had accidentally discharged. It—under the chin—and he was bleeding everywhere. I had taken Em shopping. When we came home, we found him in the den.''

"Oh, Mallory, I never knew you were the one who found him."

Her eyes widened. "Why did you think I quit nursing?"

"I figured you got bored with it. With your money, you don't have to work."

She leaped off the bed, pacing back and forth as the full implication of what he had just said sank in. "Bored with it? Nursing was the most important thing in my life except for my husband and child." She whirled and held out her hands, her eyes flashing with anger. "Oh, Mac, why can't you look beyond my father's money to the person I am? Do you think it's fun being raised in a wealthy family? Do you think I wasn't aware of the Third World? Of all the sick and homeless?"

"I guess I never thought about it."

"Yes, you did. You just assumed I didn't care."

It was an undeniable truth, so Mac made no reply.

"When I was young I wanted to join the Peace Corps. Did you know that?"

"Why didn't you?"

"My folks came unglued. They wanted me to fulfill *their* dream, which was to marry into the *right* family and drive around in one of those fifty-thousand-dollar cars you hate so much. I was young—easily intimidated—my father is a master at intimidation. I finally compromised and went into nursing. They weren't thrilled, but it was better than my being a missionary."

She shoved her hands into her back pockets and smiled wistfully. "I met Darren in college. Miracle of miracles, he was from an *acceptable* family. We were going to make a difference, he and I, he with his law practice and me with my nursing. He and Randy planned to open a law office in Seattle, a place that would volunteer legal services to the poor. They both planned to work there in addition to jobs at a regular law firm. I worked for nothing at a low-income clinic." A bitter twist replaced the smile on her lips. "Like you said, I didn't *need* the money."

The mention of Randy made Mac glance away.

"Oh, yes, I know who you are," she blurted out. "I've known since I saw Randy's photograph at your apartment."

"Why didn't you say something?"

She hesitated before answering. "I was afraid you might walk out on me."

"Mallory…" He lifted an eyebrow. "And now?"

"Now I know you never would, no matter how badly you might hate me. You'd stay for Em. And for Keith. I didn't have enough faith in you. I apologize for that. But I was scared."

"Mallory, I don't hate you." He raked a hand through his hair. "At least not anymore."

"But you did. For years. Admit it, Mac. The very least we owe each other is the truth."

He avoided meeting her eyes. "I was wrong to blame you. It was Bettina Rawlins who hurt Randy, not you."

The fact that he couldn't look at her when he admitted it didn't make Mallory feel too hot. With a shock, she realized that he hadn't completely vindicated her yet. That hurt. Especially when she recalled their lovemaking. *Trust me, Mallory. Don't hold back.* The memories humiliated her.

"Mac…you don't *still* blame me, do you?"

"No—not—oh, hell, I don't know." He sighed. "I know now that I was wrong. But there's still this—"

"Doubt?" she supplied shrilly.

"Not doubt, exactly, just a lingering…distaste." He stared at the rug, scraping a bare spot in the nap with his toe. "I've spent fourteen years of my life hating the kind of woman you are. Bettina Rawlins destroyed my brother. He had such big dreams before meeting her. And by the time she was done with him, he was sure he wasn't good enough to be a shoe-shine boy. I had to watch his life disintegrate. All because of a no good, self-centered little piece of fluff who led him on. It's not easy to do an about-face after that. Give me some time."

"Exactly what *kind* of woman do you think I am?"

He looked distinctly uncomfortable and still avoided eye contact with her. "I always believed you were spoiled and empty-headed and selfish, like Bettina.'' The electrical silence that punctuated that admission spurred him to add, ''You *did* ask for the truth. I'm not saying that's what you *are*, only that I perceived you that way.''

Mallory fought to maintain her self-control. She had been under a lot of pressure these past few days. She knew her nerves were probably shot, and Mac's probably were as well. If they lost their tempers... She ground her teeth. Spoiled, empty-headed and selfish, was she? With biting sarcasm, she said, ''What's that saying Marines have about women? If she's ugly, put a flag over her head and do it for the glory? You've got your own version for shallow, spoiled rich women. Turn off the lights and do it for the heck of it!''

His eyes flew to hers, filled with shock. ''Mallory!''

The censure in his tone galled her. ''Don't Mallory me. How can you make love to me and then, only a few hours later, use the word *distaste* when you're referring to me?''

He stared at her, saying nothing.

''What was it? I was convenient? The pillow wasn't big enough? You wanted revenge? What?''

''I don't think that deserves an answer.''

All the stress Mallory had been under these past few days began to roil within her and surged up her throat in a wave of irrational rage. ''Do you remember when you accused *me* of using you? I think maybe it was the other way around.'' Even as she spoke, her throat tightened around the words. ''What was it, your way of avenging Randy? Daddy's little rich girl finally gets her just deserts?''

He said nothing to defend himself, which only fueled her anger.

''Randy *was* twenty-three, old enough to make his own decisions. If he fell for Bettina's lines, how can you possibly hold me accountable for it? Do you really think Darren and I didn't try to warn him? Blame me, by all means, if it makes you feel better. Blame everyone in Bellevue. I can understand your resenting me, truly I can. Especially when you didn't know me.

But I think it's gone beyond resentment when you *use* someone who cares for you for some sick sort of revenge.''

Mac leaned forward. He knew he wasn't himself right now and that he should keep his mouth shut. His nerves were raw. He was exhausted. It was no time to engage in this kind of fight. Tongues could draw blood, and when he got mad, his could be razor sharp. He didn't want to hurt Mallory. He had hurt her enough already. But after everything he had tried to do, all the risks he had taken, how could she accuse him of using her? "Don't sling garbage unless you want it slung back. I didn't *use* you, lady. You were panting for it, *begging* for it. I turned you down once. What do you think I'm made of, rock? *Love me, Mac.* Isn't that what you said? Not to mention the fact that you were *crawling* all over me. *Used* you? Don't make me laugh. As for Randy, let's leave him out of this, shall we? Without me, where will you and Em be? Up the creek, that's where.''

Mallory's legs were shaking so badly that she thought she might fall. She looked at him beseechingly, unwilling to believe he really meant what he'd just said.

Mac cradled his head in his hands. After a long while, he said, "I didn't mean that. I couldn't walk out on you and Em.''

She wrapped her arms around herself. "I know that," she said softly. "Do you think I would sleep with a man I thought was heartless?''

He shot her a glare. "You must think I'm pretty heartless if you think last night was my way of getting back at you.''

"What was it then? If you still blame me, you can't *like* me, let alone have any deeper feelings. What is sex without feeling? What did last night mean to you? Anything?''

That did it. Mac shot up off the bed. "You tell me! You're so good at analysis. I suppose you studied it in school.''

"Another count against me, hmm? A college education. I think you're so confused, you don't know what you think. Guilt has a way of doing that to you.''

"And what would you know about guilt? Give me a break.''

"I know plenty. I quit nursing, didn't I?''

"What's that mean?"

"It means—" Her voice broke. "It means I thought it was partly my fault Darren died."

He froze midstride.

"Don't look at me like that. Do you think you're the only person who lost someone and blamed himself? I not only wasn't there when he needed me, but I couldn't help him when I finally got there. I couldn't stop the bleeding. And I was a *trained* nurse."

"He was pumped full of anticoagulant."

"I didn't know that!" She turned away from him. "My first thought was to slow the bleeding before I called an ambulance. I wasted precious time. I thought I knew what to do, that *I* could take the preliminary steps to help save him. And he died."

Mac touched her shoulder, and she jerked away.

"He bled to death in my arms. After that, I thought of all the things I *should* have done. Sound familiar? I started to lose confidence in my abilities. I felt panicky when I was left alone with an injured patient. Finally one afternoon after a man was brought into the clinic after a car wreck, I quit. Threw my hat and pin into the trash and just walked out. I didn't want another life on my conscience." She passed a hand over her eyes. "I was afraid. Afraid that I wasn't good enough. And so are you."

Mac chose to ignore that comment. "So you quit doing what you loved. I saw you in action with Mark, remember. You're a natural, an excellent nurse."

"I thought I was once." She dashed tears from her cheeks. "Who knows. Maybe now, I can try again."

"Maybe?"

"You think *I* should do an about-face more easily than you did?"

He rolled his eyes. "Mallory, you don't fight fair."

"And you don't judge fairly. I'd say that makes us even."

"I never meant to judge you. And that crack about distaste, I didn't mean it the way it sounded. It's just that—"

"Yes?"

"The money gets in my way."

"It didn't last night."

His eyes narrowed. "Last night, the last thing on my mind was how much money you had. You were terrified for your daughter. You needed me."

Her daughter. A wave of guilt washed over Mallory. Nothing should matter to her right now but Emily. Confused by the myriad emotions washing over her, she couldn't make sense of anything. She only knew that Mac had insinuated himself into her world and become as important to her as the air she breathed. That feeling in no way distracted her from her concerns about Emily. Somehow, Mac wasn't peripheral to her love for her daughter anymore but, inexplicably, a part of it. "I can get rid of the money, you know. Or only use it for helping people."

The plea in her eyes was unmistakable. Mac longed to take her in his arms, but to do so would have been dishonest. If he and Mallory were to have a future together, and his mind emphasized the *if*, then they'd have to find equal ground to build it on. He couldn't let her throw her money away because of him, but he couldn't accept the fact that she had it. It seemed an insurmountable obstacle, especially now, when both of them were so consumed with finding her daughter. There wasn't time to worry about their relationship right now, to sort it out, to make sense of it. And until there was time, it was better to say nothing.

"I'm already using it to help people," she told him, her gaze still clinging to his. "Remember the office Darren and Randy planned to open, the legal-aid center for the poor? Darren opened it after he passed the bar. I've funded it since his death so it wouldn't close down. *Christiani and Watts*, after Darren and Randy. That's where I told Danno he could get on-the-job training."

Mac could only stare at her for what seemed endless minutes. "Darren opened a firm and named it after my brother? Why didn't Keith ever tell me?"

Mac averted his face. He knew why Keith had never told

him. Keith had wanted him to work his way through the bitterness on his own. To find his own truth, however long it took, however painful the healing might be. In the end, it had taken the kidnapping of a child to get through to him; and, of course, getting to know Mallory. Seeing how desperately she loved her daughter. Sharing in her pain. Tasting her panic.

If only things were as simple as they looked on the surface. Was Mallory right? Was he afraid he wasn't good enough? *Yes.* Not good enough for her and not good enough to be a parent to her child. Until he ironed out his feelings, how could he and Mallory continue in a relationship? Every time he looked at her, he saw something to remind him of how inadequate he was and remembered Randy's heartbreak.

"What do you say we let things ride until this is over? We're both exhausted. We have a lot of planning to do. What's between us will still be there later."

"Unfortunately." Mallory swallowed back any further retort. He was right about putting everything on hold. They had Em to think of. Their relationship, whatever remained of it, could be examined later.

They left it at that, but the unspoken was still there between them. Mac sat back down on the bed and began studying the documents again. "You name it, Carmichael has a finger in it. Illegal betting, stolen merchandise, collecting protection money. Murder. Pimping."

"What should we do about the two men still after us?"

"See they get their comeuppance. What else?" A lazy smile curved his mouth. "Sit down, Mallory. What do you think of this plan?"

Mallory lowered herself into the chair, acutely aware that he was still avoiding eye contact with her. The tension between them left her feeling shattered. She had grown so dependent upon his strength. Now she felt as though he had withdrawn his support. Just when she needed him the most—when the situation with Em was finally reaching a critical point.

"I'm going to take the package to my office and put it in my combination safe. Then we'll slip back into your house in the morning to wait for Carmichael's call, just as we planned. I'll arrange a meeting with him, to exchange the package for Emily, at the Seattle City Center, by that big round fountain.''

She knew the place. "How can you do that if the package is in your safe?"

"Just listen. I'll be the go-between and carry the package to Carmichael. While Em walks to you around one side of the fountain, I'll walk to him around the other. When I reach him, I'll tell him I'm carrying a dummy package, that only I know where the real package is. I'll take Em's place as hostage. You run with Em into the crowd. Carmichael won't dare shoot in the crowd, and he won't want to kill me until he gets that package, right? I'll tell him it might fall into the wrong hands if something should happen to me. That will ensure that you and Em can get out of there safely. I'll make arrangements with Shelby to get you both out of town before I agree to take Carmichael to the package, and Shelby will keep you safe until everything is over."

"No!" Mallory shot up from her chair. "You'll end up dead. No way, Mac."

"I already have an escape plan. And once I'm away from Carmichael, I'll go to my office, get the evidence and take it to the authorities. Happy ending."

"It's too risky. What if you can't escape?"

"I've been in tighter spots. I'll get away. And if I can't find a way out, I can always take him to the safe and give him the package, Mallory. That would mean you and I would have to take Em and go into hiding, but it would be better than dying. Trust me, I don't have a death wish." At last he looked deeply into her eyes. "Mallory, use your head. You have Em's safety to think of. Carmichael will be more willing to go along if I'm the hostage. I'm a professional. I'm more of a threat to him than you are. He'll figure you'll do as you're told, no questions. I might play the hero, make trouble."

"She's *my* daughter." Mallory doubled her hands into fists. She knew he couldn't really have an escape plan. There were too many variables. "I'll be the go-between."

"No," Mac replied stubbornly. "Em needs you. So, we either do it my way, or we don't do it at all."

She knew arguing with him wouldn't do any good. His pride would never let him stand aside while she went to Carmichael. As noble a gesture as it was, there was no way she could just let him do it. There had to be something she could do to help him get away once Em was safe.

Mac stood and reached for his jacket where it was draped over the back of the chair. After slipping it on, he began gathering the papers on the bed.

"Where do you think you're going?"

"To put this in my safe."

"Not without me, you aren't."

He groaned. "Mallory, I'd like to keep you out of this for now. The less you know, the safer you are."

"You can't keep me out of it. I'm already in up to my neck. Em's *my* daughter, not yours."

"Do you realize how dangerous this could be?" he asked. "Just getting to my office will be a feat in itself. We're not only going to have to make certain we're not tailed, but after we get there, we have to be sure no one's staking out the building."

"Then I'll come in handy, won't I? You'll be needing a second pair of eyes. As for anyone who might be watching the building? If we see someone we'll just call the police and report a nut case in the building who's wearing nothing but a raincoat who's hiding and leaping out at women. Not even Lucetti's goons would be stupid enough to make a move on us when the place is crawling with cops."

Mac couldn't keep from grinning. "You have a devious streak, don't you?"

"You're just now realizing that? Either you're slow, Mac, or I haven't been performing up to my usual standards since we've been hanging around together."

A HALF HOUR LATER, Mac was sitting at his desk, addressing a large manila envelope to Scotty Herman. Inside were copies of the ledgers, which Mallory had helped make, and all of Miles's correspondence to Keith, which was self-explanatory. Mac knew he could count on Scotty to get the evidence into the right hands. And with mail time delaying things, Scotty wouldn't receive it until well after Em and Mallory were safely away. There was no risk this way of cops on the take reporting back to Carmichael and endangering either of them.

Mac tossed his pen on his desk and rose from his chair. He had sent Mallory up the hall to a pop machine so he could fill out the address on the envelope while she was out of the room. She'd be back soon. Picking up the package, he hurried out into the hall and dropped the envelope into the mail drop. Because Mallory had insisted on coming, Mac had had no choice but to let her know he had made copies, but he didn't dare tell her who he was sending them to. Number one, she'd be upset, fearing the wrong people in the precinct would get hold of them. And he also had to think of Scotty's safety. If something went wrong and Mallory didn't escape with Em, Carmichael was probably an expert at making people talk. As long as Mallory didn't know who would receive the copies, Scotty wouldn't be endangered.

Returning to the office, Mac gave the room a long, slow study, committing it to memory. This might be the last time he ever stood in here. He had a lot of good memories. His gaze drifted to the clutter on top of his desk. If he had time, he would clean it up. Less mess for someone else to sort through. A grin tilted his mouth. Might as well go out like he had lived. Why disappoint everybody?

He sighed and glanced at the telephone. It reminded him he still had to get to a pay phone and call Shelby. He was the one person Mac trusted enough to take care of Em and Mallory.

"ANY PROBLEMS?" Mallory stepped into the room just as Mac glanced away from the phone. She popped the seal on a can of Coke and set it on the desk for him.

Mac avoided looking at her. He had never been good at deceptions. "None. One package is in the mail. The other is in the safe. All I have left to do is make arrangements with Shelby.''

''Who did you send the copies to?''

Mac smiled ruefully. Count on Mallory to ask the one question he had hoped she wouldn't. ''I can't tell you that.''

He expected an argument, but to his surprise, Mallory nodded. ''Good precaution. What I don't know, I can't repeat.'' Catching the surprise in his expression, she added, ''I want to help, Mac. And I want to know what's going on. But not when it serves no good purpose or jeopardizes someone's safety. What sort of arrangements are you making with Shelby?''

He handed her a piece of paper. ''That's his address. I'll make sure he'll be there waiting for you and Em tomorrow. I don't want him anywhere near the center, just in case Carmichael or his goons spotted him. When you arrive at Shelby's, he'll take you out of Seattle to that mountain cabin I told you about. After you're both safe, he'll call my answering machine at the office and leave the number of a phone booth near the hideout so I'll be able to contact him later. Carmichael will have to let me call if I tell him that's the only way he'll get the package. I can call my answering machine and get the number after the twenty-four hours are up. That way I'll know you're safe before I make my break. Once I'm free I'll call Shelby. We'll set a time for him to be waiting at his end.''

Mallory felt slightly sick. Mac's plan was nearly in motion, and it looked as if it could work. But what if it backfired?

''We'll arrange the exchange in the late afternoon so the Seattle City Center will be packed with people. This time of year, there should be crowds of vacationers. Carmichael won't want any trouble if he's afoot. And I'm going to demand he come himself.''

''But then he'll know that we know his true identity.''

''He already does. We've seen the ledgers, remember? He's got to know that. I want the weasel there, Mallory, so there won't be any surprises. He'll be too worried about his own skin to play any tricks.''

"Oh, Mac." Despite their recent argument, Mallory set her can of pop down and hurried around the desk to him.

To her surprise, he enfolded her in his arms without hesitation. "Nothing'll happen. Think about you and Em and Keith all being together again."

How could she make him see that for her the picture no longer seemed idyllic without him being included?

Chapter Fifteen

The next nine hours passed as slowly for Mallory as cold molasses dripping through a pinhole. Mac, being the kind man he was, tried to set their differences aside and be supportive of her, but nothing could really lessen her anguish. She spent the night sitting up in bed, a slat in the headboard crushing her spine, her gaze fastened on shadows as she thought about Emily and all the things that could go wrong during the exchange. She was also trying desperately to come up with a plan to rescue Mac once *he* became Carmichael's hostage. Mac lay beside her, awake most of the time, her hand cradled in his, his thumb making circles on her skin.

Long before dawn, they drove to her place. As he had once before, Mac drove up and down the side streets near her house looking for watchers before pulling into the cul-de-sac. Mallory scanned the neighborhood for any suspicious movements in the shrubs while Mac searched for strange cars. They saw nothing. They broke the police seals on her garage door to sneak inside the house to await Carmichael's phone call. Since they couldn't afford to be seen, they had to sit there in the semidarkness for hours.

When it grew light enough, Mac passed some of the time showing her how to use his gun, a Smith & Wesson .38 Chief's Special. Mallory swallowed down her aversion to firearms. If her becoming proficient with a gun would increase Emily's chances, then Mallory was determined to cooperate. She did exactly as Mac instructed: loading, snapping the cylinder into place and taking a firing stance to grip the gun with both hands to aim. When she sighted down the barrel, she imagined Carmichael's face as a target. Could she kill someone? Sweat trickled down her spine. For Emily's sake, Mallory knew she could do almost anything.

They repeated the procedure with the gun until Mallory could do it by rote. When they were finished, Mac gave her six extra cartridges to carry in her jeans pocket. She didn't ask why. She didn't want to know. After the gun lesson, they went over their plans again, step by step, so she would know exactly how to reach Shelby once the exchange had taken place. She could tell by the expression in Mac's eyes that he didn't expect to meet her at the hiding place in two days as he claimed he would. Fear coiled within her like a poisonous snake and seeped its venom into her system. She wouldn't let him die. Not after all he'd done for her and Emily. She *wouldn't*.

When the phone finally rang, she was shaking. Until now, Carmichael had called most of the shots. Now she and Mac were going to make demands. There was no way they could anticipate Carmichael's reaction, whether it would be angry or retaliatory. Mallory couldn't help but be frightened. It wasn't her own life she was gambling with, but her daughter's.

Mac stood beside her while she answered the phone. Mallory took a deep breath, sent up a prayer and then said, "Hello?"

"You have it?"

"Yes, Mr. Carmichael, I have it." There was complete silence after she said his name. Licking her lips, Mallory rushed on. "I'll meet you by the fountain at the Seattle City Center, one o'clock. You, Mr. Carmichael, not a stand-in. You may bring one man with you, no more. If you send someone in your place or if I see you've brought more than one man, I'll leave. I'll stand on the west side of the fountain, you on the east."

To her surprise, Carmichael didn't argue. "You'll come alone, no police."

"I'm bringing Mr. Mac Phearson. He's going to be the go-between. As he walks toward you around one side of the fountain with the package, I want my daughter walking alone toward me around the other side.''

"That sounds fair. If Mac Phearson's going to be there, I want him in plain view so I can keep an eye on him.''

"So it's agreed? One o'clock this afternoon?''

"Agreed.''

Mac grabbed the phone from Mallory's hands. "Carmichael? One more thing. If you expect this exchange to go off without a hitch, you'd better call off your goons, Paisley, Fields and Godbey, whichever two of them are still alive. After going through Miles's correspondence last night, we have reason to believe they're the men who have been trying to kill Mrs. Christiani. The one who died, in fact, was electrocuted the night before last after breaking into her house. They don't want you seeing those ledgers because the evidence Miles recorded incriminates them. They worked with Miles, skimming your profits. Miles doctored your books so you wouldn't suspect.''

Another long silence ensued on Carmichael's end. "Rest assured, they won't be bothering Mrs. Christiani anymore.''

Mac nodded. "And now the child? I'd like to speak with her.''

"I anticipated that.''

Mac heard a rustling sound, then Em said, "Mommy?'' Mac smiled and handed the phone over to Mallory. The glow that washed over her face upon hearing her daughter's voice made Mac's heart catch. Love like that, so perfect, so selfless, was rare. Mac had never been self-sacrificing and he certainly harbored no suicidal tendencies, but bringing Emily home to her mother was something he was willing to risk his life for. Even though the odds were stacked against him.

TWELVE FIFTY-THREE. Mallory glanced from her watch to the opposite side of the fountain, her heart slamming like a sledgehammer as she scanned the milling crowd. *Emily.* It seemed like years since she had seen her, held her in her arms. Seven more minutes. What if Carmichael didn't come? What if he planned a double cross? What if he had planned one all along?

What if Em was already dead? Mallory's legs began to shake. She had a sudden, painful urge to go to the ladies' room. When she tried to pray, the words jumbled in her head.

"Here they come," Mac whispered.

Mallory was suddenly conscious of the pistol Mac had given her that was stuck in her waistband. She pulled her sweater to be sure it was covered, and turned to gaze across the expanse of water. Coming in the entrance gate, she saw Carmichael. She recognized him immediately from pictures she had seen of him in newspapers. He was a tall, attractive man with brown hair, very refined looking and well dressed, not at all what one would expect. Beside him walked a shorter, gray-haired man, also dressed in a suit. Criminals? Killers? Kidnappers? It didn't seem possible. Her gaze dropped to the amber-haired child in a red-plaid school jumper who walked between them. Tears rushed to Mallory's eyes. Em, alive and well. *Thank you, God.*

Mac turned slightly and placed a hand on her shoulder. When she looked up, she found his eyes intent on her face. "Mallory, just in case…once they get here, I may not have another chance to tell you that…" His voice trailed off and he cleared his throat. "I just want you to know…" His expression became taut. Very quickly, he bent his head and brushed his lips across hers. "I'll never forget. I'll treasure the memory of being with you as long as I live."

She caught his sleeve before he could turn away. Tears rolled down her cheeks, leaving cold trails on her skin. She felt her face contorting, her mouth twisting. "Thank you. For bringing her back to me. Thank you so much."

He cupped her cheek in his hand. "When you get to Shelby's, would you do something for me? Tell him this one is a ringer. He'll know what it means."

She dashed the wetness from her cheeks. "A ringer. Yes, I'll tell him."

Mac repositioned the manila envelope under his arm and turned to watch Carmichael's approach. Taking a deep breath, he steeled himself to start around the fountain. A few more steps and Carmichael would reach his destination. Mac lowered his gaze to the child and feasted his eyes on her for a moment. A miniature of Mallory. Even at this distance, her eyes looked as big as dinner plates in her elfin face.

Carmichael looked nervous as he drew to a stop. He checked Mac over to be sure he had the package. Mac lifted his jacket to show that he wasn't armed. Carmichael nodded and scanned the surrounding area for any sign of police. When at last he seemed satisfied, he gave another nod and released his hold on Em's hand. Mac started walking. For a moment the child just stood there, seemingly unaware that her mother was nearby. She had her head tipped back to study the Space Needle, the tallest structure in the city center. Carmichael said something to her and pointed. Em leaned sideways to see around the spiral of orange metal in the center of the fountain, her gaze following the direction of Carmichael's finger. The next instant, her small face lit up with delight. "Mommy!"

Before Carmichael could react, Em bolted in the wrong direction and came around the south side of the fountain toward Mac. Mac's guts coiled into icy knots.

"Freeze, Mac Phearson!" Carmichael yelled.

Mac stepped away from the fountain and held his arms out from his sides. *Please, God, don't let him panic.* Carmichael reached under his jacket, his attention riveted on the fleeing child. *Don't let him shoot. Please, not at the kid.* Mac tensed, ready to knock Em to the ground as she passed if Carmichael drew his weapon. The little girl sped by, so close Mac could have touched her, her big brown eyes riveted on her mother, her face aglow with anticipation. "Mommy?"

"Em," Mallory cried. "Oh, Em!"

Standing where he was, Mac was afforded a view of Mallory as she caught her daughter up in her arms. It was a moment he was glad he hadn't missed. Mallory sobbing, Em chattering like a magpie, every few words interrupted by a giggle. For just an instant, Mac allowed himself to drink in the sight of them, amber heads glinting in the sunshine, their faces shimmering. Then he forced himself to turn and start walking. When next he glanced back, Mallory and her child had disappeared into the crowd.

MALLORY'S HANDS SHOOK as she shoved the key into the ignition of the Honda. She had checked for explosives before getting into the car, but that didn't mean there was no one nearby, sighting on them with a rifle. She was so panicked that she forgot to depress the clutch and the car lurched when she started the engine. Em, perched on the passenger seat, fastened wide eyes on her.

"Mommy, why did you lay on the ground before we got in? You're shivering. This isn't our car. Did you buy a new one? Is Gramps okay?"

Mallory got the car started. A thick line of traffic had her momentarily boxed in. Keeping the clutch depressed, she leaned sideways and gave her daughter another swift hug, afraid to linger for fear Carmichael might have set a trap. Em clung to her like a little octopus, her plump arms squeezing Mallory's neck. Prying her loose, Mallory smoothed her hair and flashed what she knew was an unconvincing smile. "Oh, darling, yes, Gramps is okay. I'm just in a hurry, that's all. We're going to meet a new friend. His name is Shelby, and he's expecting us. If we're late, he may worry."

"I thought your new friend was named Mac."

"Yes. Shelby is another new friend. We can have more than one new friend, can't we? How are you, princess? Did those people treat you nice? They weren't—" Mallory tightened her hold on the steering wheel. "Were they cross or anything?"

There was still no break in the line of traffic. Mallory watched her rearview mirror.

"No. They were nice. There was a cat named Peaches and a parakeet. Can we have a parakeet? They can learn to talk, you know. I watched lots of movies. Ruthie, the lady, rented some dumb ones, though."

"But she was nice to you?"

"Yes, except for when I let the bird loose and Peaches tried to eat him." Em's small face puckered in a frown. "Mommy, why did you leave me there if you thought Ruthie wouldn't treat me nice? I liked it better at Beth's house."

"I didn't—" Mallory flashed her daughter a too-bright smile. "It's been a busy week. I'm glad Ruthie was nice. Peaches didn't hurt the bird, I hope."

Em grinned. "Nope, but he made snags in the curtains climbing up them. Ruthie's face turned purple and her eyes bugged at me. I thought she might spank me, but she didn't."

Mallory swerved out when a break in traffic gave her the opportunity. Then she forced herself to concentrate on driving. Em was safe. At least, she soon would be. *Think, Mallory.* She checked her mirrors, glanced out the side windows. *No tail.* Without signaling, she swung across two lanes and took a sharp left turn. After being around Mac, she knew better than to drive directly to Shelby's. No way. If Carmichael had someone following her, she'd give them a merry chase or die trying.

"Mommy, you just went on a red light."

Mallory laughed softly and nodded. "I did, didn't I? Wonders never cease. Are you buckled in? Good girl. If I tell you to, Em, you undo your belt and get on the floorboard, okay? We're going to play *running from bad guys.* Sound fun?"

"Not very."

"Well, fun or not, humor me."

"Okay. What kind of bad guys?"

"The kind we don't want to catch us. *Bad* bad guys."

"Are we going to play it until we get to Shelby's?"

"Yes, darling, until we get to Shelby's."

SHELBY LIVED in a new high rise on the west side. Mallory parked on the street and glanced at the paper she'd pulled from her pocket. His was apartment 1410. She climbed out of the car and tipped her head back to look up at the building. Would he welcome them? Be hostile? Recalling the conversation she had overheard between him and Mac, she fought off apprehension. Mac trusted Shelby. He had extracted her promise that she would come here. It was too late to change arrangements at this point.

Mallory helped her daughter from the car and then drew her toward the high-rise entrance, holding tightly to her small hand. *Please, let him be nice.* If he was unpleasant—if he so much as *seemed* reluctant to help them—how could she possibly leave Em with him?

"Mommy, is Shelby nice?"

"Mmm, yes, very nice." Mallory wasn't sure who she was trying to convince, Em or herself. She pressed the elevator button. "He's Mac's best friend, so he has to be a nice man."

"Do you like Mac a lot?"

Mallory had forgotten how many questions Emily could ask. She smiled as she pulled her into the elevator. "I like him very much."

The elevator jerked and then began its ascent. Em grasped the handrail. "Very *very* much?"

Dropping to her knees, Mallory wrapped both arms around her daughter. This was the first opportunity she had had to simply hold her, to *absorb* the fact that she was actually here and in one piece. Unshed tears ached behind her eyes. Em, of course, didn't realize how close she had come to dying so Mallory had to play down her own relief to avoid frightening her. This wasn't the first time that she and Mallory had been separated, so Em couldn't see what the big deal was. Mallory was grateful to Carmichael for that. The man had *some* good in him.

"Yes, Em, I like Mac very very much. But not as much as you."

"Silly, you *love* me."

The elevator doors slid open. Mallory took Emily's hand in hers again. Together, they exited into a plushly carpeted hall. Arrows indicated that Shelby's apartment was to her right. Mallory turned, tugging Em along beside her. Apartment 1410 was only a few doors down. Mallory halted before the door and took a deep, bracing breath. Here went nothing. She rapped softly. Seconds later, she heard a chain rasp and the portal opened a crack. A tall black man with a mustache and dimples peered out. There was a hard, rough edge to his features, but he had twinkling eyes that glowed warm and friendly from his brown face.

"Are you Shelby?"

"That's my name. You must be Mallory." The door swung wide. "And *you* must be—Ellen? Or was it Etta? Esther? Emma?"

Emily giggled as she and Mallory stepped across the threshold. "You're getting warmer. I'm—"

Shelby held up a hand. "No, no, don't give it away! If I can't get it right, I have to pay off with a banana split from the Dairy Queen. House rule around here if you forget somebody's name. You *do* like banana splits?"

"Yummy. My favorite."

"Oh, that's good. We wouldn't have hit it off at all if you didn't." Shelby shut the door and fastened the chain. Meeting Mallory's gaze over the top of Em's head, his expression grew suddenly serious. "Did everything go all right?"

What could she say? Yes, it went fine? A lump rose in Mallory's throat. "He—um—yes, well enough. He gave me a message for you. He said to tell you this one was a ringer."

Shelby smiled slowly. He ran his gaze over her and lifted a quizzical eyebrow. "Oh, he did, did he?" His smile dimpled his cheeks. "Well, now, isn't that a mind-blowing development?"

Mallory wasn't quite sure what that meant. Since Shelby seemed to find it amusing, she relaxed a bit. "It's not bad news then?"

"It depends on how you look at it, I guess. Is your name Erica?" Shelby hunkered down in front of Em. "Evelyn? None of those, hmm? I can't believe this. I'm usually very good at remembering names. Especially when the owner is so pretty. Erin?" He heaved a theatrical sigh. "Egghead?"

Emily was clearly disarmed by Shelby's teasing grin. "Shall I tell you? I'm afraid you aren't going to guess."

"Well, it means I'm out the money for a trip to the Dairy Queen, but I reckon I have to give up. Tell me."

"Emily."

Shelby clapped his hand to his forehead. "Emily! Of course. I remember now. I came close with Emma. I think we should *share* a banana split."

"Oh, no. You didn't guess it! And it's *your* rule."

"True," Shelby conceded. "Close is only good in horseshoes. How about I let you eat three-fourths?"

"Nope, you owe me a whole one."

Shelby cupped the child's chin in his hand. "My goodness! I never saw so many freckles on one little nose in all my life. How do you do it? I can stay out in the sun until I'm cooked to the bone and I can't get a single one."

Emily found that hilarious and giggled with delight. "*You* can't get freckles."

"I can't?"

"Nope. But don't feel sad. You'd hate them once you had some. They won't wash off, you know."

"They're too pretty to wash off. If I can guess how many freckles you've got, will you call us even?"

"Nope. I want my banana split. Besides, I'd starve by the time you got all *my* freckles counted. I've got 'em all over."

Mallory had to look away because her eyes were filling with tears. She should have known Shelby would be wonderful. He was Mac's best friend, so he had to be. He clearly loved children. Em would not only be safe with him, but as happy as a bug. Now all that remained for her to do was be certain Shelby's plan of escape was fail-safe and then to inform him of her own plans. Glancing at her watch, she did some quick calculations. Mac planned to stall Carmichael for twenty-four hours before taking him to the safe at his office and giving him the package. That didn't give her much time. She hoped Shelby didn't decide to be difficult.

TWO HOURS LATER, after Mallory had grilled Shelby mercilessly to satisfy herself that he was capable and that his plans for fleeing Seattle had no holes in them that might endanger her daughter, she told him her intentions.

"You're gonna *what?*"

Until this moment, she had thought Shelby had very nice eyes. Now, however, they looked a little wild. "I'm going to bargain for Mac's release," she repeated, peeking into the living room to be sure Em was still happily absorbed in the movie they had been watching on Shelby's VCR. Shelby wasn't exactly whispering. "Please don't be difficult, Shelby. I'm going to do it no matter what you say, and you'll only waste precious time."

"Oh, no, you ain't!"

She pursed her lips. Shelby's grammar became nonexistent when he got upset. "I'm perfectly capable, you know. I've got it all planned out. And when it boils right down to it, you haven't got much to say about it."

"Once you get to know me better, you'll find out I always got plenty to say about everything. No. That's *N-O*, as in absolutely not. Mac sent you here for me to watch out for you. Soon as it's dark, we're gonna get in my car and head east over the mountains to that cabin where nobody can find us. If I let you do otherwise, when he finds out, I'll think I'm grass and he's a lawn mower. No way. It'd be different if I could go with you, but I can't. So just put it out of your pretty little head."

Mallory felt her temper rising. Her pretty little head? She planted her hands on her hips. "Look into my eyes. Do you see a vacancy sign? Don't talk to me like I have feathers between my ears."

He jutted his chin at her. "Feathers? I think all you got up there is air. Those boys don't play nice. Do you understand what I'm saying? They pack weapons that fire *real* bullets." He motioned toward the living room with his thumb. "I'm taking you and sweet thing to eastern Washington. That's it. No arguments."

"Shelby, I love him. Can't you understand? If he dies, how will I live with it? Now that I know Em will be okay, I have to do something. When Mac calls you tomorrow, just tell him I'm with you."

He groaned, rolled his eyes and did a half turn away from her. "I'm not lyin' to him. No way. Forget that idea."

"You'll have to. Otherwise, he'll do something foolish before I can make my move. You don't want him dead, do you?"

"Mac's no dummy. He'll get himself out of it. He told me over the phone that he had a plan."

"He lied. His only plan was to exchange himself for Em. Don't you see? Look at her, Shelby. Could you let her die? He decided to take her place. He *lied* to you."

Shelby groaned. "It was his choice. I promised him, Mallory. You know that message he sent me? About the ringer? *You're* the ringer. It's a name we came up with years ago. Over in Nam. I was engaged to be married, and Mac called my girl a ringer because of the engagement ring I bought her. I got hurt over there—bad hurt—and he promised me if I didn't make it, he'd take care of her. You understand? He sent that message in case he didn't come back. He wanted me to look out for you."

Mallory's throat tightened. *Oh, Mac.* "You'll be taking care of Em. That's the most important thing. As soon as it's dark, you'll leave and head east over the mountains. She'll be safe over there. Carmichael won't be able to find her. Day after tomorrow, Mac and I will join you."

"And what if something goes wrong? What happens to her?"

"My parents will raise her if Keith isn't able. Believe me, the thought of that is enough to keep me on my toes. Trust me, Shelby. I've been planning this since last night. I won't leave room for mistakes."

She could see that Shelby was weakening. She spoke to him quietly for several minutes then showed him the note she'd composed and planned to leave for Carmichael.

He read it carefully then nodded once, convinced. She smiled tremulously and turned toward the living room to say goodbye to Em. Leaving her daughter was going to be the hardest thing she had ever done in her life.

Em reacted to Mallory's announcement that she was leaving

with only momentary sadness. "I get to go camping with Shelby? And pretty soon you and Mac are coming? That'll be radical."

Mallory scooped the child into her arms and clung to her, fighting back a deluge of tears. "Oh, Em, I love you so much, darling. Do you have any idea how I've missed you?"

Em squeezed her back and craned her neck to see what Spock was doing. Mallory had clearly interrupted her during a suspenseful moment in the movie. "I missed you, too, Mommy. Shelby! Come and watch! Spock's going to get killed."

Shelby, clearly reluctant to horn in on such an emotion-packed farewell, obliged the child, throwing Mallory an apologetic glance. Mallory forced herself to release her hold on her daughter, trying to comfort herself with the realization that this was a difficult parting only for her.

Rising to her feet, she swiped at a stray tear on her cheek. Shelby smiled and gripped her shoulder. "You take care. Don't go gettin' yourself hurt. He'll never forgive me." His face tightened. "And now that I know you, I'm afraid I'd never forgive myself, either."

Chapter Sixteen

Mallory left Shelby's apartment and drove directly to Mac's office building. Breaking and entering in broad daylight wasn't her idea of fun, especially when she had never in her life broken in anywhere. But she didn't dare wait until dark. Just in case Carmichael somehow managed to make Mac reveal the whereabouts of the package sooner than planned, she wanted that safe to be empty. Except, of course, for the note she'd shown Shelby.

Mac's office door had a window in the top half. That helped. All she had to do was break the glass. No need to pick the lock, thank goodness. The only trick would be to break the glass so quietly that no one called the police. She had watched enough television to know she needed tape. Going to a store for it would waste time. She cast a dubious glance at her attire. Maybe, just maybe, since Mac was so haphazard about everything else, someone in a neighboring office would believe his new secretary came to work dressed in jeans and athletic shoes.

Repositioning the shoulder strap of her purse, Mallory took off down the hall. Several offices away, she looked through a door window similar to Mac's and saw a woman bent over an adding machine. Mallory pasted on a smile and stepped inside. "Hi, there. I'm Mallory, the new secretary up the hall. I work for Bud Mac Phearson. Could you save the day and lend me a roll of tape for about five minutes? I forgot to get some, and I'd really rather not be fired my second day on the job."

"Oh, sure, no problem. As if Mac ever fired anyone." She threw Mallory a conspiratorial smile. "He just drives people crazy until they quit. He's having a good day if he comes in wearing socks that match." She shoved the tape dispenser forward, her eyes alight with laughter. "You aren't going to do anything foolish, like straighten his desk, are you? It completely throws him off stride. Believe it or not, he knows where everything is in that jungle he calls an office."

Mallory remembered the condition of Mac's Volvo and chuckled. "What the man needs is a wife."

The other woman rolled her eyes. "Isn't he a doll? I wouldn't kick him out of bed for eating crackers, that's for sure. Hang in there, kiddo. If I wasn't already married..."

Mallory picked up the tape. "Thanks. I'll be right back."

Her heart slammed all the way back up the hall. She quickly crisscrossed Mac's door window with tape, then used the tape dispenser to whack it. Glass splintered in both directions, and not very quietly. She winced and wiggled one foot to dislodge several errant slivers from her shoe. Nothing ever worked the way it did on television. After returning the tape with a cheerful thank-you, she raced back to Mac's office. *Hurry, hurry.* Reaching through the broken window, she unlocked the door, shoved it inward and then kicked the scattered glass across the threshold so nobody would see it.

Mac's filing system, if there was one, left much to be desired. How did he ever find anything in all these piles of papers? She focused on the safe, which sat in one corner of the room, serving as the stand for a drip coffee maker. As she stepped across the room, she reached in her purse for the note she had already composed. Grabbing the safe dial, she worked the combination, which she had committed to memory when she had seen Mac open it earlier. To her relief, the door swung open after her first try. She removed the familiar manila envelope. Very quickly, she scanned the note one more time to be sure she hadn't left anything out. Carmichael should get it tomorrow, when Mac brought him to pick up the package.

Mr. Carmichael: -
If you want your precious package, meet me tonight at
the Mukilteo ferry at 12:55. If you're late, I will take your
package directly to the police and it will be in their hands
by 1:30. I want you, no one else, to walk to the ferry ramp
with Mr. Mac Phearson. I will be waiting for you there.
As Mac Phearson steps onto the ferry, I will hand you the
package. You will return to your men; I and Mr. Mac
Phearson will depart on the ferry to Whidbey Island. No
tricks. Keep Mac Phearson in good health if you value
your freedom.

She had signed it with her full name.

Mallory's hands shook as she laid the note on the floor of
the safe and closed the door. She was trusting Mac's assess-
ment of Carmichael's character. If he was right, she knew that
the moment Carmichael read her note, he would fly into a rage.
She wanted him angry—so angry that he became careless. A
lone woman, and a not very astute one at that, against his army
of trained professionals? Carmichael would believe that getting
the package from her would be as simple as taking candy from
a baby.

Mallory had news for him. She would be the first to admit
that she had been out of her element these past few days. She
wasn't much good at playing duck in a shooting gallery. And
threats against her daughter's life reduced her to sniveling terror. But Em was safe now. No more mindless panic. No more
feeling powerless. Carmichael was about to learn a very bitter
lesson, that muscle could never take the place of brains.

Mallory had planned carefully. The hardest part had been to
forget what Mallory Christiani might do and start thinking like
Carmichael would. Last night, when she had first conceived
this idea, she had tried to put herself inside his skin and anticipate his every move. It hadn't been too difficult once she
started getting the hang of it. For instance, the very first thing
she had imagined him doing was to assess the situation from
all angles and study the layout of the area that she had chosen

for the exchange. He would instantly realize that an island like Whidbey could become a death trap. The last ferry run was at 1:00 a.m., so once she and Mac went over to Clinton Landing and disembarked, they would have only one escape route off Whidbey, the Deception Pass Bridge, which connected into the mainland at the north end. Carmichael would be ecstatic when he realized that. Because it would be dark, he wouldn't even have to worry about witnesses identifying him.

To saturate him with false security, that was her aim. She had deliberately chosen a place where he could close off every avenue of escape. He would station snipers at strategic spots around both ferry landings. If his men couldn't nail her and Mac at the ferry dock on the mainland, they would try again after she and Mac disembarked at Clinton Landing over on the island. And, just in case that failed, Carmichael would have both ends of the Deception Pass Bridge covered. Oh, yes, he would think of everything. And feel utterly confident that she was a stupid little broad who was playing right into his hands. Which was exactly what she wanted him to think. That he was shrewd, that she was as good as had, that it was only a matter of time. Oh, yes…let him feel cocky. He would never expect her to pull a switchback like this, to outsmart him at his own game. Let him forget that she came from the upper crust world of politics and wheeler-dealer big business. She had grown up watching her father grind much better men than Carmichael under his heel.

"A piece of cake," she whispered, thinking of Mac as she shut the safe with an ominous little click. He had been her rock for days, watching out for her, taking care of her, lending her his strength, thinking for her when she couldn't think for herself. Well, now it was her turn to carry the ball.

Striding to the desk, Mallory picked up the phone and dialed her bank. A woman named Sarah answered. "Yes, Sarah, this is Mallory Christiani." Mallory recited her account numbers. "I'd like to arrange for withdrawal of my funds by morning."

Sarah hesitated. "All of them? Less than twenty-four hours isn't much time to give us."

"I'm sorry. It's an emergency."

"Have you become dissatisfied with our service?"

"Not at all. I simply need a lot of cash."

"If we liquidate your market bonds, you'll lose large sums of money."

"I don't care. I want the cash—three thousand in small bills, the remainder in large denominations, so it will be easier to carry. See to it, please?"

Mallory hung up and pulled her list of things to do from her pocket. She only had until tomorrow night, so every second had to count. Some of this stuff simply couldn't be done today, though. Not until she had withdrawn all her funds from the bank. She sighed and ran a hand over her eyes. If she forgot one minor detail, she and Mac might pay for it with their lives. The first thing tomorrow morning, before banking hours, she would have to drive to the hospital and exchange Trudy's Honda for her Mercedes. Then she'd park her Mercedes at the Mukilteo ferry landing and take a cab into Everett to rent a dark-colored car, preferably one with plenty of horsepower, in case she needed speed.

Tomorrow afternoon after withdrawing her money from the bank, she would put the cash in the trunk of the rental car and take the vehicle over to Whidbey Island on the ferry, park it up the road from the landing where it wouldn't be conspicuous, and then return to the mainland as a walk-on ferry passenger. Once that was done, she would drive her Mercedes down to Tacoma and rent still another car, which she would leave parked near the marina slips there. Today, all she had left to do was some shopping. She needed a box of large heavy-duty freezer bags, a sturdy leather belt, an extra key chain and a suitcase in which to carry the cash.

It was going to be the slowest day and night of her life waiting for tomorrow night to finally arrive. Mallory picked up the phone and dialed the hospital to get the good news about Em to Keith. No sense in both of them waiting in agony. She wanted to make sure he knew Em was safe.

TWENTY-EIGHT HOURS later, the longest hours of Mac's whole life, he hung up the phone after speaking to Shelby. He'd been all too aware of Carmichael, who was squeezed into the phone booth behind him, jabbing him in the back with a gun. Mac figured he might survive the loss of one kidney, but he wasn't too sure what else a bullet there might blow away. He'd have to wait for a better opportunity to make an escape attempt. At least now that he had spoken to Shelby, he knew Em and Mallory were safe in eastern Washington. From here on in, all he had to worry about was himself.

"Satisfied?" Carmichael snarled.

Mac turned slightly. "Yes."

"Then take me to the package. And no tricks."

"No tricks. It's hidden in my office building."

Carmichael backed out of the phone booth, keeping the gun trained on Mac.

MAC KNEW SOMETHING was wrong the moment he approached the door of his office. The window had been broken. A chill of apprehension inched up his spine. Wouldn't it be just his luck if vandals had stripped the place? The first thing they would steal was a safe. He unlocked the door, put his hand on the knob, gave it a twist, stepped inside. *Relief.* The safe was still in the corner. He looked over his shoulder at the three armed men behind him. He wasn't going to get out of this one. Carmichael was going to plant a slug between his eyes the minute he got his hands on that package. The building was empty at this time of night, so no one would hear the shot.

Mac cast a panicked glance around him. No place to hide. nowhere to run. This was it. He tried to pray as he walked to the safe, but the only prayer he could remember was a dinner blessing he had learned as a child—*bless us, oh Lord, and these, Thy gifts.* Somehow it didn't seem fitting. So as he grasped the safe dial, he resorted to the basics, a straight-from the heart plea. *Please, God.* He didn't know for sure what he was requesting. Rescue would be nice. A bolt of lightning that struck everyone in the room but him, maybe? Salvation was less appealing, but it was certainly a thought, given the fact that he was about to meet the Grim Reaper.

"Hurry it up!" Carmichael shoved the barrel of his gun against Mac's temple. "You're stalling."

One more number. Mac heard a click. The safe door swung open. His legs wobbled a bit. Sweat was running down his face. *Come on, Mac, where's your pride?* He took a deep breath and tensed, trying to prepare himself for the explosion of noise, for the sudden pain that would surely come, even if only for an instant. In his mind's eye, he pictured Mallory's face, then Em's. Knowing they were together made everything worthwhile, all of it, even dying.

"What the hell? Where is it? I told you, no tricks!"

Mac focused on the inside of the safe. His guts clenched. *No package?* He stared at the small piece of white paper lying there, unable to believe his eyes. "It isn't a trick. I left it here. I swear it." He had an insane urge to laugh.

Carmichael snatched up the paper to read what was written on it. Mac swiped at his upper lip, relieved that the gun was no longer pointed at his skull.

"That stupid little—" Carmichael butted the safe door with the heel of his hand and whirled to glare at his men. "The Christiani woman has taken the package. Can you believe it? The naive little twit thinks she can play power games with me?"

Now Mac's legs felt *really* wobbly. Mallory? She was supposed to be in eastern Washington. Less than thirty minutes ago, Shelby had said, "Don't worry, Mac. Em and Mallory are both okay." Shelby had never lied to him. Well, maybe *never* was too strong a word, but he certainly didn't make a habit of it. Surely he wouldn't have started now. Or would he? A wave of nausea rolled over him. *Damn.* Mallory had stayed in Seattle? Like an idiot, he had brought her to the office and let her see him open the safe. She must have memorized the combination and come here to take the package, probably to try to bargain for his release. He couldn't bear the thought that she might end up getting herself killed for him.

Carmichael started roaring orders. "We have to meet her down at the Mukilteo ferry at twelve fifty-five. There isn't much time. I want every available man on this."

THE FORLORN CRIES of the gulls drifted on the night breeze, a lonely, spine-chilling sound. Mac climbed from the brown sedan and gazed toward the *Kitsap*, which was already docked. He ignored the bulge of the gun under Carmichael's jacket. At this point, Mac sincerely wished it had all ended back there in the office with a bullet between his eyes. He couldn't see any way Mallory could pull this off, not against a pro like Carmichael. The man had every base covered. There were men here, men across the sound at Clinton Landing, men at the north end of the island on the Deception Pass Bridge. She was trapped with no way out.

"It's time," Carmichael hissed. "Start walking. No funny stuff. Think of it this way. If you behave yourself until we get to her, she can die in your arms. Touching, don't you agree? Lovers forevermore."

Mac yearned to bash the creep's face in. He set off walking, the parking lot a blur around him, only the ferry in focus. Mallory, where was she? Didn't she know there were a half-dozen high-powered scopes trained on him? The moment she showed herself to give Carmichael the package, they would mow her down. Never in all his life had Mac been so scared. *The little fool.* He loved her so much. And now she was going to die.

As they drew near the ferry ramp, Mac spotted the red Mercedes's gleaming rear fenders, the last car in the far right parking lane. No sign of Mallory. Carmichael swore under his breath. Mac sent up a silent prayer of thanks. Closer, closer. His heart began to slam. His throat constricted until he could scarcely breathe. She was here someplace, but where? *Stay hidden, sweetheart. Change your mind. Don't take a stupid chance like this. I'm not worth it.*

"Stop walking, Carmichael!" Mallory's voice rang out from somewhere in front of the car. "No sudden moves."

Carmichael froze. Mac stopped beside him. His stomach flipped and plummeted to the region of his knees. The loading lanes inside the ferry were lit up. If she showed herself, even for a second, one of the snipers would pick her off. He glimpsed amber hair, just a flash, behind the left front fender of the car. At least she was keeping out of sight. To his utter amazement, his Smith & Wesson, gripped by a small, white hand, appeared.

"Toss your weapon, Carmichael! Hurry it up. Into the water."

Carmichael did as he was told, then turned back, his expression grim.

"Signal your men not to shoot. I mean it, Carmichael. And you'd better make it convincing. Don't make the mistake of thinking I can't hit you before they get me. Remember that gun collection of my husband's? I'm an ace shot."

Carmichael pivoted and waved his arms, then spun back. "I want that package. You can't run far enough, I promise you that. I'll find you."

Mallory's head inched up. "You'll get your package. Put your hands up and start walking, very slowly. Hurry, before the ferry attendants come forward to put up the guard lines."

Mac's legs shook with each step. He and Carmichael reached the ferry and stopped.

"Okay, Mac, come aboard," Mallory called.

Mac stepped on board. As he did, a manila envelope arced through the air and plopped, then skidded, up to Carmichael's feet.

"Don't move! Keep those hands up or I'll shoot!" Mallory's voice dripped such venom that Mac scarcely recognized it. "Hurry, Mac, dive for cover."

Mac didn't have to be told twice. He ran in a crouch to join her at the front of the car.

"Okay, Carmichael, you stand right there. Understand? Until the ferry is well away from the dock. Don't move. Don't even breathe. I'll have this gun trained on you every second."

Two ferry operators were coming forward to tie off the safety ropes. When they saw Mallory, they stopped walking.

"It's all right. Go on about your business," she instructed them.

Since she was holding a gun, they hastened to comply, giving the Mercedes a wide berth. Mac figured they'd hightail it to the bridge and radio for the authorities the first chance they got. The ferry engines began to roar. He felt the vessel begin to move. Mallory didn't take her eyes off Carmichael until the ferry had moved a safe distance away from the dock. Then she let out a rush of pent-up air and turned to throw her arms around his neck. It was testimony to how scared he was that he didn't even flinch when he felt the barrel of his .38 bang against the back of his head. If he had to die, he couldn't think of a better way to do it than with Mallory in his arms.

"Mallory, you sweet, wonderful little idiot."

She laughed almost hysterically. "Oh, Mac, you're all right. I *did* it! I did it!"

He hated to burst her bubble. "Honey, we're not going to make it! Clinton Landing is crawling with his men. And even if we make it past them, he's got the bridge covered. We'll never get off the island, probably not even off the ferry. Why did you do this? Why? I thought we agreed the most important thing was getting Em to safety?" He tightened his arms around her, wishing he could hold her like that forever, protect her, but he knew he couldn't. If only she had stayed with Shelby. "Didn't you know he'd cover all the escape routes? I could wring your neck, dammit. How *could* you do something so totally—"

"Em is fine. Shelby called me this morning at my motel to let me know they had arrived safely." She rained kisses on his face, then pulled away. "I have it all figured out. Trust me." She plucked a large freezer bag off the floor, three layers thick, two bags inserted inside the exterior one. She put the gun into the plastic and sealed it, grinning brightly as she handed it over. "Watertight. If you aren't a good swimmer, I can carry it."

"A good *what?* Mallory, we can't swim across the sound."

"We aren't going to swim *across* it, just partway. Trust me, Mac." She stood and offered him a hand. "Come on, we have to hurry. I can't explain it all now."

He rose to his feet and zigzagged through cars with her to the other side of the ferry. When they reached the rail, she began unlacing her shoes. "Hurry up. We don't have much time. You'd better shed that jacket. You *can* swim, I hope. I've done some lifeguarding, but it'll be quite a distance to haul you."

"You do realize these are orca waters?"

"Oh, come on, Mac. Have you ever heard of a killer whale attack in this area? Hurry! We have to be ready to jump at just the right moment."

He kicked off a shoe and shot a leery glance over the side into the inky black water. Unreasoning anger roiled within him. She was going to end up dead, and there was nothing he could do to save her this time. "I hope you know what you're getting us into."

"Out of. I'm getting us out of trouble. Home free, Mac. We'll pick up Em tomorrow and then we're off."

"To where?"

"To anywhere. The Bahamas. Hawaii, maybe? Florida? Mexico would be fun. What suits you?" She peeled off her socks and braced her hands on the rail to look over. "Oh, my, it's a long way down, isn't it?"

She sounded a little shaky. He curled his toes to keep them off the cold cement. "You just noticed? How's *Atlantis* strike you? Need I mention that the ferry engines could suck us up? I've never seen a ferry engine, mind you, but if they have propellers, we'll be minced into orca appetizers."

"We'll just have to swim like the devil, that's all." Her voice sounded tight. She looked toward the dark hulking outline of Whidbey. The scattered lights twinkled like diamonds. "It won't be too long now."

With a sinking feeling, Mac seconded that. It wouldn't be long. Fifteen minutes, max. He had wanted so desperately to keep her safe. The thought of what awaited them made him feel sick. Even if they swam to shore and managed to elude Carmichael's men for a while, they couldn't do it for long. Whidbey wasn't that big. He threw a worried glance over his shoulder to make sure no one was approaching, then stuffed the plastic-wrapped gun into his shoulder holster and snaked an arm around her waist to haul her against him. Giving her a fierce hug, he bent his head and buried his face in his favorite spot, the sweet curve of her neck. It was as good a way to pass the time as any—the best way. Minutes slipped past.

She was trembling, the only outward sign of how truly frightened she was. With a stab of remorse, he realized how much it had cost her to pull this harebrained stunt. And here he was, making cracks. Why? Because he had tried to protect her, and she had muffed it up trying to do the same for him. He hugged her more tightly. He couldn't stand the thought of her dying.

But it was done. She had risked everything for him, and the least he could do was make the best of it. Maybe, just maybe, they could squeak through alive. He lifted his head and watched the black outline of Whidbey coming closer. She stiffened in his arms.

"It's about time, don't you think?" She craned her neck to see his face. "See that light just to the left of the landing? Head toward it. That's where I parked the rental car."

Mac stifled a groan. There was no way to *drive* off the island. "Okay, I'm ready." He gave her a quick kiss. "If something happens and I sink, this may be my last chance to tell you that you're quite some lady. Words don't seem enough."

She turned and looped her arms around his neck. "Oh, Mac, if I did this a hundred times over, it'd never make us even. My little girl is safe and happy. I'm the one who doesn't know how to express my gratitude. Shelby was so wonderful. Em didn't even care when I left her with him."

"Yeah, that's Shelby for you." Mac was going to take him apart if he ever got his hands on him. "He's a great guy. Loves kids. Well, it's time to jump."

He set her away from him to peel off his jacket. They

climbed up on the rail together, tensing for the dive. Mac looked over at her, and suddenly, he knew he couldn't push off without telling her one more thing. Not even his memories of Randy could stop the words from coming. "I love you, Mallory."

There were tears sparkling on her cheeks. "I know you do."

The next instant, she dived off into the blackness. Panic filled Mac when he lost sight of her. He launched himself into the air. Ice-cold water enveloped him, dragging him down to what seemed like fathomless depths. He fought to reach the surface, but the current dragged him back. *Mallory.* She was so small. She'd never have the strength— His chest felt as though it might explode. Then, like a cork, he bobbed to the top, shooting from the water to spew and gasp. *No Mallory.*

He spun in the water, horribly aware of how close the ferry was. He could feel the current sucking at him, trying to drag him under the broad underside of the vessel. "Mallory!" he screamed. "Mallory, answer me!"

Chapter Seventeen

Only the surging of the water and the roar of the huge engines answered him. Mac thrashed his arms, swimming first one direction, then another. Where was she? *Oh, please, God, please.* He couldn't see far. He thought he heard something and struck off swimming. Blackness. Nothingness. He was swimming away from land.

"Mallory!" he yelled. "Mallory!"

Suddenly the water seemed like a living thing, bottomless, monstrous, an overwhelming enemy. And it had literally swallowed up the woman he loved. His breath whined in his lungs. The cold made him feel numb. Frantic, he thought about diving to find her, but he knew there was too large an area and the water was far too deep. He was already tired. The ferry was pulling farther away. If he didn't head inland soon, he'd never make it.

"Mallory!" A sob tore up his throat. He couldn't swim away. He wouldn't. He'd rather drown with her than leave her. "Mallory! Mallory, answer me!" He was screaming and the ferry engines were no longer nearby to drown out the noise. His voice would carry across the water. Let them hear him. He didn't care. He had to find her. "Mallory!"

"Mac! Over here!"

Joy ripped through him. He flailed in the water, choking, blinking, trying to see her. "Where are you?"

"Here!"

He saw the black outline of her arm waving and struck off toward her. When he reached her, they clung to each other, almost sinking. He started to laugh. ''You scared the living hell out of me, lady.''

''*I* scared *you*?'' She pulled away and started doing a breast stroke. ''Come on before you become whale feed.''

They swam in tandem. It was a long way to shore. When they could finally touch bottom, they were both so exhausted they staggered from the water, their clothes pouring water. Up by the landing, Mac could see Carmichael's men swarming forward on the ferry dock, waiting for the boat. Mallory took his hand and led him up a steep bank. They had to fight their way through underbrush. When at last they broke through to the road, they had to walk quite a distance to reach the car. She unfastened a key chain from her belt and unlocked the doors.

''I'll drive. I know where we're heading.''

Mac nearly protested, but stopped himself. She had brought them this far. He climbed in and fastened his seat belt. She drove toward the south end of the island and pulled into a winding, overgrown driveway that twisted down to a beach house.

''It belongs to friends. I called them and they said we could borrow the boat. They keep it gassed up. They left the keys hidden on deck. We'll have plenty of fuel to reach the Tacoma marina. I have a rental car waiting for us there.''

A boat? A boat! Of course, a boat. It was perfect. Carmichael would never have thought of them finding a pleasure craft this swiftly. He climbed from the car, feeling suddenly elated. A boat! She had planned this right down to the last detail. He watched her run around to the trunk. Throwing it open, she dragged out a suitcase.

''Money,'' she explained as she led the way down to the boat house. ''Enough to take us anywhere.''

''How much is that?''

''Give or take a few thousand, a little over eight.''

Mac nodded. They could hide out a few weeks on that. Then

it hit him what she had said. When speaking of less than ten grand, one didn't say "give or take a few thousand." He stopped dead in the path. "Not eight *hundred* thousand?"

Mallory giggled. "Isn't that enough?"

Eight hundred thousand. Mac knew he should be pleased, but instead he just felt shocked. He had roughly twelve hundred in savings after paying last quarter's tuition for Danno and Mark. He followed on her heels, saying nothing. And then she opened a boat house the size of a barn and he found himself staring up at the biggest monstrosity of a yacht he had ever seen in his life. "Mallory, honey, this is *not* a boat. This is a *ship.*"

She was already scaling the ladder. "A beauty, isn't she?"

"I can't drive this." His voice rang like a death knell and bounced off the aluminum walls.

"You don't *drive* it, you navigate it. Throw open the doors for me, would you?"

He shook his head. "I can't *navigate* it then. I'm serious, Mallory. Hold up. Isn't there a *little* boat around here?"

Her wet head appeared over the side. "Mac, I can handle the boat. Just open the doors."

"Ship."

"Ship then. Open the doors and loosen the ties."

Dubious, he slid the doors wide, struggled to unfasten simple-looking knots that managed to become intricate under his clumsy touch, then climbed aboard, convinced that she wasn't *big* enough to handle something so gigantic. To his surprise, she backed it out of the slip like a pro and before he knew it, they were gliding through the black waters of Puget Sound toward Tacoma. Several minutes later, after taking a tour of the *ship,* which had more rooms than his apartment, he stood beside her at the helm, looking out the cabin windows at the city lights of Seattle twinkling along the coastline.

"Home free," she said softly.

Mac wanted nothing more than to take her into his arms, but seeing her at the wheel of such an expensive craft brought it home to him how impossibly distanced their two worlds were.

She came to him all wrapped up in a bow with eight *hundred* thousand dollars resting at her feet, and probably more where that came from.

"I have one question. Who received the package? Will he get it to the police so Carmichael will go to prison for killing Darren? If not, we'll never be able to return to Seattle. We know who he really is."

Mac quickly relieved her of that notion.

"You mean you sent it to Scotty? So we can just stay in the mountains for a while and wait until everyone involved is arrested?"

"Yeah. No trip to the Bahamas or Florida or Mexico. All you get is a dirty old cabin."

Her eyes lit up with happiness. "Oh, Mac!" With a cry of delight, she flipped a switch on the control panel and turned loose of the wheel to launch herself into his arms. "Oh, Mac, I love you! That was brilliant, sending Scotty copies."

"Mallory…" He pressed his face into her hair. With all his heart, he wished he could hold her forever.

Something in his voice made Mallory draw back. Looking up at him, she felt a sinking sensation. His eyes were dark with emotion, and it wasn't happiness. "Mac? What is it?"

"Just that I let myself fall in love with you. But there's no future for us, Mallory."

She stiffened. "After everything I've done, you still—" She licked her lips. "What do you mean, Mac?"

He glanced around the cabin. "*This!* We're nothing alike. I could never measure up." He raked a hand through his hair and moved farther away from her. "I could *never* make enough money. You'd hate me within a year. You don't want that for Em. You want to stick her in a middle-income apartment and give her a dad who can't spell elaborate? Give me a break."

"Mac…I'm sure you can spell elaborate."

"If I can, there's something else I *can't* spell." He turned and flashed her a grin exactly like Danno's. It was a grin that told her more than a thousand words might have. A vulnerable grin, calculated to hide his feelings. He lifted an eyebrow.

"Imagine taking me home to your mother? Or the two of us going to one of your charity shindigs. I didn't even make it through my sophomore year of high school. I lied about my age and joined the Marines at fifteen. I'd embarrass you. I'd embarrass your daughter as soon as she got old enough to re-alize what I really am. And after a month or so, I'd bore you to tears, too. You need a man who can stimulate you."

"I found you wonderfully stimulating."

He rolled his eyes. "You need someone to share your inter-ests, to *talk* to you on your own level."

"Is it because of Randy?" she asked hollowly.

He groaned. "No. I realize how wrong I was about that."

"Oh, really? But now you'll turn your back on me because I'm the little rich girl from Bellevue? Why can't you open your eyes and see me for what I am? I love you. Sell the Mercedes. Give me a red Volkswagen and I'll be happy. I don't care if you can spell elaborate! I don't care if you can spell I love you, just as long as you can say it."

"It'd never work."

"So you say. Well, let me tell you something. *I* was the one born to money, not Em. And I hated it. My father could never show me affection, so he bought me expensive cars and pretty clothes and sent me to schools I hated. And all my mother cared about was making me into the perfect little lady. I want better than that for my daughter. My life was miserable. And now *you're* going to toss me back because you don't think *you* measure up? If I could give my daughter a father like you who would hug her and hold her when she cried, that would matter. Not what he could buy her! It's *what* a parent says to a child, not how *well* he says it." She grabbed up the suitcase. "I'll show you what I think of my dad's money, anybody's money."

"What—Mallory!" Mac raced out the cabin door after her and caught the suitcase in midair, barely saving it from a one-way trip into the sound. He nearly collapsed on the deck when he had it safely in his arms. He put it down behind himself and stared at her. "Are you out of your mind?"

"No, I'm furious!"

"Raving mad, more like. Do you know how many kids this would put through college?"

"Fine, put kids through college with it! Just don't throw it in my face. I've had it thrown in my face for thirty-four years. Take it! I don't need it. I don't *want* it. It was an escape route for us, nothing more. Why do you think there's so much of it? Because I never *spent* it." She brushed angrily at the tears streaming down her cheeks. "Put *yourself* through college with it. Go learn how to spell elaborate if it will make you feel better. I can work as a nurse and buy my own red Volkswagen."

Mac sighed. There was no doubt at all, she was right. Now he had to find a way to let her know he was convinced. "Mallory, shouldn't one of us be driving the boat? We might crash."

"Who cares?"

"I do. If I plan to marry you, I have to survive the trip."

"It's on automatic pilot." She took one last swipe at her nose and blinked. "What did you say?"

"You heard me." He caught her up in his arms. Leaning back, he studied her, his eyes glistening in the moonlight. "Are you sure? We *could* date for a while, you know, try each other out for size. You have no idea what a slob I am."

She grinned. "Nobody's perfect. As for trying you on for size, I already have. And you, sir, are a perfect fit."

"Will you marry me?"

"I thought you'd never ask."

He chuckled. "You won't want an *elaborate* wedding, I hope?" She encircled his neck with her arms and hung on tight. He buried his face in the curve of her neck and rocked her to and fro. His foot bumped the suitcase and he smiled. "One nice thing, if it doesn't work out, I can sue you for alimony."

She nipped his earlobe. "No way. Keith would keep you tied up in court for years. They told me yesterday that he's improving, and I have a hunch he'll like having you in the family so well that he won't let you get away without a fight."

He groaned happily. ''I guess I'm stuck with you forever then.''

''And don't you ever forget it.''

nocturne™

HER BLOOD WAS POISON TO HIM...

MICHELE HAUF

FROM THE DARK

Michael is a man with a secret. He's a vampire
struggling to fight the darkness of his nature.
It looks like a losing battle—until he meets
Jane, the only woman who can understand his
conflicted nature. And the only woman who can
destroy him—through love.

On sale November 2006.

nocturne™

USA TODAY bestselling author

MAUREEN CHILD

ETERNALLY

He was a guardian. An immortal fighter of evil,
out to destroy a demon, and she was his next
target. He knew joining with her would make
him strong enough to defeat any demon.
But the cost might be losing the woman
who was his true salvation.

On sale November, wherever books are sold.

REQUEST YOUR FREE BOOKS!

2 FREE NOVELS
PLUS 2 FREE GIFTS!

Silhouette® Romantic

SUSPENSE

Sparked by Danger, Fueled by Passion!

SPECIAL EDITION™

Silhouette Special Edition brings you a
heartwarming new story from the *New York Times*
bestselling author of *McKettrick's Choice*

LINDA LAEL MILLER

Sierra's Homecoming

Sierra's Homecoming
follows the parallel lives
of two McKettrick women,
living their lives in the
same house but
generations apart,
each with a special son
and an unlikely new
romance.

December 2006

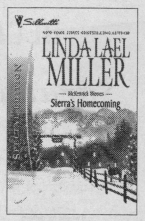